FROZEN TALONS

MICHAEL WARREN LUCAS

Tilted Windmill Press

ACKNOWLEDGEMENTS

Roger Zelazny has been dead for decades, but he helped me out of a serious jam.

One dismal damp night when the caffeine hadn't quite worn off but the allergy meds were kicking in hard, I realized that when Tolkien said that the elves went into the west, he meant that they emigrated to America. Clearly, the dwarves would follow—and, later, orcs. I wrote a goofy story about bootlegging orcs in 1927 Detroit.

Folks demanded more. I wrote them.

To my vast annoyance, the short stories started to form a larger arc. Starting a long arc is a promise that the author will finish the arc. It's difficult to wrap up a large saga in a short story, or even a series of short stories. It can be done. Writers I admire have done it. I'm not yet that skilled.

That's when Roger Zelazny's ghost whispered in my ear: *Dilvish the Damned*. A collection of popular short stories about a sorcerer-swordsman who broke out of Hell to avenge himself, followed by a novel that finishes the tale. I facepalmed, hard, and started writing *Frozen Talons*.

I must thank the fine folks who read earlier versions of this work and pointed out my boneheaded problems: ZZ Claybourne, Brigid Collins, Ron Collins, and Laura Ware, in addition to a few folks who wisely preferred to remain nameless.

I must thank my Patronizers for their ongoing monthly support. Yes, *must*. Our covenant declares that I will do so, and I will not be the one to break it and suffer the ghastly karmic penalties declared therein. Kate Ebneter, Stefan Johnson, Jeff Marraccini, Eirik Øverby, and Phil Vuchetich throw so much cash at me, I thank them in in the ebook and print versions of everything. If you also desire blame for everything I do, check out https://patronizemwl.com.

The *Prohibition Orcs* omnibus and *Frozen Talons* are the first fiction projects I published with Kickstarter support. At the end, you'll find a list of the fantastic folks who are willing to admit that they helped me drag these two books into the world.

Also check out Roger Zelazny's standalone novels like *Lord of Light*, *Doorways in the Sand*, and of course Dilvish's tales. I hope to one day tell stories as well as Zelazny, or at least create a character as daemonically delightful as Black.

This book is for Liz.

December held her world with soft cruelty.

Puffy flakes of snow drifted from the black sky, settling over rooftops and the empty parking lot alike. Uruk-Tai's new flat cap was large enough to tug over the tips of his ears and thick enough that his scalp felt as steamy as June, but the gentle, steady wind sucked all warmth from his face and crept through his canvas pants, making his frozen calves itch. He wore his heavily patched wool coat buttoned tight, but December slipped her frozen breath up from the bottom and between the buttons every time he moved. Even in 1927 Detroit, nobody made a good orc coat. The spiked brass knuckles on his hand absorbed the cold, feeding it straight into his blood.

December had spent days cloaking everything with soft death. The tiny parking lot had been sloppily shoveled, making space for six or seven Model T's, but the drifts up against the brick stores on either side rose up to Uruk's waist. At the back of the lot, the speakeasy's sloped roof shed most of the snow, but a good six or eight inches still burdened the shingles. Heavy clouds hid the Moon and the nameless stars. Streetlights reflecting from those same clouds gave the snow sparkle.

Uruk sometimes thought that December was softer to orcs than any other race. Those drifts would trap a man and smother a dwarf, but an orc could break a path through them exactly as he trudged through any other day. If he ever dared speak such a thought, though, December would correct him. An orc could never mistake softness for kindness. Not with December, and not with America.

He needed to stop dreaming and focus on tonight's war. Deliver the Canadian Club, split the money with Sanford, and return to the clan victorious.

Sanford's beat-up, borrowed truck, backed into the lot, grumbled as the engine idled. If they shut it off in this cold, the cantankerous engine might not start again. The stink of exhaust penetrated Uruk's frozen nose. Even through the heavy leather gloves, his talons were beginning to absorb the cold. Uruk kept his talons trimmed short so that he couldn't accidentally claw open a wall or a throat, but they were thick enough to hold the cold and send ice into his blood. When the night's work was over and he could warm himself over a radiator, his talons would be the last bit of him to thaw.

Grandpa said that in the Old Country orcs grew their talons not only for war, but so in winter they could rest the tips against the hot rocks surrounding the fire. The heat would slowly counter the cold. Touch the rocks for too long and your talons would grow too hot, burning your blood. Grandpa's platoon had amused themselves by challenging each other to see who could scorch their talons the longest, all knowing the pain would not arrive until after.

Grandpa's war wasn't bootlegging, though. Bootlegging was a new war, demanding new weapons and new leadership.

And uncomfortable alliances. Like Sanford.

The human stood next to him, hands stuffed into the pockets of his *over-coat*. More human strangeness. An orc might wear two or three shirts to fend off December. Humans did much the same, but made different shirts for each layer. Uruk knew too much about human clothing, *under-shirts* and shirts and jackets and, now, *over-coats*. Uruk could wear his cleanest shirt closest to his hide, but if Sanford's *under-shirt* was soiled and his buttoned shirt clean, Sanford still had to put the soiled cloth next to his skin. Ridiculous. Not as ridiculous as being a paper man, a human who worked with the writings humans treasured, but an added ridiculousness.

Sanford's clothes did keep him warmer than Uruk. Even in night-sight, only Sanford's face shone. Warmth glimmered around his wrists, and his pants had a dull sheen that would disappear even ten feet away. December swallowed night-sight.

The thought made him glance across the parking lot. The customer had not yet come out of the speakeasy.

Sanford said, "We could demand an extra hundred if you wore the suit."

Sanford had insisted that Uruk own a human-style suit. An orc might wear a jacket over his canvas or denim, but a suit was not merely un-orcish—it was *human*. Sanford had considered it so important that he had taken Uruk to his own *tailor* and paid for it. Uruk had gone along for the sake of their alliance.

Owning it did not mean wearing it, though.

The man listened better than most humans, which meant that Uruk needed repeat himself only twenty or thirty times. "It is dark. He cannot admire *cut* or *fit* in this cold."

"He would see that you wore an overcoat," Sanford said. "It would be enough."

"It is at home." Reginald the tailor said he had spent more time on that suit than anything else he had sewn. The texture of a man's suit repelled Uruk, so the tailor had unearthed a scratchy wool much more suitable than the delicate horrors men liked. Reginald had cut and sewn over three visits so that the suit even moved like an orc, bending with his hips and shoulders and knees. Uruk had been forced to admit that Reginald had done the impossible, sewn an orcish suit.

Except suits were un-orcish.

Uruk had taken one long look at the thing, stuffed it back in its bag, and crammed the whole thing in the corner behind Grandpa's chair.

"I had a second suit made," Sanford said. "It's in the box in the back of the truck. You could —"

Uruk's indignation swelled. "I said that I would wear it when I *needed* it."

"I *need* us to make as much money as we can," Sanford said.

How much more could they need? In five weeks, the clan had made almost two thousand dollars bootlegging. Uruk had pried up a second and then a third floorboard to make enough space to hide their share. Sanford might be correct, but not in a way that mattered. The suit might make him need to pry up a fourth board before the end of the week, but Uruk would rather be a proper orc.

Uruk did not know how to explain any of that to Sanford. The man's need for money had brought the paper man to Uruk, the clan's need for money kept Uruk with Sanford, and now money and marrow feud with the elves bound them together. Even if Uruk wanted to abandon the war, the elves had killed another clan of Tai for bootlegging. Uruk and his brothers had retaliated by hijacking a truckload of mirovar, the elvish holy wine, and exchanged it for the orcish draught taken by the elves. That might seem even, but in that fight Uruk and his brothers had captured an elf-enchanted Tommy gun and used it to kill an elven wizard.

Elves survived for centuries, pallid lives without color or joy or rage. But they treasured all their pointless years. They would balance the death of one elf with thousands of orcish corpses.

The clan *needed* this stone-headed man.

Perhaps his brother Tara could squeeze the idea into Sanford's head. Tara was almost un-orcishly pensive, but Uruk had learned to trust his thoughts.

Night-sight showed a sudden rectangular glimmer of warmth in the speakeasy's wall. "The door is opening."

"About time," Sanford grumbled. "Making us wait is a silly power game."

Silly power game? All games were silly, but how could you play games with power? Light bulbs shone when you flipped the switch, but no light had come from the speakeasy. Only humans would taunt power.

Three men shuffled forward, barely visible even in night-sight. Their heavy, long coats held warmth almost as well as Sanford's. Maybe Uruk should take some of the money and find someone to make a proper orcish coat.

No, a foolish distraction.

Consider a new coat tomorrow.

The man in front was built almost like an orc. Broad shoulders, a heavy waist, the biggest hands of any man Uruk had ever seen. He had hair on his head, though, and that silly little wart that humans called a nose. His face shone in night-sight, and when he smiled his teeth gleamed. "Mr. Smith! How delightful to see you!"

Sanford had explained the brain-numbing idea of a false name more than once. Uruk understood that the police couldn't easily find you if they didn't have your real name, but how could you build a reputation if *nobody* knew your real name? Orcs lived under constant threat from the police. Bootlegging was no different. A false name was only for the police, and then only to protect the clan.

Sanford seemed content that *Smith* carry any reputation he earned. "Jake! A pleasure as always." Happy words and bared teeth, the start of every human respect chant. "Permit me to introduce my partner —" he coughed "—Urka-Tai."

So much wrong there. To orcs, *my* was a powerful word. It meant that you would fight to the death for what you claimed. Humans spread *my* like manure in a cattle pen. Sanford claiming to fight for Uruk was like a child fighting the great cannon of President Commander Coolidge's Navy. The man would be swept aside.

And then, Uruk's name. Sanford had struggled to improve his pronunciation, but failed every time. A human throat could not form orcish names. Sanford's greatest efforts could only fail, so Uruk bared only his Lesser Tusks. "Uruk-Tai."

"So it's true," Jake said. "You work with orcs."

"Steady partners," Sanford said. "Completely trustworthy."

Jake rubbed his chin, meeting Uruk's gaze. "And you're with this Thigh clan?"

Sanford opened his mouth to answer, but Uruk cut him off. "Tai." The paper man's pronunciation of the clan name was less awful than how he pronounced Uruk, but cut through by December's breath, one night before the Greatest Dark, the clan's name must be declared correctly.

"I see." Still rubbing his chin, Jake began nodding. "See, that's my worry."

The man was right to worry. Uruk could crush his skull with a slap. He would spend the rest of his life in prison if he killed a human, but Jake would still be dead.

"My orcish partner is our strength," Sanford said. "With him, we have no need to water booze. Every bottle is top-notch Canadian Club, straight from Windsor."

"What about the stories?" Jake said.

Humans always told stories about orcs, so they could justify ignoring them.

"What stories?" Sanford said.

"Up in Mount Clemens," Jake said.

"We don't serve that far yet," Sanford said. "Next year, I'm sure."

"Some folks up there bought hooch from a Thigh orc." The man was not even trying to pronounce Tai correctly. Anger at the insult bubbled in Uruk's gut, but before he could speak Jake said, "It was poisoned. Killed every one of 'em."

 2

December. The night before the Greatest Dark.

The longest night of the year was for settling disputes and ending feuds. Violate an agreement forged in the Greatest Dark and December herself would declare marrow feud on you—and persuade January to join in. No orc could stand against that. Actively feuding with another orc clan during the Greatest Dark was not merely a war. December would not allow those feuds to end until all sides joined the frozen dead.

Jake's lie demanded nothing less.

Uruk tasted blood pounding in his throat and his hands instinctively straightened to use his talons. A torrent of righteous rage at the unfair accusation dissolved the cold in his limbs and sharpened his vision.

The parking lot was suitable for a massacre.

The brick stores on either side were dark, as was the speakeasy in the back. The man Jake would have no way to escape except back into the speakeasy, and if he fled Uruk could run him down easily. Uruk's boots would have greater traction on the tamped-down snow and ice than any shoes Jake could be wearing. His talons might be trimmed, but slaughterhouses hired orcs to kill cattle with a punch between the eyes. Humans would die the same. The truck filled the narrow driveway, its canvas-tented bed obscuring the view from the road. This time of night, the road was empty. If anyone glanced into the parking lot as they passed, December's fluffy snowfall would haze the scene.

Uruk bared all his tusks. "The Tai are not poisoners!"

"Just saying what I heard." The man spoke with that wheedling tone that humans used when they wanted to declare innocence even though they knew they were guilty. That might work with other men, but orcs knew better.

"Where did you hear this?" Sanford's tone held as much iron as Uruk had ever heard from the paper man. Good. Sanford might not consider Uruk a true partner, not in the pit of his heart, but the man hadn't missed the implied insult.

"One of the drivers last night." Jake seemed perfectly relaxed, as if he hadn't just stood in full view of December and offered mortal insult. "Then a couple guys from the stockyards said it."

"This is unacceptable," Sanford said. "We provide a top-quality, unadulterated product." His gaze flickered at Uruk. "We need the names of those people."

"I ain't squealing out my customers," Jake said.

"They are liars," Uruk said. Only humans would need to be told that.

"They have impugned our reputation," Sanford said. "I'm not going to turn them over to the police, but I—*we* must know who is slandering us."

"So you can set your orc on them?" Jake sneered.

"If they're human, a lawsuit for slander should settle the issue." He held a hand towards Uruk. "In the unlikely event that an orc is responsible, my associate would handle the matter appropriately."

Uruk said, "No orc would do this." Poisoning was un-orcish. No clan would feud to defend a poisoner. An orc's own clan, no matter how widely scattered, would gather together to capture the poisoner and present him to the victim's clan.

"We will solve this," Sanford said. "In the meantime, shall we conclude our business?"

Jake scratched his ear. "See, you're pretty steep. What with these rumors, I don't know that I want to pay your prices for what might be no good."

December or not, Uruk burned to slash this Jake's face. His mouth had opened to reveal his Greater Tusks, and he had no urge to hide them again. One more insult and he would need them. "Do you *seek* feud with the Tai clan, man?"

"For tonight," Sanford said, "this is easily settled. Look in the truck. Pick one bottle, any bottle."

Jake studied Sanford, glanced at Uruk, and nodded. "All right."

"Not one right in the back," Sanford said. "Something random, from the middle."

Night-sight made it easy to watch as the man hopped up into the truck bed. His hands fumbled over the open-top boxes, finally pulling out a fifth. His other hand reached for a second bottle, as if he thought the darkness concealed his perfidy.

Uruk gave a tiny growl.

The man hurriedly let go of the second bottle and climbed back out.

"Thank you," Sanford said. How could the paper man be grateful to someone who had insulted them so badly, who even tried to rob them? "You see it's full, don't you? Give it to me, if you please."

Sanford deftly broke the seal and raised the bottle as if to toast. "To successful business dealings." Without a pause he put the bottle to his lips and swigged a shot. The feeble whiskey made him cough, adding a brief sharpness to the air before December blew it away. Paper men couldn't handle even feeble human liquor.

"You ain't a whiskey man, are you?" Jake said.

"I enjoy a shot," Sanford said. "Barkeeps rarely let me go straight from the bottle, though." He held the bottle out to Uruk. "Would you care to finish this?"

Uruk snatched the bottle and tipped it back, pouring it straight down his throat. It had a pleasant burn, like the embers of last night's fire. Maybe it would thaw his legs.

"Clearly," Sanford said, "we would not indulge if we were not absolutely certain of the quality of our product. Perhaps now we can proceed?"

A few drops remained in the bottom. Uruk thrust the bottle at Jake, daring the man to challenge him again.

Jake took the bottle and sniffed, eyebrows raising. The dregs would be a good shot for a human, but the man wouldn't drink after Uruk. Then again, Sanford had been certain to get the first drink as well. Men would rather waste precious liquor than share a bottle with an orc.

Jake lowered the bottle. "Yeah. All right."

The man did not know enough to even offer reparations for his words? After those lies, he expected Uruk to sell him liquor?

"Have your men carry the crates inside," Sanford said, "and you and I will settle up."

"Get your orc to carry them," Jake said.

The thought of prison didn't stop Uruk's hands from trembling with rage. He held himself to another low growl.

"He is not my *orc*," Sanford said. "He is my *partner*, and your accusation insulted him and his clan. I don't think he's in the mood to help your men carry your whiskey."

Sanford understood. A little. Good.

"Maybe if you apologized," Sanford said.

December would bring apples before a man apologized to an orc. Uruk let a little more of his Greater Tusks show.

Jake scowled. "Get them, George."

"So let's settle up before we freeze," Sanford said.

The other two men began hauling whiskey crates, while Jake pulled a money clip from his pocket. "As agreed—minus the bottle you drank, of course."

Uruk let his growl grow louder.

Jake glanced at Uruk, but this time shrank a little.

"We drank that bottle at your insistence," Sanford said. "You don't think I habitually drink while conducting business, do you? I had hoped to share a shot around afterwards to celebrate, but the mood has left us." He held out a hand. "The full agreed-upon amount."

Jake scowled and added another bill.

Uruk grunted.

"Thank you, sir," Sanford said. "I trust that you will tell your friends how we provided top-quality whiskey, with no hint of impurities, and how we stood by every detail of our arrangement." His voice lost its cheer. "Every. Detail."

"George!" Jake said. "I'm not paying you to dawdle. Get on with it."

Uruk could contain himself no more. "Who told those lies?"

"Told you," Jake said. "I'm not ratting out my customers."

"I will be making inquiries," Sanford said. "If this rumor has roots, I will find them. If it turns out there is no rumor beyond your establishment, we will return to discuss the matter." He offered Jake a broad human smile. "Or, at least—my partner will."

Even in night-sight, Jake's face grew pale.

Good.

He couldn't have the man's blood. Uruk would have to be satisfied with the man's fear.

The truck cab stank of years of garlic and cabbage and putrid human sweat. To close the door Uruk had to squeeze his knees high against the dashboard and crank his neck to the side, then pull his shoulders in to give Sanford space to work the gearshift. Glass all around held December's icy breath at bay, but the tiny carriage heater couldn't keep frost and fog from the windows. The seat was too short, the ancient straw padding crushed beneath his bulk.

Uruk had modified the clan's beat-up Model T to fit an orc, but bootleggers needed a truck.

Every time Uruk and Sanford delivered whiskey or draught, the truck reminded him that America was not built for orcs. Nobody would ever build a truck meant to be driven by an orc. Orcs had to squeeze themselves down to fit. The only things built to orc scale were the guns.

Sanford had borrowed this truck many times from Lord Dodge, and Uruk had learned to fit in it.

He would have preferred to ride in the back of the truck, where wind whistled between gaps in the canvas and road slush splashed up between working floorboards. He could straighten his legs there, and sit up straight. A partner would ride in the cab, however. The carriage heater's meager warmth didn't make up for being squeezed until every breath cramped, but if Uruk did not behave as a partner Sanford might forget that he was one.

Large fluffy snowflakes swirled around the windows, sometimes striking the glass and holding their form for a heartbeat before dissolving and sliding down to join the slush at the base of the window. Uruk's night-sight showed steam pluming from the hood, where flakes fought the powerful engine and lost.

Individual flakes might be lost, but if December chose she could smother the truck as she did the rest of the world. For now, though, Uruk had a solid roof between him and December.

Sanford settled into the driver's seat. The cabbage smell grew stronger. Had the paper man been eating that disgusting vegetable for dinner? Bootlegging had brought Sanford as much wealth as it had brought the clan. He could afford decent porridge or pig or even cow. With a man's puny appetite, he could afford to eat sweet cow muscle and nothing else for every meal. Why would a man make himself suffer by eating vegetables?

The paper man's food was not Uruk's concern.

Even if his diet made the truck stink like a stockyard.

Sanford drew and let out a deep breath. Maybe men enjoyed that smell? "That man lied," Uruk said.

Sanford put the truck in gear. "A man lied. Either Jake thought that he could squeeze our price down, or someone is spreading rumors about us."

"We will not sell to him again," Uruk said.

Sanford hesitated. Was he concentrating on getting the balky truck up to speed, or was he deciding to argue with Uruk? Uruk did not have the patience to be dismissed by his "partner" tonight. Not after Jake's torrent of insults. Sanford shifted the truck into second gear and said, "Very well. Our customers need to know that if they insult you, we won't deal with them."

Good.

"I'm more concerned about this rumor, though," Sanford said.

"No Tai orc would poison whiskey," Uruk said.

"I believe you," Sanford said. "You have always been honest with me. And we provide quality whiskey."

Uruk grunted.

Sanford said, "We're starting to get a reputation for being able to deliver, and for straight dealing. Our competitors might start rumors to knock us down. I'll check the papers for any stories about poisoned hooch. A reporter wouldn't be able to resist that kind of story, especially with a nonhuman angle."

Nonhuman? Elves got whatever they wanted. Dwarves brewed their own drink in their halls, where the ceilings were so short that a human would have to crawl and orcs could only dream of invading. Did Sanford believe the legends of hobble-folk? No, he must be obeying some human strangeness that Uruk couldn't care about. "We agreed to talk before and after every war. Find the liar and we will talk."

"Our best defense against rumor is quality product, delivered on time, at a fair price." Sanford's face tightened. "Those who buy from us come back for more. That's what makes a business successful."

Human babble. They loved their words. He and Sanford had agreed weeks ago how they would bootleg. After weeks of these nightly wars, Uruk did not believe that Sanford spoke to change how they worked. He spoke to remind himself, to strengthen their agreement in his own mind.

Uruk grunted. He had to tolerate human weakness for the good of the clan.

After a moment of silence, Sanford said, "We do need to discuss the future."

For all of the man's claims of partnership, Uruk had been expecting this. "You wish to end our alliance." Even if a human had to work with orcs, he wouldn't want to for long.

"No!" Sanford took his hand off the gearshift to swipe fog from the inside of the windshield. "No, our alliance works well. I place the orders and work with the buyers. Your clan brings the whiskey over. We deliver it together. If anything, it's working too well."

Only a human could think that a war went too well. "We will find places to hide the money."

"That's not —" Sanford took a deep breath. "I borrowed this truck from Mr. Dodge. We use my brother's boat to cross the river. It's time for us to get our own truck, and our own boat."

"Your own brother will not share his boat?" Uruk might fight with his brothers to maintain leadership of the clan, or to slap foolishness out of one, but any Tai would offer all he had to support the clan. Was Sanford feuding with his own brother? Perhaps Uruk should reconsider this alliance—no, most ink-weakened paper men would not deal with Uruk. The clan still needed Sanford.

"It's about risk," Sanford said. "What do you know about the law?"

"If a police says that an orc has broken the law, that orc goes to prison."

Sanford was silent for a moment. "I'm sure that's how it looks to you. If the police catch us bootlegging in my brother's boat, though, then a judge will send my brother to prison."

The clan reaped the rewards, and the clan shared the risks. That was proper.

Sanford said, "If they stop this truck while we have whiskey in the back, then Mr. Dodge will have trouble."

Ah. Sanford served Lord Dodge, and Sanford was performing extra labor. Your labor could not endanger your lord. "You must separate from Lord Dodge or end these wars."

"I've already turned in my notice to Mister Dodge. Celebrimble will not forget that I defended Mister Dodge from his takeover," Sanford said. "And I'm sure he remembered that your shaman broke the curse he put on my wife."

Detroit's elven lord forgot nothing and forgave less. "You broke it," Uruk growled. "Even a paper man must claim his victories."

Sanford drew a deep breath through his nose. "All right. *I* broke it—but your shaman showed me it was there, showed me the way. I must have money to defend my family. The more successful we are, the more we bootleg, the easier it will be for Celebrimble to catch us."

Uruk hadn't expected Sanford to think of that. He grunted.

"We must... The bootlegging wars must continue. We need equipment to bootleg. We need a truck and a boat. With that, we can bring enough whiskey over that we'll need a place to store it. And perhaps a second truck. If we were to grow larger, how many orcs could you hire? Orcs that you, personally, trust?"

The greater Tai clan had members crammed into tenements across the city. They all had honorable work, mostly as laborers down in the Port of Detroit. How could he lure them away from such work?

Uruk blinked.

The clan had so much money, he didn't know where to hide it.

The best place to hide a clan's treasure was in other parts of the clan.

The thought felt uncomfortable. Orc clans shared treasures taken in wars, though, and what was bootlegging but a war without cannons? Uruk could pay orcs twice what they made as laborers, and still afford the wool for his woman to make himself and all his brothers fine new coats.

"Twenty," he said slowly. Probably more.

Did Sanford relax? "Good. That's one problem we won't have. Tell me, have you ever heard of a *corporation*?"

Another foolish human word. "No."

"A corporation is a kind of business," Sanford said. "It can take in money and own property, and it's owned by people. All the big businesses you see? They're all corporations."

Not even humans could be that stupid. "This is a paper man thing."

Sanford laughed. He had started to learn when someone insulted Uruk, but he still ignored insult to himself. "I do—*did*—corporate law for Mister Dodge. Corporations are why humans have lawyers. There were other reasons, but corporations are how we organize money."

Humans could do anything they wanted with their money. Uruk was going to spend some of his on wool for new coats. He grunted.

Sanford said, "And it's how the United States government organizes money. Once you start to make a lot of money, the government pays attention to you. If they don't like the way you have your money organized, they take your money and put you in prison."

Uruk was so surprised that he coughed out an orcish curse before catching himself. How could someone with that much money go to prison? Was Sanford lying? No, he needed the clan. Their first war together had proven that to Sanford. The man might be wrong about the suit, but his skills had kept President Commander Coolidge's Department of Treasury from dragging him and Uruk's clan to prison. Lord Dodge would not employ Sanford unless he was a competent paper man. Uruk's brain still struggled with the idea. Eventually he said, "Money is power. How can humans with power go to prison?"

"Money *is* power," Sanford said. "Money is power, and the government wants power. Once you have enough money, you have to give a piece of it to the government. You need to organize your money to make it easy for them to claim that piece."

Would they come into the tenement and pry up floorboards? "We could bury it."

"People have tried, but the government is very good at finding buried money." Was Sanford hiding a laugh? "One of the things they look for is when you buy something. If we buy a truck and a boat and start paying a bunch of orcs and a few men, they will come to us and want their share."

Weaker clans within a greater clan often gave small gifts to stronger families. Stronger families protected those families, especially when they faded out and only the aged remained. But *demanding* such gifts was un-orcish. Every orc knew what they owned and who was strong.

A clan was only a tiny piece of America, though.

And humans could lie. Elves could lie and make humans like it. The lifeless elven perfection made men and dwarves treat them like they were special, when orcs could see that elves persisted rather than lived.

"It's called *taxes*," Sanford said. "People with money pay the government, and the government builds roads and pays policeman and teachers."

"Stupid," Uruk said.

"Many men would agree," Sanford said. "You and I, we can't change it. We need to work with it. That means we need to organize our money so that the government thinks we're legitimate. Nobody must notice us."

Nobody, meaning men. Every orc in the tenement would notice each of the Tai brothers in their new coats. It still sounded like a trick, though. Uruk needed to be alert. Humans were arrogant, and did not hesitate to rob orcs. "How is this done?"

Sanford said, "We form a corporation, owned equally by you and I. The corporation owns our truck and our boat, and it will pay the rent on whatever storage space we need. It will hire everyone we need. Any money it needs, you and I put in equally."

Only humans could come up with such a ridiculous system. "This *cor-por-a-tion*." The name was equally ridiculous. "How do we *form* it?"

"I file a paper with the government. The owners—you and I—both sign it."

The paper man wanted Uruk to sign paper. Predictable.

"It says who we are and what we do," Sanford said.

Sanford knew law, but he knew nothing of war. "You would tell the government that we are *bootleggers*?"

"Of course not!" Sanford said. "We will tell them that we are in transportation services. During the day, we hire a man and an orc to deliver cargo around Detroit. It all looks perfectly legal. After hours, we use the truck for real business."

Uruk said, "Complicated plans fail."

"I would not suggest this if we didn't need it," Sanford said. "The government makes a lot of noise about bootlegging, but very little attention. They pay a lot of attention to money. Not paying taxes will put us both in prison. If I knew a less complicated way to do it, I would. In the last month, I've made more money bootlegging than Mister Dodge paid me in a year. I'm not sure how much you make working at the docks, but I would wager that your family are some of the best-paid orcs in Detroit."

Uruk grunted.

"I don't know what you've done with all that cash," Sanford said. "It's not my business."

It wasn't.

"I'm sure you hid it somewhere. Probably still in cash."

Sanford knew he was being rude, and he kept *doing* it? Uruk let his Lesser Tusks creep out and gave a tiny growl.

Sanford raised a hand. "I don't want to know. I don't even want to guess. I just want you to think about a question. Don't answer me, just think about it. If we keep making this much money—or if we start making a lot more money? Think about how big that pile will be."

Three floorboards a month. That would be six by the end of January, and nine by the end of February. How many floorboards were in his family's apartment? In all the apartments of all his brothers?

Sanford said, "We will be known as bootleggers. People, men and orcs, and probably elves and dwarves too, they will all know we have money. We are doing this for our families. Once it's known that we are successful, criminals—human criminals—will try to rob us. It's going to happen. I don't know about orcs. Would one orc clan steal money from another?"

Uruk expected raids, one day. Orc clans would raid one another on any excuse. Uruk tried to imagine having so much money that it wouldn't fit under the floorboards. Stacks of bills everywhere in the apartment. Grandpa sleeping on a pile of dollar bills and sawbucks. "Yes." The word tasted bitter.

His clan could not stand against every other family, every other clan in the tenement. If the pile grew that large, they might have to.

How could Uruk even be thinking about having that kind of money? What orcs could have labor that brought such riches? Even imagining it was un-orcish.

If December could see him now, she would freeze his marrow in a breath.

"A corporation will let us hide our money in ways that cannot be robbed from us," Sanford said. "We will have to pay a small amount to the Feds every year, but the money will be safe and we won't have rivals attacking us for it. When the time comes, the corporation can even buy new homes for us."

"Buy a home?" An orc family with their own home? Families from several orc clans always lived together in a single cavern, usually a tenement here in America. A home like Sanford's, but only for Uruk, his brothers, and their wives and children? It was harder to imagine than Grandpa's old armchair heaped in dollar bills.

Sanford babbled on, ignorant of the pressure in Uruk's head. "It seems like you treat your brothers well, for orcs. You'd probably want to buy a home for each of their families as well."

Impossible. How could any orc live that way? Uruk could never walk under open sky again.

Sanford seemed to notice Uruk's silence. "The corporation can spend money for us, reducing the amount of taxes we have to pay. It is in the interest of the corporation that the owners spend their time running the corporation rather than maintaining homes, so the corporation will buy them housing. It is in the interest of the corporation that the owners have reliable transportation, so the corporation will buy them new cars. Those words, *it is in the interest of the corporation*, are magic."

Uruk's befuddled brain grabbed hold of that word. *Magic.* This was paper man magic. He had to decide if he would trust it, or not.

Every orc knew that gods never gave, only took.

The corporation didn't matter.

Could human magic stand against orcish gods?

Perhaps for humans. Never for an orc.

But Uruk needed to protect the clan from all threats, including humans. "I will think on this."

"Good." Sanford eased the truck onto Gratiot. "And I will investigate these rumors."

Sanford held silent until the truck reached Uruk's Hamtramck tenement, where he pulled to the side of the road and dropped the transmission out of gear. With practiced fingers, he counted out the liar's money and handed Uruk his share. "Not tomorrow, but the night after."

Uruk grunted and swung his door open. "Yes." He shut the door gently, to not break the fragile glass, and turned away before Sanford even put the truck back in gear. The sky was bleeding pink as the sun approached dawn, but December's wind still burned through Uruk. Sleep would be good. Uruk missed sleeping next to his woman, but the war demanded it. His Vara would have warm water for him to drink and wash with. He would eat his dinner as Vara and their sons broke their fast, then he could climb beneath the ragged warm blankets and sleep past noon.

And tomorrow night, his family and his brothers would thank December for the Greatest Dark. Uruk would remind himself of why he fought this war.

He opened the tenement door, and the snarls and shrieks of orcs about to fight flooded out.

 4

Mha spasmed awake like she'd been stabbed.

The old groom's quarters were both cramped and cavernous. If she hauled the bed frame with its taut canvas mattress and the rusty coal stove and the two heavy oak stumps, the one she sat on and the one nobody would ever sit on again, hauled everything out into the rest of the neglected horse barn, she could cross the room in four steps. Thirty years ago it would have been three, but age had shrunken her stride just as it had shriveled her spine and stolen her strength. Mha barely fit between all that furniture. Cramped.

Cavernous, because a second orc should share that space with her.

That orc was not gone. She had sacrificed *that* orc's name with his death offerings, and would never even think it again. His final gifts remained, though. She had a fine new leather tunic that reached to her ankles, its smoothness lined by every scar *that* orc lived with. With another couple hours of work, she would have the most solid boots she had ever owned. Her feet would be warm and comfortable for the rest of her life. Once she had the boots she would meld his thigh bones into a staff, locking them end-to-end the way her long-dead mother had taught her. If Mha went out through the barn and into the sturdy closet she claimed as a pantry, she would find curing ham on shelves and fresh sausage dangling from the ceiling. Enough that she could have a bite of meat every day for the rest of her life.

That life might last too long.

Mha had no children to eat her. Her son Kha had been crushed by a falling crane at the Port of Detroit, and Nork had died in the Great War. Her daughters had all been claimed by other clans. Mha and *that* orc had defended them well, forcing their would-be husbands to prove they could protect their wives against all threats.

Her warrior's family, dead years before.

None of her daughters would recognize her now. She would not shame them, or herself, by seeking them out.

The gods would keep her alive for a long time, every day her muscles weaker than the day before. Because they could.

A lifetime ago, during the Spanish-American War, she and *that* orc had saved Lieutenant Harrison's life. When they had lost everything, Lieutenant Harrison had given them a place to live. *That* orc was dead. Lieutenant Harrison was dead. Only Mha and Harrison's woman Thorn remained.

Mha had no labor but helping Thorn.

The help Thorn wanted?

Drinking *tea*.

Eating *cookies*.

Listening as Thorn shared the senseless saga of her life, and offering her own sagas in return. Mha doubted Thorn understood her sagas any better than Mha understood Thorn's, but speaking her saga to someone, even a human, gave Mha a sense that her life had had worth, nonsensical as that was. It gave her a chance to go over the decades of her life. She had so much more past than she had future, and the past had been so much better, that living there felt comfortable.

Mha needed a saga for today. A short one, so she could return to the barn and finish her boots. Perhaps the Yam Skull Battle? That had been hilarious, especially the bit where the giant python had caught a man-soldier in its coils and *that* orc had tried to pry the snake off with a crowbar and had dislocated the soldier's jaw instead and the snake had thrashed about so hard that everyone got knocked off the boat and into the swamp. Thorn would laugh at all the wrong places, but savoring the memory would thaw Mha's heart.

No, not the Yam Skull. On the shortest day before the Longest Night, Mha needed a saga to remind herself of her clan's strength. Perhaps Vara's marriage war. Vara had been her youngest daughter, and the last one taken. Mha had demanded more of her suitor than any other, relenting only after knocking the foolish young Tai down the stairs five times in five different ways.

Mha had known the shape of her own fate then. She and *that* orc would age together. One would die first. The other would die alone.

Mha could have slashed Uruk-Tai's throat instead. A declaration that none would take her daughter. Some orcs claimed their youngest child that way, so that they would have company in their old age. Mha and *that* orc had placed their Vara's life above their own.

Mha gladly paid for that decision, every single day.

Wishing she could know that her daughters were well wasn't a hope. A hope was something that might happen. But knowing they were well would ease one strangling knot around her heart.

The coal stove still radiated enough warmth that Mha couldn't see her breath, even as outside Sun-Eater December's breath solved all orc problems. The walls of her room were snug, especially where *that* orc had nailed scrap lumber over the cracks and stuffed greasy rags as old as Mha into popped-out knotholes. *That* orc had done everything he could to make the room the most comfortable orcs could hope for. The dusty smell of coal ash mingled with the sharper scents of curing meat and old rust.

What had wakened her?

Not an attack. She would never forget the Spanish-American War, but war had forgotten her.

Not an intruder. The only sounds were December's wind and her own rickety heart.

Mha blinked. Feeble gray light seeped through the narrow horizontal window up near the ceiling, declaring dawn of the shortest day. Up on the shelf beneath the window, four hollow skulls looked down on her. Three were yellowed from decades out in the light, the tusks fragile and cheekbones chipped by the pinky-thick steel chain run through them. The fourth gleamed white, meticulously cleaned less than a month ago. She had spent hours on that fourth skull, treating it more respectfully and tenderly than she did her own hide. Three rejected suitors and *that* orc, all witness to her pathetic end.

It wasn't bad enough that her crumbling body demanded naps during the day, or that she plunged into sleep after dinner. Sleep wasn't bad. It wasn't death, but it was better than sitting behind the barn watching the wind swirl snow through the branches hour after hour. It wasn't bad enough that an orc should be surrounded by her clan on the shortest day, watching them argue and struggle and tussle and exchange tributes before the Greatest Dark claimed them all.

She had *overslept*.

Instinct wanted to fling her to her feet, but if she moved too quickly that bad hip would give out on her again. She eased herself out of bed to gently stretch sleep-tightened muscles. Movement would loosen her joints, but instead of the Army's morning jerks she would walk and dress and cross the yard to the farmhouse.

Her tongue tasted like earthworms.

The good part of tea: it washed the night off her teeth.

At least she had the comfort of her treasured new tunic. She had finished sewing it yesterday, and it had come out well. Before tanning, the hide had undergone decades of beating and cutting and scarring, leaving the leather intricately mottled. Mha knew the scars in that leather as well as she knew the wart on the back of her left thumb, and she loved them more than her wart or her thumb. Perhaps today, she could finish the boots.

Not unless she caught up, though.

She had pridefully demanded labor. The gods had given her work worthy of a worn-out, broken-down, age-crippled ruin of an orcess.

Mha dressed carefully, tying her aching feet into her worn-out boots that the Army had released her in all those decades ago. The cardboard-lined ruins had to last only one more day. Today she would finish the new boots. *That* orc's gift would protect her feet for the rest of her life. Her shawl, stiff with three layers of burlap, would keep the snow out of her collar and hide the shameful *hair* from December.

Perhaps Thorn was not yet awake. Oversleeping had already shamed Mha before December. To have a decaying human woman claim Mha's only labor and make her own *tea* would be a greater shame than she had known her entire life.

Her aching hip put a lurch in her step as she tromped through the drafty barn and ached as she ground the old carriage door open against fresh snowfall. The rising Sun gleamed through bare-trunked trees, giving the shin-deep drifts glitter and sheen. Untouched snow covered the thirty feet to the farmhouse's back door. December Sun-Eater's breath had taken away the path Mha had trudged through yesterday, just as she would claim this day's path tonight. A few scattered snowflakes still drifted down, but the thinning clouds declared that December had finished her storm. Dark smoke rose from the farmhouse's crumbling chimney, torn to tatters by the breeze.

Mha had failed.

Thorn was awake.

The Sun gleamed off a dark shape by the farmhouse. A car. A big four-door one, not the tiny thing Thorn's nephew drove when he came out to insult his elder. The delivery man drove a truck. That car did not belong here, with abandoned dying women who had nobody to eat them.

Movement past the farmhouse caught her eye. She lifted a hand to shield her old eyes from the Sun's fierce light, surrendering their warmth to December so she could get a better look.

Three humans, out by the road. Two poked in the snowy ditch with sticks. The third stood at the back of another car, rummaging through the open trunk.

A tiny flame of hope flickered in her heart.

Mha watched for a breath, until she could be certain that she recognized the uniforms.

She turned back into the barn, moving as quickly as she could to collect her skulls and fasten their chain around her bony hips. Ancient habits guided her as she deftly bit her right thumb at the base of the talon. Even her blood looked weak. She couldn't smell it. Had her blood failed, or her nose? No, no time. She smeared the pads of her thumbs and marked the oldest skull, snarling a charm that had been ancient when her grandmother's grandmother had used it. "Mine." The skulls were hers. She would fight for them. The suitors she had rejected in her youth, and *that* orc.

Humans would not understand her skulls, but an orcess needed them to face the police.

5

Uruk charged up the tenement's claustrophobic stairs.

Humans, generations ago, had built the tenement for their comfort. The stairwell had been plastered, but young orcs had carved them down to the bare lath. Holes every few feet showed where women had punched gaps to reach long-harvested bounties of rats within. The stinks of dust and mold and slow-decaying hardwood filled Uruk's nose. The balls of Uruk's feet barely fit on the narrow plank treads, and the rise was so shallow that Uruk normally skipped every other step. The snarls and shrieks from upstairs dragged him so fiercely that he almost slipped trying to take three at a time.

At the second floor, the Don women had gathered in the hall to peer up the stairs. Their clan was young, the oldest child still clutching his mother's leg and just losing his soft birth talons. Mothers bared their Lesser Tusks as he passed, warning Uruk to keep moving. The Don brothers must have a lot of work if Uruk could smell warm lard from the stairwell.

The shouting overhead grew fiercer. Had someone dared declare a feud on the shortest day? Who would be such a fool as to brawl right before the Greatest Dark?

A lone voice punched through the chaos. "Tai!"

His brother, Kaba.

Uruk's blood heated. Had Daka done something extra stupid and compelled Kaba to correct him? No, too many throats fed the noise for it to be purely within the clan. If Daka had returned from last night's run across the river and immediately started a feud, Uruk was going to break his ribs one at a time until he learned to behave properly. Or had Daka been so thoughtless that Uruk must let another clan beat him? If Daka had shamed the clan, Uruk would add broken ribs to whatever beating his brother had earned.

An answering shriek echoed down the stairs. "Norkosh!"

The four Norkosh brothers lived on the sixth floor. Had one of them trespassed onto the Tai's fifth? Uruk climbed as fast as he dared, cursing the clumsy human stairs the whole way. At the next landing, he snatched the brass knuckles from his pocket and shoved them on. The one-inch spikes were no replacement for proper orcish talons, but far better than the filed-off stubs American orcs endured.

He rounded the last turn of the stairs to see Kaba filling the fifth-floor landing, Daka at his back. Uruk glimpsed orcs facing Kaba on the stairs further up. The oldest Norkosh brother stood only a few stairs up the landing, just far enough up that Kaba's long arms couldn't claw him. The Norkosh had one hand on the wall for balance, but the fingers of his other hand were extended, the natural position for an orc ready to slash with his talons, and all his tusks fully exposed. Uruk glimpsed more orcs behind him.

On this shortest day, the Norkosh were ready for war.

Kaba filled the landing, so Uruk had to stop a few steps short. "Kaba! Who chants for war?"

Kaba did not turn from the Norkosh. "The Norkosh think they can come for us."

"Tai blood!" a Norkosh further up the stairs screeched. "Tai blood! Tai blood!"

Sanford had predicted jealous raids. Uruk had not expected them so soon, and especially not on the shortest day.

Uruk shoved Kaba aside. The leading Norkosh made to leap into the space on the landing, but Uruk squeezed in first. "My clan! Mine! If you declare war, you do it to me!"

The stairs and halls were too narrow for orcs to fight side-by-side, and the narrow treads made balance precarious. If Uruk and Kaba could hold the landing, they might have an advantage as single Norkosh came down. If not, one orc would fight one orc, each exhausted victor facing a fresh enemy in a brutal chain of brawls. Norkosh were a few inches shorter than Tai, but just as strong. Four Norkosh against Uruk and two of his brothers? Even victory would cost. For a heartbeat Uruk regretted allowing Tara to take a home closer to his work, but he shoved the unworthy thought aside and glared into the leading Norkosh's eyes.

It wasn't a random angry Norkosh leading the attack—Kuru-Norkosh commanded the seventh floor, Uruk's peer. He stank of rage, his purple-green skin flushed with hot blood. "War? You do not deserve war! We will wash the walls with your blood!"

Behind Uruk, a woman hissed. His Vara must be back there, and Daka's woman Kovo as well. Their fine boys were at school. If they returned to find fresh blood soaking the floorboards, they would be deeply disappointed to have missed the war. If the Norkosh wiped out the Tai, Uruk had to be sure to leave Norkosh corpses amidst their own so his boys would know who to avenge them on. Uruk raised his hands, displaying the brass knuckles. The spikes glittered in the light seeping through the narrow, filthy window. "Declare your cause, and the Tai will answer you." Let Norkosh say aloud that he was jealous, that he would declare a feud over another clan's prosperity. December would not care who started the war, but the Sun would remember Norkosh greed forever.

"My brother's daughter should be an adult today," Norkosh snarled. "Your draught poisoned her!"

6

Mha let herself in the farmhouse's back door, exactly as instructed.

Despite the late hour, the teakettle sat on its shelf. Light poured through the windows, highlighting the lacy panels Thorn had draped over them. The useless lace didn't stop the light, but did make it impossible to see the yard. An enemy could walk unobserved right up to the kitchen window. The pan and the skillet hung on their hooks, the stockpot gleamed beneath the hard-used wooden table. The unscratched metal sink shone, and the stink of the dried leaves dangled from hooks on the wall.

But every morning, Thorn brushed up against them saying *don't they smell lovely* when Mha needed no reminder of their revolting stench. They didn't stink so bad today. The drinking water bucket Mha had filled last night was untouched.

Thorn had not performed Mha's labor.

But even in Mha's weak eyes, the muddy man-sized boot prints stood out against the brightly polished tile floor. They had gone to the coal stove, lit it, and retreated into the *parlor* without putting on water or starting to cook.

Mha declared, "Thorn. I am here."

No answer.

Had the police awoken Thorn? Was Thorn dead? No, Mha recognized the squeak of Thorn's voice drifting from the front of the house, broken up by a voice humans would call deep. Had Mha failed in her labor of serving the old woman, making Thorn call for police to take Mha away? Mha would not mind the police taking her away—it wouldn't be a proper ending, but it would be *an* ending.

She would miss telling the saga of Vara's marriage war, though.

Mha wiped her feet on the rug just inside the back door until her boots would not soil the floor. The worn-out soles slipped on the tile unless perfectly dry. Mha was already pathetic enough. She had no wish to break a bone and become even less useful. If she couldn't perform feeble labor like making *tea*, not even October the Devourer would let her die.

Thorn hated dirt on her floors. Mha felt confident that Thorn had instructed any police to wipe their feet.

Unlike men, an orc could follow instructions.

Mha caught her fingers brushing against *that* orc's skull chained to her waist. She snatched her hand back up. Was she expecting comfort from a skull? That's why she wore *that* orc's skull, to remind her that there was no comfort. She was alone. She would always be alone. When she died, she would rot in the barn until Thorn noticed her failure to make *tea* and sent her insulting nephew to search for her. Her meat would go to waste.

Mha tested her boots against the tile. They were dry enough to hold. Did Thorn still want her tea? Tea or not, the house needed warm water. Mha carefully filled the fragile steel teapot from the bucket and put it on the stove. The stove felt less hot than usual. Mha licked her pinky and touched the stove top, but her spit didn't even sizzle. Whoever set this fire had starved it. She opened the door and placed another four coals atop the blaze.

"Mantis?" Thorn called. "Is that you?"

Human mouths could not form orcish names. At least the Army had called them all *orc*, with a duty or rank added when needed, but civilians insisted upon insulting them by trying. "Mha n'Tass. Yes, Thorn."

"Come on out here, Mantis," Thorn said. "There's a young man here who would like to meet you."

A male human replied, "You're the only one round here what thinks I'm young."

Mha straightened, smothered the urge to caress *that* orc's skull again, and tromped out to the front room.

The room Thorn called a *parlor* could comfortably hold a dozen relaxing orcs. They'd have to get rid of the couches first—they were covered in brightly colored fabric that would stain at the first fart, and those spindly legs would snap under a ten-year-old's weight. The matching chairs were even more fragile, and too snug for any child older than five. The long low table might be useful as firewood, so long as you only wanted warmth. The smoke from burning the heavy varnish would poison any food cooked over it. A glass cabinet almost tall enough for Mha to rest her elbows on comfortably was stuffed to overflowing with figurines and icons in delicate glass and porcelain, each painted as finely as human skill permitted. Thorn dusted them every day, cradling each in her crabbed fingers and murmuring senseless fragments of words over them. Mha didn't know if they were from the human church, or perhaps trophies from Thorn's past. Mha did know that if she sneezed within ten feet of the cabinet, it and its contents would shatter into sand, so she stayed as far from it as possible.

This morning, Thorn had forsaken her rocking chair in front of the fireplace for the broader, padded armchair. It was placed where it could command everyone's attention, but no orcish clan chief would sit on anything so plushly padded. The intricate carvings covering the dark wood of the legs and frame stank of human pride. Thorn perched on the throne like she belonged there, her hands relaxed on the arms, legs crossed at the ankles. She had abandoned her usual housedress for a boastful blue wool dress decorated everywhere with white flowers, and wore shiny leather boots too short to cover her ankles instead of her shapeless slippers.

A man sat on the couch opposite, studying Mha with cool eyes. He wore the black pants and button-up coat of a police officer, but his coat bore extra gold braid around his wrists. He carried himself like one of the competent Army officers, able to make decisions and certain they would be obeyed. A younger henchman stood behind him, waiting with his hands behind his back. The way the henchman stiffened and straightened as Mha entered told her that he did not expect to be obeyed.

"Sheriff," Thorn said, "this is Mantis."

"Mha n'Tass."

Thorn continued like Mha had not spoken. "Her husband saved mine during the Great War, and now she does for me." She looked at Mha. "This is Sheriff Baxter. You and I seem to have slept through some excitement last night."

A *sheriff* was like an Army captain, but for times without war. The police made sure that orcs behaved as powerful humans wanted them to, but the sheriff made sure that the police obeyed the powerful men. Humans were not smart enough to obey power, so they needed sheriffs to keep order.

The Army had taught Mha about rightful authority. Whatever orders or insults the sheriff offered, she had to accept. Only hot-blooded fools who had never served a nation's war argued with authority.

Baxter met Mha's gaze easily. "No blood today, orc."

At least Baxter knew not to disrespect her name, and offered a proper greeting. "No blood today."

Baxter's henchman gave that snort humans used when they failed to hide disrespect. "We had blood."

Baxter turned on his henchman. An orc would rebuke another with a snarl, but Baxter didn't raise his voice at all. "Have you ever dealt with orcs before, Saul?"

The henchman—Saul?—shook his head.

"Then keep your mouth shut while I ask questions." A better rebuke than Mha expected any human to offer an underling. Baxter turned back to Mha. "How long have you lived here, orc?"

"Three summers."

Baxter turned to Thorn. "Your neighbors worry about you, you know. Living out here all alone, with nothing but an orc for company."

The neighbors shouldn't worry. Mha was not Thorn's problem. They should scorn that insulting nephew and distant son for their refusal to honor their elder, heaping insult and humiliation upon those children until they did right and ate Thorn, but they shouldn't *worry*.

Thorn rolled her fingers into a loose fist, knuckles popping like gunshots, and stuck a finger at Baxter. "It's that boy Hank Neville, isn't it? He's had his eye on my property for forty years now, and he's gonna have to wait for it a while longer yet. I've got my friend to look out for me, and I don't need no busybody trying to drive me out of the home my Bristol built for us. He just wants to cut down all my lovely woods. Those trees were here before that Neville was born, and I daresay that they'll still be here when he's feeding worms."

"Didn't say it was any neighbor in particular," Baxter said.

Thorn gave a sniff. "You didn't have to." She jabbed the finger at Mha. "My Mantis does the heavy things, then she keeps me company. We have a nice cup of tea every morning. Don't we, Mantis?"

"Mha N'Tass," Mha said. "Tea, with a trade of sagas."

Baxter studied Mha's face. Did he understand what Mha thought of tea? "You could have Miss Brown come by more often."

Thorn laughed. "My Mantis is fine, so long as you don't ask her to pick up fine china. She's harmless."

Bile throbbed in Mha's gut.

She was older than any orc should be asked to live. She had lost everything. But to be told she was harmless? Pure insult.

Even worse than the insult? Such offense should make her blood boil. She should scream and leap, slashing the enemy's face with the one talon she kept sharp. Instead, her tired heart picked up a few extra beats and her face grew warm, but more with shame than anger.

Mha had lived so long, she was no longer an orc.

"I don't know about that." Baxter kept his gaze on Thorn. "I think if someone threatened you, you'd find out that your orc could be more dangerous than you think."

Was the sheriff *defending* her?

Thorn cackled, slapping her knee. "We'd show them, all right! How about that, Mantis? Someone gives us what-for, I'll hit him low, you hit them high? It's what I keep the frypan for, after all."

"Mha N'Tass." Was her voice weak? "I will defend this cavern with my breath and bone."

Baxter studied Mha. "You know, Thorn, they told us in the Army that orcs prefer to be called by their job title, or just *orc*. Our mouths aren't shaped to say their names correctly."

He *had* been defending her! Or at least, he was offering a shred of proper respect. Mha's throat tightened.

Thorn said, "Oh, we're too old for that kind of formality. Her husband saved mine back in the war, you know. That puts us on a first-name basis. She has a home here as long as she lives and breathes."

Mha forced a breath out.

Thorn would give Mha labor and listen to Mha's sagas, both comforts in her last days, but the ancient humaness believed that orcs were big humans. She would never accept that the respect due a man did not fit on an orc.

And Mha ached for the simple respect of someone pronouncing her name correctly. Someone who would not only listen to her sagas, but understand them.

The morning sunlight through the high, narrow, filthy window lit the stairwell no better than a torch. Uruk had lived his entire life in this tenement, trudging across this landing and down the stairs every day he could remember. As a boy under Grandpa's leadership, the clan had brawled with the seventh floor Norkoshes to answer their insults right here on this landing. He now led the clan. That responsibility quickened his breath and made him more aware than ever of the crumbling walls and scarred floor and the narrow halls.

Behind Uruk, his brother Kaba growled and shifted his weight. Further back, but in front of Vara and Daka's Kovo, Daka keened with the need to answer lies with blood. Floorboards groaned underfoot, as if the decrepit tenement was unable to contain so much orcish rage. The cramped landing stank of sweating orcs.

If the clan died today, it would be because Uruk failed them.

Uruk's heart hammered at Kuru-Norkosh's filthy accusation. "The Tai are not poisoners!"

"Tai blood!" a Norkosh brother further up the stairs screamed.

Kuru-Norkosh balanced on the narrow stairs, three inches beyond Uruk's reach and just high enough that Uruk had to crane his neck to meet his eyes. "Only the Tai dare bootleg! Proper orcs know to take what labor they are given, but the Tai raise themselves! Tai arrogance killed our daughter, and we will have yours for it!"

"An orc does not poison!" Uruk said. "If I wanted weak Norkosh blood, I would cut your throat and drink from it!"

"Men do not run draught!" Kuru-Norkosh spat.

"We do not sell you draught!" Uruk said.

"The Tai do not deserve our money," Kuru-Norkosh said. "We buy from a man who buys from you!"

"Even foolish Norkosh should know that an orc does not poison!" Uruk said. "Look to the man who sold it to you."

"No man could fake an orcish seal," Kuru-Norkosh said.

"Are Norkosh as thick-skulled as men?" Uruk hissed. "The Tai do not poison." Would they declare marrow feud today of all days?

"And the Norkosh know that they do." Kuru-Norkosh straightened. "Blood is not enough. The Tai do not deserve an honest war. I will fight you alone!"

"Tai!" If Uruk's breath came any harder, he would blow the window out. He refused to show his dismay. "The Norkosh dare claim that their worthless leader can defeat me." The Norkosh clan worked in a slaughterhouse, killing cattle with a punch to the head. Uruk's years at the docks had made him strong, but he was no practiced killer. A clan leader could never admit that worry clawed at his guts, though. "Prepare to scour their apartments and claim their worthless treasures before the Greatest Dark claims us."

"Norkosh!" Kuru-Norkosh didn't look away from Uruk. "Prepare to drive the Tai into the street, naked and broken."

"Put a spike on the hood of the Model T." If Uruk was to win, he had to defeat his own fear first. "Kuru-Norkosh's head will show the world that the Tai are proper orcs, as December embraces their bare hides."

"We will toy with your carcass as we bury our daughter," Kuru-Norkosh sneered. "We will leave your soiled meat on her grave, so all know what happens to poisoners."

Fury at the insult would give Uruk strength and speed.

But if Uruk lost this war, the clan would lose everything. Their homes. Their clothes. Their friends. Not even other Tai would take them in. Uruk's death would leave the clan in the care of December, during the Greatest Dark.

8

If Mha had not pridefully demanded labor while making *that* orc's final sacrifice, perhaps she could have wound up serving the sheriff. The sheriff did not try to say her name.

But the sheriff would not pretend to listen to Mha's sagas—and if he ever asked for one, he would not pretend to understand it. The sheriff would not offer his own sagas in exchange. The sheriff would not offer *tea*. Mha did not appreciate the leafy flavor, but it was part of the human respect chant and it was warm. Coffee was better, but Thorn had no coffee.

And the ceiling was high enough that Mha did not have to worry about her nasty hair gouging the plaster.

Mha did not belong in the *parlor*. Thorn lived alone, yet she had flimsy couches and tables and chairs for a dozen humans. The wooden floor gleamed in the brilliant morning sunlight pouring through the windows, highlighting its perfectly polished sheen. Even with trimmed toe talons, barefoot orcs would scratch that glassy perfection beyond repair in a week. A few branches crackled in the fireplace. Pine and sweet flowers hung in the air, as if Thorn had a small magic to defy December and bring a tiny slice of spring into her home. The white plaster walls had curved with age, but were unmarked. How could anything grow old without scars? Who would want to live without collecting scars to remind them of their struggles and loves?

The only way America let an orc be an orc was to claim a tiny space and fight to hold it.

Thorn sat in her chair as if she was in charge. Perhaps she was. She had dismissed everything the sheriff had said. Was Thorn so powerful that the police answered to her? Why would she not send them after her insulting nephew, then? And if Thorn was in charge, why did the sheriff have a henchman?

Sheriff Baxter turned his attention to Mha. "Tell me, orc. Did you see or hear anything in the night?"

"The wind. The barn creaks."

"Nothing unusual?" Baxter said.

"No, man."

Baxter grunted. "Too much to hope for. You both slept through it."

Thorn said, "You missed it, Mantis. The sheriff was telling me that someone was killed on the road outside the house."

There had been a war, and Mha had missed it? If she had heard the noise, she could have gone out to join in. Even if the battling humans had united against her, a last war would have been joyful. But her useless old meat had surrendered her to sleep instead. Mha was not fit even to stand watch.

"We don't know that he was killed there," Baxter said. "He was *found* there."

It didn't matter if the war had been here or elsewhere. Mha would have slept through it.

The henchman said, "I thought orcs didn't sleep."

"Orcs sleep just like everyone," Baxter said. "They can stay awake a couple days at a time, but then you gotta let them rest a day or two. No different from us."

Why would a human stay awake for two days when they had orcs to do it for them?

"Besides," Baxter said, "this orc is old. I bet she either doesn't sleep at all, or sleeps like the dead."

Not enough like the dead. The sheriff seemed to be expecting an answer, but he hadn't asked a question. Even the most tolerable humans didn't know how to speak.

The Army had taught Mha how to make humans say something else. "Man."

It worked. "We're done with you, orc."

Hope flared. If she could go back to the barn, she could finish her new boots.

"Stay a bit, Mantis," Thorn said.

If Mha hadn't made the mistake of hoping, she wouldn't be so disappointed.

Thorn said, "I'll finish up with the sheriff here, and we can have our tea. I thought I might bake biscuits this morning."

Biscuits were better than cookies or—worse—*muffins*. How did humans eat so much disgusting sugar? If it made an orc's blood hum it should make men explode, but they seemed to gulp it down without remorse. She would need a solid porridge to settle her stomach after a muffin. A link of orc sausage would help as well.

"I don't think you have anything to worry about," Baxter said. "My money says that man was at the Pickle Barrel last night. Probably got his hands on some bad hooch and wandered out in the cold. Sad when these things happen."

Freezing to death wasn't a war. December welcomed wanderers.

Thorn leaned forward. "Your boy told me he'd been shot."

It *had* been a war! It had been a war, and Mha had slept through it! Was December taunting Mha now?

Baxter glared at his henchman.

The henchman tried to shrink without moving. The youngest un-blooded orc would face a charging battalion with more bravery. "I didn't know it was a secret."

"We'll talk later." Baxter held the henchman's eye for another beat, then turned back to Thorn. "There's no sign of a fight here. The victim's not local, and you're not that far from the Pickle Barrel."

"So you told the truth," Thorn said, "but you weren't honest."

"There's nothing for you to worry about," Baxter said.

"I wasn't going to worry," Thorn said. "Gangsters don't come out to Clinton Township. And if they do, they don't visit old ladies, more's the pity. But if gangsters came out here and started shooting, Mantis and I would give them a proper greeting and give you a ring to pick up what's left."

Thorn asked Mha every week what food she wanted delivered, and encouraged her every time to order things no orc would willingly stomach. Could Mha get some of these *gangsters*?

"While I'm here," Baxter said.

"Here it comes," Thorn said, waving a hand. "I'm not moving in with my nephew, I'm not moving all the way out to New York City with my boy, and I don't want to listen to anybody else snoring all night. Does that answer your question?"

"I wasn't going to say any of that," Baxter said.

Thorn said, "You'd be the first."

"What I was going to say," Baxter said, "is that your barn isn't a good place for an orc. The next big wind we have is gonna knock it right over."

December would not be so kind.

"The wind hasn't knocked me over yet," Thorn said, "and that barn's younger than me."

Baxter's gaze fixed on Mha again. "I could take your orc somewhere where she could be with other orcs. Someplace where she'd have a good home. Where you wouldn't have to worry about her."

Mha's pulse fluttered.

Any man who understood how to talk to orcs would know that the world had no place for a worn-out orcess.

The sheriff was young. He probably didn't know that old orcs should be eaten. But perhaps—maybe—had December sent him? A drive to some quiet place distant from the farm. Standing in the snow. A pulled gun, one last lunge with bare talons, a flash of gunpowder.

It would hurt less then waking up without *that* orc.

She could tell the saga of Vara's wedding war on the way.

"Don't be silly," Thorn said. "Two old war widows can rub along together just fine."

Mha didn't know if she was disappointed or pleased.

Baxter and Thorn spoke that meaningless human separation ritual, declaring allegiances neither would keep, and the police left. Thorn rubbed her hands together. "Well, isn't that a fine start to a day?"

Mha could say nothing to such a senseless question, but Thorn always expected answers. "Yes, Thorn."

A war. Out front.

Thorn braced her kindling arms on her throne and struggled to her feet. "After all that, we need more than biscuits. I still have a jar of blueberry preserves. I'm thinking... *muffins*."

 9

The tenement's basement could hold forty orcs, if they all huddled together. A dozen split between the stairwells left a vast span of buckling concrete between them. Water stains mottled the cinderblock walls, and the air smelled thick with old mold and the ancient building's rotting bones. Uruk-Tai bent his knees to avoid cracking his skull on the low rafters, but passing beneath the rust-stained but still sturdy steel support beams required ducking. A single light bulb, always on, struggled against the space and left the corners gray shadows. Other than the shaman Azok-Snaka's nest of blankets beneath the looming boiler and the three squat brass braziers he used for rituals, the floor was swept clean. Black smears of ash streaked the ceiling, still smelling of pine.

Outside the basement, America made orcs struggle to be orcs.

In this basement, America surrendered to orcish law.

Despite the sun having risen on the shortest day, Azok-Snaka remained wrapped in his blankets. The shaman wasn't as old as Grandpa but in the windowless basement day felt no different than night. He always rose when needed.

Uruk's brothers Daka and Kaba, plus his Vara and Daka's Kovo, stood against the west stairs, spread out enough to fight but far enough back to let Uruk stand for the clan. Grandpa was still hobbling down, but war would not wait for him.

The Norkosh had come down the east stairs. The liar Kuru-Norkosh stood in front, while his three brothers and a woman with a child at her breast lurked behind him. The newborn would not last long in December, but Kuru should have thought of that before starting a war on the shortest day.

No. Such thoughts would destroy the clan.

Kuru-Norkosh's wrong-headed anger bloated his arrogance, and had led Uruk into arrogance of his own. If he let himself grow confident, he would die. If he failed to control his worry for his boys and his woman and his clan, he would die. Kuru-Norkosh had strength and balance. He could break a cow's skull with one punch between the eyes. Uruk needed to make sure that that punch never landed. Move quickly. Strike fast. Use every trick Grandpa had ever spoken of. Claw the throat. Rip the balls. If they break your tusk, use the stub to gouge out an eye.

Uruk could already taste blood.

Before he could speak Kuru-Norkosh shouted "Azok-Snaka! The Tai clan are poisoners, and I demand their leader answer for them!"

"The Norkosh are liars!" Uruk said. "What is theirs is ours by right! We shall piss on their corpses and leave them to rot."

Azok's blankets stirred.

Disquiet tightened Uruk's guts. The shaman should be on his feet by now, placing himself between the clans and defining the law of this war. Instead, he dragged himself upright with a bubbling breath.

Azok was ill. The illness had crawled down into his lungs to die, and would take the shaman with it. Behind Azok, the orphan boy who served him got to his feet, almost dancing with impatience.

Uruk's blood chilled.

A shaman who could not stand on his own could not serve his tenement.

If the shaman lacked the strength to sanctify a battle between Uruk and Kuru, it would spread. Norkosh in other tenements would declare marrow feud against all Tai anywhere. The Tai would know that the feud had started because Uruk had failed to end it here. Uruk and Vara would be dead, and his fine boys would lose the respect of their own clan. They would not *read*. The only work they would find would be at the sewer plant.

Uruk had to answer Kuru-Norkosh's challenge. "Azok-Snaka! Mark Kuru-Norkosh's face, so that all know his dishonor. Or bind us to this war, so that all will know the truth before the Greatest Dark rises!"

The orphan boy shuffled his feet, but did not move. A child whose clan had died out had no home. This one had been chosen by Azok-Snaka as his student. He only had a home as long as he learned his lessons, or as long as Azok-Snaka survived.

Azok-Snaka took his feet. He opened his mouth to speak, and immediately erupted in a cough so fierce that he spewed a brown sticky lump eight feet across the floor. His purple-green skin was pale, with sweat running down his forehead and gluing his shirt to his chest. So many American orcs died of age-sickness, but Azok-Snaka might win the Old Country dream of dying in war.

At least Kuru-Norkosh had the decency to let the shaman steady himself.

Uruk watched Kuru-Norkosh, not willing to shame the shaman by witnessing his weakness.

Battles between leaders were set in legend. Azok-Snaka would call on Kuru-Norkosh to state his claim, and then call on Uruk to respond. He would draw a circle of brazier ash and his own blood on the floor, big enough for the two to brawl, and declare that the last orc alive in the circle had won. Sagas told of these wars, especially when the victor showed true contempt by throwing the other out of the circle while still alive.

No, put that thought aside. To enter the circle intending to leave his enemy alive was nothing but pride, or—worse—hope. Uruk had to kill Kuru-Norkosh as quickly as possible, exactly as he would haul the last crate of the day onto a docked ship. A labor. Nothing more. Nothing to be excited over.

Azok-Snaka heaved a bubbling breath. He stood within arm's reach of the massive boiler, as if he might fail them all and lean against it. "Kuru-Norkosh. Uruk-Tai. To me."

Confusion flashed through Uruk, and was mirrored on his enemy's face.

Behind Uruk, his clan fell silent.

"Norkosh. Tai." Azok-Snaka coughed another wad on the floor. "To me, I said."

A shaman only broke the rituals of war for a greater war. What could he have that was more important than two entire floors of the tenement threatening to wipe each other out on the shortest day? Uruk stomped forward, never looking away from Kuru-Norkosh.

"Hold," Azok-Snaka wheezed. "Obey your shaman. Hold."

Uruk grunted. "Shaman."

Kuru-Norkosh's gaze did not flicker from Uruk. "I obey."

"Yesterday." Azok-Snaka wobbled on his feet. Uruk thought for a moment that he might put a hand on the boiler, but the shaman steadied himself. "Yesterday night, the *landlord* comes to me." His words bubbled and scratched as they clawed their way out of his throat. "He tells me that the Lord Mayor has declared this building unworthy. The land lord has sold the cavern. It will be knocked down at the end of January."

The tenement unworthy? How could a building be unworthy?

"We will burn Tai clothes for warmth," Kuru-Norkosh hissed.

"Listen!" Azok-Snaka snarled. "Obey, and listen."

Uruk did not let his glee at the rebuke reach his face.

"And this morning," Azok-Snaka said, "a Norkosh drank poison draught."

"The Tai do not poison!" Uruk said.

"Listen!" The force of Azok-Snaka's shout ripped another brown mouthful from the shaman's lungs. "Multiple attacks! The death of a child. Poison. The Lord Mayor. All at once. Someone has declared war on the cavern."

Elves. A hiss escaped Uruk. Would they never stop?

"Kuru-Norkosh," Azok-Snaka said. "What new things have the Norkosh clan done this winter?"

"We work as we always have," Kuru-Norkosh spat. "At the slaughterhouses. No Norkosh would put himself forward."

Azok-Snaka nodded and turned to Uruk. "Then it is the Tai clan's feud with the elves that has started this war."

A roar of protest erupted from Uruk, echoed by the Tai behind him. Kuru-Norkosh let out his own bellow, as if he'd been proven right. The Norkosh clan let out their own feeble snarls.

An ear-splitting screech ripped through the shouts.

Azok-Snaka had reached for the boiler, but only to scratch a talon along it. "Obey!" Azok-Snaka shouted. He spat more filth. "Obey! Listen."

The shouts had just started to quiet when Kuru-Norkosh said, "A proper orc takes what work he can find. He does not surrender to human greed or Elvish pride."

"And there would be no draught!" Uruk said.

Azok-Snaka said, "If the Tai had not brought us draught, another clan would. We must have draught."

Uruk raised his chin in vindication.

Kuru-Norkosh couldn't bare his tusks any further.

"And perhaps," Azok-Snaka said, "that other clan would have not made enemies doing so."

Kuru-Norkosh barked a laugh.

"When other Tai sought draught only so our children could become adults," Uruk said, "elves killed them and took the draught." A war of leaders would be easier than standing here not ripping out the other orc's throat. "They have always been our enemy, and a proper orc refuses to die without a fight."

"Obey!" Azok-Snaka said. "Enemies attack the cavern. We need every orc to defend it. Your war must wait."

Uruk couldn't restrain a hiss. Were the Tai expected to hold that insult?

Kuru-Norkosh keened at the ceiling, mirroring Uruk's frustration.

"*My* cavern!" Azok-Snaka snarled. "Many clans, but my cavern!"

Illness would claim Azok-Snaka soon, and he declared he would fight to keep the cavern? A tenement without a shaman would slaughter itself in days, though. When Azok-Snaka died, his orphan boy would call for his replacement. The new shaman would arrive within hours and claim Azok-Snaka's wars as his own. He might keep the orphan as a student; he might not.

Grandpa always claimed that a dying shaman was more dangerous than any other. They would not fear to cast their bindings with the whole strength of their lives, so that their cavern would outlive them.

And if the tenement was destroyed, Uruk's tiny clan would have no place to shelter.

Marrow seething, Uruk stilled himself. "I obey."

Kuru-Norkosh howled.

Azok-Snaka jabbed a little finger towards Kuru-Norkosh.

Kuru-Norkosh coughed like he'd been punched in the belly.

Uruk didn't even try to hide his satisfaction. The shaman still had strength, but only Kuru-Norkosh had made him waste it.

With a single deft swipe, Azok-Snaka slashed his palm against a Lesser Tusk. Rich red blood welled from the gash and seeped down towards his wrist. "Uruk-Tai. Kuru-Norkosh. To me."

A blood oath with the liar? Did Azok-Snaka expect Uruk to ally with orcs who made filthy accusations? But Kuru-Norkosh was walking forward, and Uruk would not do less.

Azok-Snaka slashed his other palm.

Uruk had seen a blood oath when he was a child. He hadn't yet understood what was happening, but Grandpa had demanded he and his brothers witness it. He stopped a yard from Azok-Snaka and held up his hands, palms out and open. Eyes on the shaman, Kuru-Norkosh's presence at the edge of his vision felt heavier than a bull. Kuru-Norkosh trembled with fury, but held his hands out as well.

Azok-Snaka snatched Kuru-Norkosh's hands. Tusks flashed, scoring shallow wounds into Kuru-Norkosh's hands. Kuru-Norkosh's eyes flared for a heartbeat and his jaw set.

Uruk choked a laugh. If a simple cut like that could disturb Kuru-Norkosh, the Tai could have slaughtered their whole annoying clan years ago.

He had barely finished the thought before the shaman seized his wrists and slashed one palm, then the other, with his tusks.

Hot fire branded across each palm.

These weren't cuts. The tusks scored like acid, then molten lead. Electric shivers shot up into his shoulders and down his spine and made his dick try to crawl up inside him. Uruk had never doubted Azok-Snaka's power, but having it try to squeeze the air from his lungs made him understand it. Uruk kept his face still, and didn't flinch—but a snort of surprise escaped.

Kuru-Norkosh grew a superior smirk.

Before Uruk could slap Kuru, Azok-Snaka grabbed Uruk's hand. Blood touched blood, sending a shriek up into Uruk's bones. His lungs shuddered for breath and the floor seemed to rock.

"Kuru," Azok-Snaka said. "Uruk. Take each other's free hand."

Shaman's fire still danced through Uruk's guts, but Kuru-Norkosh looked stunned. Uruk snatched his enemy's hand, baring his tusks at the minor victory.

The shrieking fire scrubbed that grin away, pouring from Azok-Snaka into Uruk and out into Kuru-Norkosh, then reversing. Rage at the death of a child sloshed through Uruk, resonating with his own fury at the unjust accusation echoing back into him, Kuru-Norkosh's lust for justice as strong as his own.

But stronger than both together, Azok-Snaka's will.

"You will work together to defend the cavern," Azok-Snaka hissed.

Uruk had guessed that those hard words were coming, but they still burned as fierce as the shaman's fire. The blood echoed Kuru-Norkosh's matching anger.

Azok-Snaka said, "You will follow the trail of poison until you discover our attackers and destroy them. You will use each clan's hoard for victory."

Uruk could not have released Kuru-Norkosh without tearing off his own hand. His other arm would break off at the shoulder before he could free himself from Azok-Snaka's grip. The shaman's chain of fire and blood whirled through him like a broken rope through a loaded winch, hissing and flying and never-ending.

"You will unify for this war, leading your clans against those who would crush us. Until I declare the cavern safe, blows you would make against the other will echo back onto you tenfold." Azok-Snaka coughed. "My cavern. Mine!"

The chain snapped.

Uruk stumbled backwards, gasping for breath. Fire lingered in his bones. His wobbling knees threatened to buckle. Uruk demanded that they hold, demanded that his spine straighten and his chin stay high. It was like his own tenth birthday, when Grandpa had ordered him to drink a bottle of draught and all the men of the clan had gathered in a circle to shove him back-and-forth, laughing as they tried to make him fall. Every child became an orc that way. Shaman's fire was stronger than any draught, and more treacherous—but he had not fallen then, and he would not fall now.

In two staggered steps, Uruk steadied himself.

Kuru-Norkosh's fury was a tight knot in the back of his mind, embers of the other orc's rage.

The slices on his hands had closed. In their place, his palms bore the throbbing brown-and-red rune of a blood oath. Looking at them, he felt Azok-Snaka's burning will in his veins.

To Uruk's shock, he could also feel the weakness of Azok-Snaka's life.

The shaman's death would break the blood oath.

In that second, Kuru and the entire Norkosh clan would go to war.

Azok-Snaka studied Kuru for a breath, nodded at Uruk, and stepped back to his nest of blankets without turning his back. "Go." The ancient shaman couldn't completely hide his trembling as he lowered himself to sit cross-legged. "Both of you. Leave this cavern. Track our enemy to its nest." A bout of coughing threatened to rip the shaman in half. "Destroy them."

Kuru met Uruk's gaze and smiled.

 10

December's cold eye burned down on the world.

An insistent breeze sent loose snow skittering across the hard frozen crust of ice covering the drifts that had swallowed the ground. The two-lane road of black asphalt had defeated the crust, but every Model T or shiny new Dodge or Oldsmobile wallowed through filthy gray slush. All those men journeying from their homes to labor for their lords filled the air with exhaust, but the clean sharp smell of December's breath underlay everything.

Facing Kuru and Azok-Snaka, Uruk had sweated through his shirt. Every wisp of air that slipped down his collar or up the bottom of his battered wool coat felt like an icicle against his skin. The sun had climbed above the roof of the crumbling warehouse next door, and after the long night the bright morning sunlight hurt his eyes. Uruk's hollow gut reminded him that Vara would have made a warm meal for him. His feet steamed in his boots while his bare fingers froze. The brass knuckles would have made them even colder. He would have preferred that cold. The police would arrest an armed orc, though, so the brass knuckles remained in his coat pocket.

The tenement's six floors loomed over him. Their tenement was no better or worse than any other orcish tenement. The hollow sockets that had once held glass windows were either boarded over or blocked from within, so men and dwarves could not witness orcish life. An elf would not deign to notice the most worthy orcish tenement. How could the Lord Mayor declare a building unworthy? What made a building unworthy? Were they supposed to paint the old red brick in bright colors, the way humans did? Should they sweep away years of bird's nests from ledges?

December knew. But she spoke only in frozen blood.

And even sparrows needed a place to raise their young.

Kuru tromped out seconds after Uruk, buttoning his coat up around his neck. Kuru's coat was no better than Uruk's, but Uruk's new flat cap was obviously thicker and warmer than Kuru's threadbare old rag.

Uruk adjusted the edge of his cap, tugging it a nail's width further over his ears.

Kuru's eyes flashed. "We must find the source of the poison. Where does the Tai clan keep their draught?" He clapped his hands together un-orcishly and bared his Lesser Tusks.

"That draught did not come from us," Uruk hissed. "Even a Norkosh should be able to understand."

The palms of Uruk's hands erupted in pain.

Uruk choked back a growl of surprise and fisted his hands until his trimmed talons dug into the meat of his palms. Peeling a hand open, he could see the bloodstained rune twitching. Even outside the tenement, he felt a distant echo of Azok-Snaka's will. Was Uruk not even allowed to defend himself?

Kuru peeled his hands apart and glared at Uruk.

Uruk could also feel Kuru's fury—less strongly than when the shaman had chained them together with his fire, but like a war cry from a mile away instead of across the street. Uruk would have to do the thinking, as well as tolerating Kuru's insults. "Where is the Norkosh speakeasy?"

Kuru bared his teeth. "I will not give you Norkosh secrets."

Rage had made Kuru stupider. Uruk said, "We must find out where your bartender got the draught."

Kuru opened his mouth to answer and immediately clutched his hands closed.

Uruk had learned from one lesson. Stupid Kuru needed more.

Kuru breathed in through clenched teeth. "Our bartender had no draught. The Tai do not sell to clans allied with the Norkosh."

"Why would we sell to clans who would accuse us of —" A flare of shaman's fire ripped through the bones of Uruk's hands, stopping his breath and making his eyes water.

Even standing beneath December's gaze, Uruk was not allowed to defend the clan.

Out on the road, a Model T tooted its horn. The Oldsmobile in front of it had started to slide in the slush. The Model T slowed, coasting, giving the Oldsmobile space to slip and swerve. A breath later, the Olds' front tires sailed into the muddy easement and sank.

The Model T veered to glide past and went on its way.

Uruk needed to be the Model T, not the Oldsmobile. He must keep his head clear. He must not give Kuru the pleasure of goading him into testing the blood oath. December would see Uruk following the shaman's will, as Kuru tortured himself by defying it.

The shortest day would end soon, and the Longest Night begin.

Uruk picked words before speaking. "Where did you get the draught?"

"From a man who —" Kuru clenched his hands and shuddered.

Uruk let himself smile. "I will drive. You tell me where to find him."

"No!" Kuru said. "I will drive. Speaking to you sickens me."

Perhaps Kuru would die defending the tenement. Uruk would take great pleasure in watching his blood steam in the snow.

 11

Uruk had never seen a speakeasy so broken-down that orcs would not drink there, but the decaying building Kuru drove them to might be the first. A wooden sign bore the faded icon of a fish, above a handful of incomprehensible human letters. The roof sagged like the back of a worn-out horse that deserved to be eaten and savored after a long life of labor. Boards were nailed up over where windows had been, the rag-stuffed gaps declaring that the glass beneath had been broken out. December's bright morning exposed every rotted-out board in the walls. Tiny feet had left trails in the fresh snow across the roof, where squirrels had nested beneath one of the holes. Larger tracks declared that raccoons occupied the chimney.

The place even stank of old fish. If someone wanted to mend this building enough to rent it to orcs, they would have to burn it down first. How could the tenement be unworthy when this building stood?

No other Detroit neighborhood would tolerate this ruin. The slaughterhouse across the road stank of blood, though, and whatever was in the crumbling warehouse next door gave off a rotten stench Uruk had never imagined, not even in the filthiest freighters. Last night's snow had hidden older footprints, but a trench in the drifts showed where people had trudged from the road to the fish building.

An orc endured. But Uruk would not hurry to deliver whiskey or draught or even mirovar to this house of rotten fish, no matter how much money was offered.

Not that they would deliver here. Sanford found their customers, and paper men disliked smells as mild as a fart.

The breeze brought a deeper whiff of gore from across the street. "Humans will drink anywhere," Uruk said.

"Not even humans drink here," Kuru said. "Man Dick only sells."

"Man Dick?" Uruk said. "Does he show it off?"

Kuru snorted. "He says it's his name."

What kind of human would bear a name like that, Uruk wondered. No—not his turd, not his toilet. An orc focused on important matters. December's breath was too cold, capturing every shred of the Sun's warmth before it reached his face. He couldn't defend the Tai clan against Kuru's lies until Azok-Snaka broke the blood oath itching in his palms.

A man who made a building like this his cavern could not have power.

Perhaps Uruk would act out the old orcish joke, laying a Dick across the bar and punching it.

Kuru was already stomping through the snow to the door. Uruk's thoughts had let Kuru take an unearned lead. Uruk leapt forward. Kuru blocked him from claiming the lead, but they reached the door side-by-side.

Human homes were always rickety, but dry rot held this ruin one good fart from collapse. Kuru did not knock, though, instead grabbing the knob and swinging the door in. "Man Dick!" Kuru shouted as he stepped inside. "This liar—" Kuru hissed, fisting his hands.

Uruk smiled. "Man Dick! We must speak of draught." An orc did not enter a human space uninvited, but Kuru had not hesitated. Uruk followed.

Inside was lit only by slivers of light slipping between boards over the windows. The air felt slimy, and the stink of long-dead fish clotted in Uruk's throat. Dusty shelves lined the walls, and a low counter showed this had once been a store. Chalkboards hanging on the wall behind the counter still bore human letters scrawled in white that might be prices or curses for all Uruk knew.

"Man Dick is not here," Uruk said.

"He sleeps in the back," Kuru said.

How could even a human stand to sleep in this stink?

"I'm coming!" a muffled voice shouted through the door. "Hold your horses, I'm coming."

Dick stumbled from the stockroom. He reminded Uruk of a frog, face bulging and broad, with a mouth too wide for a man and a gleaming bald scalp. "Ugh. Orcs. Don't you know this ain't a decent time for this kind of business?"

Kuru said, "The draught you sold me yesterday. Is this the Tai that sold it to you?"

"We did *not* —" Fire flashed through Uruk's hands, scorching up into his wrists and stopping his breath for a beat. How had Kuru been able to speak that lie without pain?

Dick blinked. "You mean like a China man?"

What did draught have to do with human plates? Uruk found his breath. "You sold this orc draught yesterday."

"I don't sell out my customers," Dick said.

"Who sold it to you then?" Kuru said.

"What?" Dick said. "Stop wasting my time. You want more draught? I'm out."

Uruk switched to orcish. "Humans are slow." What would Tara say? "They can only take one little idea at a time."

Kuru growled. "Tell me what orc sold you that draught."

"I don't sell out my suppliers neither," Dick said.

Kuru bared his Greater Tusks.

Would the blood oath let Kuru attack a human? Uruk quickly said, "That draught was poisoned."

"Don't give me that noise," Dick said. "I only sell good stuff."

Kuru's growl became a hiss.

"An orc died drinking it," Uruk said. "If nobody else can answer for that death, then you can."

Dick held up flabby hands. "Hold on now, I'm an honest businessman here."

Kuru-Norkosh demands blood for blood. No, too complicated for a human. "Someone will die. Will it be you, now? Or the orc who sold you poison?"

Dick glanced between Uruk and Kuru.

"Choose," Uruk said. "Now."

"All right, all right already!" Dick said. "It was an orc."

"Which orc?" Kuru snarled. "This one?"

"Nah," Dick said. "A little taller, and his coat was white. Fancy hat, too."

What orc would wear a white coat? Even undyed wool would turn gray with labor. "His name," Uruk said. "What was his name?"

"I got no idea," Dick said. "You don't go trying to say an orc's name, it just makes them mad."

Why did humans respect orcs only when it made life more difficult?

Kuru hissed. "How do you find this orc?"

"I don't!" Sweat shone on Dick's scalp. "He shows up every few nights with a crate, and I buy them. Never had a complaint before, except from damn fool humans who think they can drink that stuff."

Kuru shuddered with anger. "Then we wait."

In orcish, Uruk said, "We can't wait."

"We wait!" Kuru snarled. "The Tai will return —" Kuru's throat bulged as he choked on the oath.

Kuru deserved that pain, but Uruk didn't let himself smile. "The tenement is at war. We cannot wait while our enemy acts. Have one of your brothers wait if you want. Or Norkosh from your greater clan."

"My brothers labor at the slaughterhouse," Kuru said.

"This orc shows up at night," Uruk said. "Let them sleep in turns here."

"Let *your* brothers sleep here," Kuru said.

"You say this orc is a Tai," Uruk said. "If he did not show up tonight, you would claim my brothers lied."

"They would," Kuru said, then winced.

Uruk would not let Kuru goad him into triggering the oath. "Then it must be your clan. They can walk here after work."

Kuru's entire body quivered with frustration. "Agreed!"

Uruk switched back to English. "Man Dick." The human was too squat to lie on the counter. He would flop over the sides, and punching him would be like punching a sack of cotton. "Norkosh orcs will guard here at night. When this orc in the white coat appears, they will take him."

Dick lowered his hands. "Hang on here. I ain't having no orc lurking around here. You do your business and get out."

"You defend these poisoners?" Kuru said.

"I ain't defending anyone!" Dick said. "This ain't my business."

"You sold the draught," Uruk said.

"They'll ruin my business," Dick said.

Kuru said, "Behind the counter. They will sleep behind the counter, and watch."

"I work here," Dick said. "I ain't having orcs stinking up the place."

"Orcs shit would make your home smell better." Uruk was too tired to explain the simplest things to human. "Orc guards tonight, or face Kuru-Norkosh now. Choose."

Dick glanced between Kuru and Uruk. "Fine! I'll figure out a place for them to sleep where they won't be in the way. But you better not breathe a word to any of my customers."

Uruk looked at Kuru.

Through clenched teeth, Kuru said, "No blood today." He whirled and stomped out.

December's fresh air called to Uruk. "No blood today." He would not flee, but he walked as quickly as he could back into the daylight.

Uruk didn't even get a chance to breathe before Kuru said, "If we must hunt, then we hunt. We will go to the docks where the Tai work, and find this *white coat*." His tone was clear; white clothing was un-orcish.

A white coat would stand out. Orcs would notice such a thing. The quickest way to prove Kuru a liar would be to go to the docks, but letting Kuru think he led made Uruk's guts knot. "First!"

"If we hunt, then we hunt!"

Uruk nodded at the slaughterhouse across the street. "You must tell your brothers to come here tonight."

"And what will the Tai do to aid the war?" Kuru sneered.

Uruk said, "I already have a human hunting for this poisoner."

12

Humans tortured blueberries.

Blueberries and strawberries and apples and all the other berries were cause for celebration. Small tart bundles of deliciousness that exploded on an orc's tongue and filled the senses. A clan that had done very well might even have its own blueberry bush or elderberry tree, allowing the clan a feast every summer. If a clan had too many berries Mha could imagine drying them for winter. Even without the juice, blueberries in porridge would make a fantastic Longest Night feast.

Humans had invented ways to preserve fruit far better than drying.

And they ruined that knowledge by adding handfuls of sugar. Berries came sweet. Why would anyone bury that flavor under a grave of sweetness? Sugar made food rot, but humans' tiny glass *preserves* jars were so powerful that the fruit survived the abuse.

The stove had started to heat, shedding warmth across the tiny kitchen. Mha sat on the low wooden bench, balancing so that some of her weight remained on her feet. The bench had been built for an orc, but by a man. If it collapsed Mha would break a bone, and December had made it clear she would not die easily. If she stretched her arms, she might break a piece of delicate stoneware or the frilly teapot or the fragile black iron pans. Instead, she sat and stomached the stinks of sugar and cinnamon and tea.

Thorn could not even give proper commands. "Would you be a dear and grab the flour for me?" "My back's a little achy this morning, dear, could you lift the rolling pin for me?" Thorn *must* know the difference between an orc and a deer. Not even a human could be that confused with age-sickness. Mha tried to be grateful for the labor she had been granted, and not constantly tell herself how much simpler it would be if Thorn would say *get the flour, fill the water bucket, hold the bowl*. Instead, Thorn had to torture her orders with extra words the way she entombed fruit in sugar.

Thorns knuckles turned even redder as she attacked a jar. "I'm a little stiff this morning, dear. Do you think you could get this lid off for us?"

Once, Mha had worked a machine gun too heavy for any man to lift. Now she unscrewed jars. The lid didn't even put up a fight. The jar popped in a disgusting waft of sugar. Her stomach twitched in revulsion. She commanded it to bear the stench.

"Mmm." Thorn fumbled the jar from Mha's grip and inhaled deeply. "Just smell those blueberries. Isn't that delightful?"

Mha had pillaged two-day-old battlefields that smelled better. Humans never understood how wrong they were. It was best to make them move on. "Yes, Thorn."

Thorn mixed flour and baking soda and foul spoonfuls of blueberry preserves, then greased a pan designed for tiny round loaves of bread. Despite Thorn's age-swollen knuckles, she deftly divided the batter between the pits. Once, Thorn must have performed this labor every day. Mha did not know how she would eat even one muffin, especially after Thorn sprinkled heavy brown sugar over each. "There," Thorn said. "I'll doctor these up with a caramelized topping, that will be lovely."

Doctor? Muffins did not need amputation, they needed to go straight to the bone heap.

"Get the oven for me, would you, dear?"

With Thorn's inedible trophies set to bake, she declared the tea ready to drink. Mha poured a tiny human cupful for Thorn, and filled the orc mug halfway. Tea was not disgusting, so long as she ignored Thorn saying "Help yourself to the sugar, dear." That was not a command. Not exactly. Mha helped herself to all the sugar she wanted.

Thorn sipped her tea. "I can't believe that we had a murder right here in front of our house."

Did Thorn believe that the sheriff lied? Mha could not think of anything to say, so she took a drink. The warmth soothed the ache where her teeth met her gums. Maybe she should heat her evening drinking water?

"It's rumrunners I'm sure, coming around and making trouble," Thorn said. "It's no matter for us, though. The police will handle it."

Police? A full war could break out in front of the farm, and the police wouldn't arrive for minutes. The police could not defend the farm.

Thorn could not defend the farm.

When Mha finished her boots, perhaps she should once again inspect the trash in the barn. Previously she and that orc had sought tools but, maybe, if she was very lucky, she needed a weapon?

The idea sent a delicious shiver through her guts.

Thorn was expecting a response. "Yes, Thorn."

"My Bristol would take me to the Pickle Barrel every Saturday night." Thorn had begun her saga. Humans did not use the word *my* the same way orcs did, but Mha could imagine a younger Thorn fighting for her husband.

"They had a band, and we would waltz the night away and drink wine and eat whatever it was they had that evening. Mister Satrap always made sure we got the VIP treatment. On good days, they would slow-cook prime rib and these wonderful baked potatoes covered with salt."

Baked potatoes were delicious. The next time Thorn insisted that Mha get something new, perhaps she should say *a potato*. She could bake it in the barn's tiny stove. Thorn had all these disgusting human ideas about food, but now and then she came out with *bacon* or *oatmeal* or *cayenne*. Salt on potatoes might be another one of those. She still had a handful of salt.

"And then pie—oh, Mantis, the pies!" Thorn raised a quivering hand.

Mha had smelled pie. She could not imagine a greater violation of fruit.

"Apple and peach, every weekend, plus pecan, you have to have pecan." Whatever Thorn was staring at wasn't in this room. "We would each get a different piece and share them, then dance another hour until I couldn't stand it anymore and demanded he bring me home."

Fleeing pie made good sense, if you couldn't bash it into oblivion and treat the baker likewise. But humans liked pie. Why did Thorn flee?

Mha reminded herself she was not required to understand Thorn's saga, any more than Thorn would understand hers. Crumbling women only needed witnesses.

Thorn set her teacup on the table. "I kept him up half the night, let me tell you. Then he would sleep through church, so I had to wake him up any way I wanted. Believe you me, I wanted him up." She leaned her face towards Mha and winked. "Well, part of him up. It was best if the rest of him lay flat."

Mha almost dropped her mug. How could Thorn speak of such things? Mha was not her family.

Perhaps solitude had hurt Thorn's mind. It happened sometimes with humans. They became dangerous. Mha would have to watch Thorn carefully. The ancient humaness could not fire a derringer without shattering every bone from her finger to her spine, but she could slip something into the tea.

"Pie would be nice," Thorn said.

The muffins were starting to bake. However bad Mha remembered them smelling, the reality was always worse.

"Tell me, dear," Thorn said. "You're still big and strong."

Humans did not know what strong meant. Before Mha could say so Thorn continued, "You move those old tools around the barn just fine, and you had no trouble with that preserves jar."

Was that what Thorn thought strength was? If Mha could not open a jar, surely even the Moon would wipe her away as a shame to orcs.

Thorn's eyes narrowed. Ancient will shone through the wrinkled wreckage of her face. "Do you think you could drag me and my old wheelchair up to the Pickle Barrel? I'll buy lunch."

Mha's heart thrummed.

A wheelchair? Through the snow? As December's breath chilled the shortest day?

Her worn-out boots with their flat soles could slip on snow crushed to ice by car tires. She might break something.

Cars and trucks raced past the farm. One could strike her.

Dragging a wheelchair through snow, even beaten-down snow, would be the fiercest labor she had performed since she and *that* orc had come to the farm. Her heart might burst.

No matter how fiercely Mha wanted, she must not hope. If she hoped, she was lost. "Yes, Thorn."

 13

A steady stream of trucks grumbled through the crossroads by the slaughterhouse, the painted fruit and meat and bottles on their sides declaring their cargo and the painted human words trumpeting which lord owned them. Exhaust stained the crusted snow, December's wind sending loose white flakes skittering across the gray. Uruk cautiously crossed to the three phone booths on the opposite corner.

The short booth for dwarves and the one for men were sturdy wooden frames filled with windows that blocked out the wind and snow. A double-hinged door provided more privacy. A man in a rich overcoat and expensive broad-brimmed hat that didn't cover his ears filled the human booth, earpiece pressed to his head, his face inches from the mouthpiece. The brand new Oldsmobile pulled to the side of the road must be his.

The orc booth was the size of the other two combined, a delicate wooden shed with the side facing the road open. Had Lord Bell decreed that the sides of orc booths should come within inches of Uruk's shoulders, and the roof come close to his head? He must have. The man looked equally uncomfortable in his minuscule phone box, and that tiny dwarf box wouldn't hold a hound. Lord Bell *must* have decreed it be so.

Lord Bell had not decreed that the orc booth stink of men's piss, or placed the coil of turd in the corner. That was entirely human. At least the open side kept the stench down.

Uruk dug into his pocket for a quarter. The man phone cost two cents, but orcs paid a quarter. Their phone was bigger and, like so many tools built by humans, orcs could wreck them with a sneeze. Lord Bell did not repair broken orc phones for months, so orcs were very careful with them. Still, some unworthy orc somewhere must break phones. Otherwise, why would calls be so expensive?

Two months ago, the thought of spending a quarter to call not just a man, but a *paper* man, would have made Uruk scoff. A phone was for calling distant cousins or the government, not a man. A quarter was the tiniest part of the clan's fortune now, and what was a fortune for if not war? Uruk pinched the tiny coin between his thumb and forefinger and eased it into the slot, drew a deep breath, then raised the earpiece and pushed the lever.

A human man declared, "Orc operator." The earpiece added a buzz to the words. This phone would die soon. "Give me the number."

If the operator claimed Uruk misspoke, he would need another quarter. "Twinbrook. Six. Eight. Nine. Six."

"Hold." The operator worked his magic. Uruk leaned back from the mouthpiece to free his breath and draw another. Breathing into the mouthpiece would make the operator hang up.

Miles away, a phone rang. It came through the earpiece as a fuzzy chime. The operator would hang up after the fourth ring. Uruk's impatience knotted his throat, but he held silence as Lord Bell demanded.

Two rings.

Three.

Four—and a click! "Sanford residence."

Uruk let out a relieved breath.

The operator said, "Orc operator. Speak your name, orc."

"Uruk-Tai."

"Thank you operator," Sanford said. "I accept the call."

Uruk waited for the *click* of the operator leaving. "Man Zhan-ford."

"What has happened?"

"Tell me you have found the poisoner."

Sanford inhaled. "You believe that man?"

Humans needed to hear the simplest ideas more than once to accept them, and Kuru-Norkosh would return from the slaughterhouse any moment. Perhaps Uruk could speed through the foolishness by repeating himself in advance? "An orc has been poisoned. An orc has been poisoned."

"Poisoned whiskey?"

"Draught."

Sanford hissed through his teeth. "Nobody else brings draught."

"And our tenement," Uruk said. "The city has declared it unworthy. We must leave."

The dying earpiece made Sanford's sharp inhalation a buzz. "It *is* war."

Uruk's blood surged. He had made a man understand!

A snarl erupted behind him.

Kuru-Norkosh stood at the edge of the road, tusks bared. In orcish: "You share our secrets!"

"What's going on?" Sanford said.

Uruk bared his own Lesser Tusks, growling in orcish. "I talk with a hunter."

"An orc war is not for men," Kuru-Norkosh growled.

Kuru was correct—but Uruk would slash Kuru's throat and bear the pain of the blood oath all the rest of his days rather than admit it. "I tell him what to hunt."

"Command him," Kuru snarled. "Give orders. Let him accept them. Then we go."

Uruk whirled, turning his back on Kuru as contemptuously as he knew how. "Zhan-ford. This poisoner. Find him."

"I made those calls already," Sanford said. "But this other attack? Your home? There is only one place it could be done. It is in the interest of the corporation that your family has a home. Call again in two hours."

Two hours? At the docks, that was the length of the gap between the start of work and Man Coffee. "Yes."

Sanford hung up.

Making two calls in one day, instead of one every few months? Phones changed war.

Uruk turned back to Kuru. "My hunter is loosed." He surprised himself using the orcish *my*—Uruk owned the hunter. He would fight to keep him.

Sanford was a strange weapon for a bizarre war.

"Then we go," Kuru sneered.

Uruk raised his chin, letting the tips of his Greater Tusks show. "I will show your claims baseless. We go to the docks."

Kuru's grin held only hunger.

The mark in Uruk's hand shuddered. Uruk did not let the quiver reach his face.

Azok-Snaka's magic faded with his life. When magic and life failed, a normal war would join this bizarre one.

14

Mha's blood surged at her first true war in years.

Her new leather tunic reached past her knees and canvas leggings shielded her calves and thighs, but her tattered wool coat stopped at her waist. At every lurching step, December gusted her frozen breath up across Mha's flanks and tire-crushed snow betrayed the stripped soles of her boots. Keeping her balance against the cold and ice and the jolting in her traitorous hip demanded complete concentration.

Mha could have balanced against the wheelchair, but it would betray her. The chair's wooden wheels had no treads, and any grease on the axle had dried years ago, leaving the wheels half-paralyzed. The ladder back rose high enough to loom over Thorn's head, but the handles mounted to its top were too low for an orc to grab. If Mha wasn't stooped with age, she would have had to crouch to draw it behind her. She could not trust it.

Besides, she would not give December the satisfaction. She would fight standing, as a proper orc.

She stepped backwards, testing her footing. This war demanded perfect tactics. Probe until she found a spot where the ice had worn thin, exposing the road beneath. Haul that side of the wheelchair to her. Shift the other foot back. Repeat. A hundred feet down the road, and the muscles of Mha's back and shoulders felt transformed into hot bands of braided barbed wire. The ache of her bad hip had risen to gnaw on her liver.

Thorn huddled in the wheelchair like a giant spider shrouded in shawls. A blanket heavier than Mha's coat protected her legs, tucked above fur-lined boots. Thorn wore two coats, one over the other, an assortment of scarves around her head and over her hat, and heavy mittens over her gloves. The mittens were far too large for Thorn's hands. They must have belonged to her husband. Humans would not accept their mates' final gifts, but Thorn must still miss her man. Why else would she have kept those ridiculously large gloves? Thorn's foggy breath plumed out through a narrow gap in a thin shawl draped across her mouth and nose.

The two-lane road was wide enough for trucks to pass each other, with comfortable space between them. Tires had worn tracks of ice, but the wind and warmth of trucks and cars had churned the surrounding snow to slush.

The road was new and straight. Nothing like the squirming tangles of Cuban roads. Even walking backwards, Mha could guide herself straight by splitting her attention between the ice underfoot and the treacherous asphalt ahead.

This morning, Mha had felt ready for death. But now, her heart pounded steady and strong against the inside of her ribs and thudded war drums in her ears. December's icy breath chilled her sweat. An orc's worth was in her labor, and no human could drag this decrepit wreck of a wheelchair down this road. It was enough to make her grin fiercely at the oncoming trucks. Bright clear skies meant a cold day and clear air, exposing the drivers' faces behind the glass. Most scowled and shouted, inaudible within their soft cabs. Mha only bared her Lesser Tusks and heaved the chair another foot.

A truck horn blared.

The thrill of defiance warmed Mha's gullet.

Thorn's voice was fuzzy through the shawls, but still distinct. "Does he expect you to roll me through the ditch?"

The human drivers saw only an inconvenient orc so yes, they would. Maybe one of the drivers would come out to berate Mha. Her decrepit tusks could still take a throat. The police might imprison her, but ending her life reminding men to respect orcs would be worthwhile. "I can carry you down the ditch."

"Don't be silly, dear. We have the same right to the road as everyone else." Thorn sounded happier than Mha had ever heard. Did she share Mha's delight?

The truck slowed further, almost matching their speed. The horn wheezed again.

The ball of Mha's foot found a clear patch of asphalt. She set her weight down—no, ice beneath the heel. If she hauled on the wheelchair, she would slip. December might still take her, but Mha would not let it trick her. The difference meant nothing to December, but everything to Mha.

"Shoo!" Thorn flapped her hand at the truck. "We're not dead yet!"

Mha slid her foot an inch to the side. Better.

Mha wasn't dead yet. She'd longed for death, she'd begged November and December alike to take her, when what she'd *needed* was labor. It wasn't just the work, though.

The driver made an obscene gesture and pulled his truck around to pass.

Even a rotting orcess could annoy the world into admitting she existed.

15

December had blown the stink of dying seaweed away from the Port of Detroit, leaving the comforting fumes of tar and diesel engines and livestock. Uruk recognized the steel-hulled passenger freighter *Manasoo* in dock despite the freezing water, its wheelhouse and the top of its stack visible over the fifteen-foot brick fence separating the port from the road. From the way the stack shifted, the ship bobbed on its lines as winches hoisted crates from its bowels. A dozen Tai orcs must be laboring on the *Manasoo's* freight alone. Chunks of ice large enough for an orc clan to dance on drifted on the water, transforming the Detroit River into a thick slurry of shifting ice. The *Manasoo* had taunted December by arriving so late—her greedy captain risking his ship and crew for the promise of a few dollars. One year, December would claim her due.

Soon, neither bootleggers nor freighter could travel the river. By January, Uruk might be able to drive his car over the ice. February might permit an entire truck.

Kuru parked his rattling rust-ridden Model T at the back of the stretch of muddy dirt reserved for orcs, in the shadow of the brick wall. Uruk knew every car parked there, each a testament to a clan of Tai who had labored to earn it and keep it running. Each was as clean as December permitted, acknowledging the Sun-Eater with only a spatter of slush along the lower body. Uruk felt confident that every one of these cars ran better than this Norkosh wreck.

Across Jefferson Avenue, the world changed.

Detroit was one of the world's greatest cities, and it all began on the other side of the road. A port was full of shout and sweat and worthy labor, but four lanes of asphalt separated all that from glass and concrete and finely dressed humans. Every building was taller than Uruk's tenement. A brightly uniformed man stood in front of most buildings, performing no labor but opening the door for any human that wanted to enter. Humans were not strong, but even the feeblest among them should have the strength to open a door! Most of the men wore dark suits and carried small suitcases, marching like they owned the world and carrying themselves with arrogant pride.

Beyond those buildings? Taller buildings. Hudson's Tower gleamed over them all. One of the dock workmen said that it was over four hundred feet tall. Who would want to climb that many stairs? Uruk would never know.

Orcs were not permitted in that part of town. The police would not imprison them. They would be shot.

Orcs belonged at the docks, doing labor that mattered.

Beyond the buildings, the shout of a dozen orcs starting their hauling chant drew Uruk. His gut knew the words, as his body knew the steps. On this beat, you pulled. On the next, you shifted your grip. On the next, you reset your feet. Then heave again. Another shout, and Uruk's feet shifted with the memory of that labor.

Bootlegging was labor. It brought the clan strength and wealth.

But his feet insisted that proper labor meant sweat, and chants, and fresh calluses on the palms every night.

Kuru cut the engine. It died like it had been stabbed in the liver, shaking and choking. "Take me to your clan."

Uruk squeezed himself out of the passenger seat. "Are you a man, to need the simplest things explained to you over and over? I will talk to *my* clan. You may follow."

Kuru bared his Greater Tusks. "I will watch you. And them."

Uruk's hand and fingers stiffened. One strike would take Kuru's eyes.

On the palm, the blood oath sizzled.

Uruk did not allow the pain to touch his face, but Kuru still smiled with satisfaction.

Kuru whirled and tromped towards the trucks idling at the long low loading dock.

A wiser orc would have looked back, rather than declaring that he led when Uruk had not agreed to follow. Or asked where orcs entered the port. Or followed one who knew. Most warehouses and factories required orcs to enter by the loading docks, but the port had a double wooden gate in the fence next to the lot instead. Uruk allowed himself the pleasure of a smile. If Kuru had used his eyes, he would have seen a well-used handle built for an orcish grip. He itched to march through the gates and disappear before Kuru noticed, but if Kuru was doubly humiliated he might become even more foolish.

Besides, this way Uruk got to watch.

Uruk could not hear the dockman yell at Kuru, but the signs the man made with his hands satisfied.

So did the way Kuru clenched his hand as the blood oath stung him.

Kuru stomped back just short of a run, all his tusks bared and eyes wide, December whipping away the quick sharp plumes of his breath. When he was fifteen feet away, Uruk swung the gate open and strode into the docks.

The dockyards ran for hundreds of feet along the shore, expanses of asphalt and cinder-covered dirt, heaps of snow and heaps of crates and open-walled cattle pens. The cold stink of water mingled with the warm stink of manure and the green stink of fodder, a blend that reassured him down to his toes.

Loss surged through Uruk.

Had his callused hands grown soft? Money was not heavy. Would hauling it sap his orcish strength? What of his fine boys? They were learning to *read*. How would they build the strength to face the world?

"Orc!" shouted the human Orc Boss. "What do you want?"

The Orc Boss was the biggest man Uruk had ever seen, but had a face so flat he must have been hit in the face with a shovel right after birth. His nose was a nearly orcish snout, but no orc would let himself grow so soft. His greatest skill was shouting loudly enough to be heard over the orcish work chant.

Kuru thudded to a halt next to Uruk. His mouth worked, but whatever foolishness or lies he wished to bleat, the approaching Orc Boss held him silent.

Men took an orc's mere shout as a threat. Uruk waited for the Orc Boss to huff closer before saying, "No blood today."

Kuru bared his Lesser Tusks. "No blood... today."

The Orc Boss frowned. "It's you, is it? Well, I got work for you, but it don't pay as well as when you quit. That's what happens when you walk off the job."

"I am not here for labor, man." Men said that all orcs looked alike, but the Orc Boss had eyes. "I must speak to my greater clan."

"You're making a social call?" the Orc Boss said.

What was the human word? "It is *em-erg-en-cy*," Uruk said.

The Orc Boss narrowed his eyes. "You know they're working, right?"

As if Uruk would interrupt work! "We wait in the lee until water break."

The Orc Boss frowned. "You can't wait until after work?"

Kuru opened his mouth.

Quick as he could Uruk said, "They all go to their homes after." The Orc Boss flinched—in his haste, Uruk had spoken too loud. He pulled his voice back. "Only here are they all together. We will not interrupt work."

"And who is this?" the Orc Boss said, looking Kuru up and down.

"I am here for the truth," Kuru said.

"No orc would interrupt work," Uruk said.

The Orc Boss bared his teeth. "Guess you wouldn't at that." He jerked a thumb. "Go straight there. Don't start no fights."

Uruk had *said* he intended no fight, but humans never heard what an orc said. "No blood today."

The Orc Boss glanced between Kuru and Uruk, then back at Kuru.

Kuru snarled, "No blood today."

The Orc Boss gave Kuru a slow nod. "I will hold you to that, orc. We have police here."

Kuru pulled his mouth shut to hide his tusks.

Police. If Uruk could goad Kuru into a rage, the police would take him—

The oath sent a white-hot spike up the bones of his arm, making Uruk's eyes water. He drew a shaky breath.

The Orc Boss studied Uruk's face, then nodded again. "You know the way, orc."

Uruk led the fuming Kuru to a spot on the river side of the smallest warehouse where two corners came together in a scrap of shelter. A roof of trash wood offered meager shade, and an ice-crusted water barrel offered refreshment. December's stray breaths found their way around the buildings, but weren't enough to carry away the reassuring stink of orc piss from the corner.

Disturbingly, someone had dragged an empty crate over next to the wall.

Kuru sneered at the crate and said in orcish, "Your clan *rests* during work?"

Why was that crate there? "No proper orc rests at work," Uruk said.

"Yes," Kuru said.

How dared Kuru call the Tai improper? Uruk's hands twitched to slash, but the blood oath ripped its own slash across his palm. He hid his pain better than Kuru had. "I do not accuse without proof. I am more of an orc than you."

Kuru grimaced as his anger woke his oath. "Only orcs bootleg draught. Only the Tai dare bootleg. I would expect even a mad Tai to understand."

"Mad?" Uruk said. "Norkosh take the filthiest labor they can find!"

"And the Tai the most dangerous," Kuru said. "You seek glory, and leave your children fatherless."

"The Tai care for our own," Uruk hissed. "Always." The world should know Kuru was a liar. Would a quick scarring slash across his face violate the blood oath? Uruk's palm twinged.

"Uruk-Tai," an orc behind Uruk said.

Uruk did not look away from Kuru. "No blood today."

The orc—Gartapsh-Tai—came up beside Uruk, his eyes fixed on Kuru. He did not return the greeting.

Uruk clenched his jaw, willed his gut to relax, and raised his hand to show the shaman's mark. "Kuru-Norkosh and I are bound by blood oath. Our cavern is under attack. Kuru—" no, if he declared that Kuru had accused the Tai of poisoning a child, Kuru would not leave the docks alive. "I must speak with all other Tai who are bootlegging."

Gartapsh studied Kuru another breath, then showed his Lesser Tusks. "No blood today."

Kuru showed his own and spat, "No blood today."

Gartapsh said to Uruk, "You bring all the draught our clan needs, and more. Why would we gather more?"

"Someone spreads lies about us," Uruk said.

"I speak the truth," Kuru said. "Poisoned draught killed my brother's daughter."

To Uruk's surprise, Gartapsh stilled. Unbound by blood oath, he should have slashed or snarled or even showed tusks.

The sight chilled Uruk's blood in a way not even December could. "Gartapsh. Speak."

Nasty triumph shone on Kuru's ugly face.

"I cannot," Gartapsh said. "Young Lortz can."

Uruk remembered Lortz-Tai joining the dock crew a month before Uruk had quit. "Orc Boss told us to remain here. When he breaks, my father's brother's son, send him."

"He breaks now." Gartapsh did not remove his eyes from Kuru.

If Lortz had his break now, why did he not arrive with Gartapsh?

"He is slow today," Gartapsh said, "but he comes."

Uruk glanced over Gartapsh's shoulder.

Lortz *was* walking to the lee, as fast as he could.

Even from yards away, Uruk could see Lortz's bruises and the limp and the hitching stance of broken ribs.

 16

Walking backwards, dragging the wheelchair against its sticking axle, Mha did not see the Pickle Barrel until the snow-covered pebbles of the parking lot ambushed her feet.

A long wooden building sat set back only a thrown grenade's distance from the road, with wings off to the left and right, and broad eaves that offered shelter from the fresh snow shivering down from thickening clouds. Windows lined the front wall, but the owners had hung heavy drapes within to hold the warmth. Humans might think they could deny December and welcome June, but the snow heaped on the roof testified to December's insistence. The building's heat would melt the snow's belly into ice, making it heavier and heavier until the roof gave in. Better to allow December a slow tithe of heat, rather than refuse her and make the Sun-Eater demand full sacrifice.

Mha had made her own sacrifice of warmth. Her bones burned with the long slow struggle to haul the wheelchair down half a mile of icy road, but the cold had gone up her tunic and seeped into her skull. Her tusks ached all the way into their roots and her age-knobbed hands felt frozen around the chair's varnish-smoothed handles. Snow had made its way through the cardboard lining her boots, icing her toes and raising steam around her ankles. The tunic held a scrap of heat around her middle, and her coat, threadbare as the rest of her, warmed her liver—but the rest of her honored December.

Thorn laughed. "We made it! I knew we could."

We. Had Thorn fought in this tiny war? "Yes, Thorn."

"Just a little further, dear. Can you smell that roast?"

Mha's attention had been on bringing air into her lungs, not tasting it. As if acknowledging her tribute, December brought Mha the sweet smell of slow-roasted cow. Her stomach growled.

"Don't worry, dear, we'll get you a nice roast." Thorn's humor evaporated. "Orcs do like beef, don't they? You must."

Mha had eaten cow three times, all during the war. She and *that* orc had once shared a whole cow thigh, roasted over a fire pit, cracking the bone and devouring the sweet marrow before leaping at each other. The memory of those two young orcs, one that had grown into *that* orc and one who'd rotted into Mha, still flared bright. "Yes, Thorn." Her breath shook on the word.

Perhaps December would take it as a sign of her labors, not the weakness in her heart.

"Almost there." Thorn thrust a finger into the air. "Onward! There's a steak calling my name!"

Dragging the wheelchair across snow-choked cinders demanded more strength than the road's smooth asphalt. The wheels turned a few inches before catching, jerking in Mha's grip, before turning free again.

"They need to do something about this parking lot," Thorn said. "Maybe if you pulled a little more smoothly?"

Pull smoothly? The ground was not smooth, the axle was not smooth, the wheelchair itself fought smoothness. Even Mha's old joints were not smooth.

Older orcs in the Army had taught Mha what to do with meaningless orders. "Yes, Thorn."

"I'm sure you're doing your best, dear."

They were only halfway across the parking lot when a man in a long coat and heavy hat that went over his ears trotted out of the Pickle Barrel's front door. "Are you all right?"

"About time!" Thorn said. "Come around this way, whoever you are."

"Are you hurt?" the man said. "Did your car break down?"

"Not at all, young man," Thorn said. "My name is Rose Harrison, but everyone calls me Thorn. And this is the orc who does for me, Mantis."

"Mha n'Tass," Mha said.

Thorn rolled right over her correction. As she—as every human—always did. "And we are here for lunch."

The man blinked. "Where did you park?"

"We live just half a mile up the road," Thorn said. "Why get out a car just to come that little way?"

Why did she say that? Thorn did not have a car. Mha would walk that without thought, if she had reason to.

"Oh." The man looked puzzled. Even Mha had understood Thorn, how could he be confused?

Thorn's commanding finger aimed at the man. "Manners, young man! I've introduced myself and my friend."

Friend?

The man straightened. "My apologies, ma'am. I am Erik Baywater, manager of the Pickle Barrel."

"Nice to meet you, Mister Buywater," Thorn said.

No human could speak an orc's name, but was Thorn also unable to speak human names?

Thorn said, "You can certainly get us nice warm seats by the fire. It's nippy out here, and we've had quite a journey. That smell, is it prime rib today?"

"It is, ma'am." Baywater glanced up at Mha. "If you'll permit me, I'll take over your chair. Your orc can go around back and wait in the furnace room. It's warm, and there's running water."

A spot by the furnace? Hope surged before Mha could squash it.

"Nonsense!" Thorn said. "Mantis will be dining with me, of course."

Mha's throat tightened. Eat with Thorn, in a human mess hall? "The furnace room is orcish." Maybe she could find an oilcan and address the wheelchair's axle.

"Missus Harrison!" Baywater straightened. "This is a quality establishment."

"Call me Thorn. And I do hope so. I would hate to think it has gone downhill since my husband and I were last here."

"I mean," Baywater said, "we are not in the habit of allowing orcs in the dining room."

Mha's tension eased. The whole world had not struck its head, only Thorn.

"I see," Thorn said. "You have a phone, do you not?"

"Of course."

Thorn's smile became predatory. "Then I suggest you call Mister Satrap and ask him who holds the mortgage on this property."

Baywater's face went even more pale. Did that mean he had lost, and Mha had to eat in the mess hall?

"Quickly, now!" Thorn hefted one of her canes to waggle the handle at him. "I want this settled before we get to the front door."

Disappointment surged. Thorn frequently told Mha to say what she wanted. Mha had said she wanted the back room, but Thorn cared more about defeating Baywater.

"Oh, and my wheelchair seems a little stiff. You'll want to have your man look at it while my Mantis and I eat."

Mha's spirits plunged. But—perhaps—she might taste cow a fourth time.

17

December's breath scoured the quay, sending fresh snow skittering over the sanded concrete and into the Detroit River's icy slurry. Heavy gray clouds sailing overhead promised more snow and storm for the Longest Night. The roughly roofed corner the Port of Detroit set aside for the orcs was sheltered enough that the edges of Uruk's coat only fluttered. Looking at the beaten orc Lortz-Tai sent a chill not from December down his spine.

The bruises were *wrong*.

Orcs fought. An orc who lost a fight would go to work the next day, beaten and broken. But even here in America, where orcs trimmed their talons, orcs brawled with blunt fingers and struck with the edges of their hands.

Lortz-Tai could be no older than thirteen. The fresh brown bruise on his purple-green face was too broad to be a grown orc's fingertips.

Large men might punch a foolish young orc who wandered where he was not welcome. An orc wouldn't dare fight back. An orc who killed a man with a slap would be in prison before sunset. This bruise was larger than a man's knuckles.

An orc might fight with a fist, but only for brass knuckles. Brass knuckles gouged and crushed flesh. Lortz had no such wound.

That bruise could only be an orcish fist. An un-orcish orcish fist.

What had *happened*?

At the edge of Uruk's vision, glee made Kuru-Norkosh's face even uglier.

Lortz's lurching gait spoke of injury, but his face showed no pain. His narrowed eyes blinked against the snow, but no more. A man so badly beaten would have *called off* work, but an orc endured.

Lortz stopped next to Gartapsh-Tai and said in orcish, "Uruk-Tai. No blood today."

"Lortz-Tai. No blood today." If only Tai had been present Uruk would have urged Lortz to sit on the upturned crate and save his strength for labor, but he would not let Lortz shame himself before Kuru.

Kuru sneered, "No blood today."

Lortz's eyes flashed and Lesser Tusks glinted between his lips.

"Kuru-Norkosh is bound by blood oath," Uruk said. "Our cavern is under attack. Speak of your war."

Lortz kept his glare fixed on Kuru for a breath, long enough to show he would fight if given reason, then dismissed Kuru. Good.

Gartapsh kept his attention on Kuru. Also good.

"Last night, at work's end." Lortz spoke in short breaths, fighting at least one broken rib. "Dockmen said an orc was delivering. At the Blind Pig. That had to be you. Dad—" Lortz did flinch then, at his child's habits bleeding into adulthood—"*Gartapsh* sent me. Thragg-Tai claims a wife this Sunday."

Claiming a wife demanded draught. "I will send three bottles," Uruk said.

Kuru opened his mouth to speak. Gartapsh growled, but Kuru's hiss and clench of fist told Uruk that whatever Kuru would have said, it would have gone against the oath.

"The Blind Pig had a truck, but." Lortz shook his head. "Not you. Not a Tai. He said he was Tai, but." He strained to squeeze a full breath between his ribs. "Not a Tai."

What orc would claim a clan not his own?

"How do you know?" Kuru demanded.

Uruk turned. "My clan!" he snarled. "I speak to *my* clan!"

"I cover your failures," Kuru said.

Uruk's hand flew up to slash Kuru's face, but a flare from the blood oath sent shivering fire all the way up his arm into his jaw. His breath froze as if December had claimed his heart. His vision dimmed. The mud and dirt under his boots swayed. Perhaps Uruk could not give Kuru the mauling he deserved—but he was not going to fall in front of any Norkosh.

Gartapsh spoke.

Kuru answered.

Uruk focused on remaining upright until the ground steadied and he could hear the horns on Jefferson Avenue over his pulse in his ears. Gartapsh demanded Kuru give more details about the attack on the tenement, filling time until Uruk could recover. Finally, Uruk was able to say, "Lortz. Go on."

"His face was wrong," Lortz said. "His skin looked greased. Even his tusks were strange. Maybe twenty or twenty-five years old. And his clothes. He said *hello*." That untranslatable last word in English.

Humans feared the sound of orcish. Speaking English around them was wisest. Uruk nodded.

"I demanded to know his clan. He said Tai."

Kuru gave a satisfied grunt.

Uruk ignored Kuru. "You gave your line and demanded his." Every orc knew their heritage, a chain of father's fathers back to the clan's founding. Two orcs of the same clan would exchange generations until each learned the depth of their shared blood.

"He refused his."

Uruk let out his own grunt of surprise.

"But a Tai," Kuru said.

"No Tai would refuse his line," Gartapsh snarled. "Even to you."

Kuru bared all his tusks.

"What more?" Uruk said to Lortz.

"He claimed the clan, but refused his line," Lortz said. "I challenged."

As was proper. Uruk nodded.

Lortz said, "He did not understand."

"What?" Uruk said.

"I challenged him again," Lortz said. "He... he said he did not understand orcish."

Uruk's thoughts stopped. Challenges were always in orcish. An orc who did not speak orcish?

Even Kuru was silent.

Lortz said, "He said that he was *sorry* he did not speak orcish."

Sorry? Another untranslatable, meaningless English word. How could such a thing happen?

"He was not an orc," Lortz said. "I defended the clan."

Lortz was not small for a thirteen-year-old, but an orc ten years his senior would have far more muscle. Such a monster must be fought, doomed as the fight might be. "Tell me the saga," Uruk said.

"I struck his face," Lortz said. "The blow—he shouted. I surprised him."

No orc would cry out from such a blow.

Gartapsh's gaze moved between Lortz and Uruk, narrowed eyes showing his worry.

Lortz said, "He even fought wrong."

"How can an orc fight wrong?" Kuru said.

Uruk choked his anger before the blood oath choked him.

Lortz, properly, ignored Kuru.

Uruk would not repeat Kuru's question. "Tell me how he fought." There—different enough to show his thoughts were his own.

"With fist and foot," Lortz said. "He kicked, but—sideways. When I struck him again. He slid sideways. Always sideways. I missed." The young orc's need to spill out the saga struggled against his shortened breath. "He tangled his arm around mine. Threw me into the wall."

Kuru snorted.

If Lortz hadn't been so badly beaten, Uruk might have scoffed as well. "Go on."

"Fists," Lortz said. "He fought like a man. Not any man fight I've seen. A strange man-fight. He moved. Never stopped."

Moved? Uruk had seen workmen fight. They brawled like orcish children, adjusting their feet but standing and punching each other until one fell.

"I lost," Lortz said. "He kicked me. In the chest. Couldn't breathe."

"You had fallen?" Uruk said.

"No," Lortz said. "I stood. His kick almost—hit my chin."

A brawling orc would kick another in the dick if offered the chance, but the chest? No orc could kick that high. What sort of monster mocked the clan?

"My breath stopped," Lortz took the deepest breath he could manage and looked into Uruk's eyes. "I fell." Shame dripped from his voice.

"You defended the clan," Uruk said—the kindest words for a fallen warrior.

"He did not speak," Lortz said. "He straightened his human clothes. Drove away."

Uruk's heart stuttered. "Human clothes?"

Lortz nodded. "Paper man clothes. A suit. Sewn for an orc."

18

Before the US Orc Army had trusted Mha with a Gatling gun, she had hauled canvas, fodder, and water barrels for human mess tents. The Pickle Barrel looked nothing like any of them.

A fieldstone fireplace dominated the middle of the dining hall. A concrete post at each corner supported the chimney, and a clever dangling mesh of fine chain imprisoned the drifting cinders without blocking the heat. Logs the size of Mha's thigh were stacked in a square so the fire could devour them inside and out. After dragging Thorn's stubborn wheelchair half a mile down the icy road, the heat felt wonderful.

The tiny tables could seat four or perhaps six men, each with their own spindly wooden chair. The Pickle Barrel could fit twice as many men if they'd use long benches and tables. They'd be warmer, too. Why waste body heat only to have a giant fire? And why polish the tables so brightly when elbows and knives would batter them?

The ravenous hardwood fire couldn't compete with the smells drifting from the kitchen. Beef was the strongest, but Mha's mouth watered at the aroma of baking potato and frying oil. The thin reek of the nasty greenery humans loved added a sour note, but not enough to turn her stomach. Mha had forgotten the stink of padded chairs that had soaked up years and years of human farts. The Army had taught her to ignore that stink, and her gut remembered that lesson.

Baywater ordered Mha and Thorn to wait just inside the door while he prepared their table, and vanished down a dark hall.

All but five of the tables were empty. Four of them had flabby paper men, in their suits and cloth nooses and platters overflowing with more bounty than a human soldier ate and fancy glasses full of rotting grape juice. The fifth was surrounded by tiny human women, their dresses marked by fur in the wrong places for warmth and lace any place they might want to hold heat. The men stared openly at Mha before turning to each other and laughing or scowling. The women glanced once and whispered to each other.

Humans didn't like orcs looking at them, but Mha found herself too tired to care. Not tired in body—hauling the wheelchair had given her strength. Tired in heart. If humans watched her, why shouldn't she look at them? Why shouldn't she look at the *paintings* hanging on the back wall? Why shouldn't she wonder why the cooks were hiding, and why there was no counter for the eaters to fetch their meals or return the empty plates?

A human woman backed out of a double-hinged door in a cloud of fry-smell, bearing a platter half her size nearly overflowing with plates buried beneath food. Mha glimpsed a gleaming kitchen beyond the door. The woman had to be strong, for a human, to hoist all that. Was she bringing food for her whole table? The woman turned and saw Mha. The platter wobbled. Her smile disappeared.

The woman knew Mha did not belong here. Would Thorn's unthinkable demand that Mha eat with her make the woman spill the food?

The woman used the other hand to stabilize the platter, and smiled again. Spilling a meal would merit anger, but why would she smile so at doing what was expected? And the clothes made no sense. Humans did everything they could to refuse December a sacrifice of heat, yet this woman and two others standing near the kitchen door wore thin tunics that ended above the knee and left their shoulders bare. Only failed clans could not clothe their own.

The woman carried her platter to the two men without food. "Here you go, gentlemen! Rare for you, sir, and medium here, am I right?"

One of the men reached around and squeezed the woman's butt.

Mha couldn't contain a growl, but the woman only hopped back. "Sir! You wouldn't want me to drop your lunch, would you?"

"Depends on what else you drop," the man who hadn't grabbed said. The grabber laughed.

Thorn said, "The best thing about getting old is that you don't have to put up with that anymore."

Mha grunted.

"Oh, my dear, I'm sure those big orc men do the same."

Mha said, "My first suitor grabbed my ass."

"Men are all the same," Thorn said.

The man who had attacked the woman glanced at Thorn with that human smirk of lying innocence.

"I ate his throat," Mha said. "His family took the leavings, but..." She caressed the oldest skull dangling from her belt. "I carry him with me."

The two men stopped laughing.

"Serves him right!" Thorn slapped the arm of her wheelchair. "Certain young ladies could learn from you."

"There you go, sir," the woman said. "Can I get you anything else?"

"No," the grabber said. "That's... fine? Thank you?"

"Just let me know." Rather than sitting down to eat with them, the woman lowered her platter and walked back towards the kitchen. Was she not eating with her people? Did this mess hall have people who only carried food for others? Someone who prepared your food offered you a gift of respect. What kind of person could not be bothered to walk across a room for respect?

The two men ate in silence. So did the men at the next table over. The women in the back stopped eating to whisper even more fiercely to each other, casting glances at Mha and Thorn.

Baywater scurried back up. He'd discarded his heavy coat and hat, revealing extra meat around his middle and his spindly neck. "This way, ma'am." He didn't even glance at Mha. "As befits a special guest such as yourself, we've prepared the private dining room for you. You have your own fire, and a personal waitress dedicated to your comfort."

"Oh, how nice," Thorn said. "Isn't that nice, Mantis?"

"Mha n'Tass," What did *nice* mean? "Yes, Thorn."

Baywater led them down the dark hall and into a broad, doorless room. Long tables more suitable for a mess hall than anything out front had been shoved against the walls. One of the feeble four-person tables sat in the middle of the room, flanked with one of those feeble chairs on either side and draped in red cloth. Were they eating with seamstresses? No, the cloth bore plates and glasses and forks and spoons. Did Baywater think that Thorn would eat without scattering crumbs? An orc did not waste food, but just this morning Mha had watched Thorn waste crumbs and precious blueberries as she attacked her *muffins*. A bare wood table could be wiped clean. Why launder a cloth?

Thorn fumbled for her canes. "Close enough, my dear Mantis. Mister Barrywater, get your man to put some grease on those wheels."

A last chance! "Mha n'Tass. I can fix the wheels, man."

Baywater looked hopeful. "If you wish—"

"Don't be silly, dear!" Thorn said. "Not that kind of silly. We're going to *eat* ourselves silly."

Baywater smiled like his bowels were stopped up. Did he need a prune? "Of course, ma'am." He raised a hand to the young human woman standing just behind him. "This is Miss Iris. She'll be taking care of you today."

Iris was dressed much as the others, in a short tunic that bared her knees and shoulders. She looked at Mha and swallowed nervously, but refused to look away. Good. The men out front could learn from her.

Baywater said, "Can I bring you—" his eyes flickered at Mha—"each a glass of the house white?"

White what?

"Young man," Thorn said, using both her canes to spider to a chair. "I ask you to look at us. Do we look like *glass of white* people?"

"Of course not, ma'am," Baywater said.

Why had he *asked*, then?

"We are having prime rib, so it must be red," Thorn said. "And a glass for me is fine, but my friend is going to need the rest of the bottle. In a big glass, of course. You do have big glasses, don't you?"

Baywater flinched. "Of course, ma'am. See to it, Iris." He pivoted on a heel and scurried away.

Iris took a deep breath, straining her tunic. Her clan had also failed to clothe her properly for December. "Welcome to the Pickle Barrel my name is Iris I'll be *happy* to take your order."

"Perfect," Thorn said. "Mantis! Sit, sit!"

"Mha n'Tass." Where was she supposed to sit? The chair looked too fragile for an orcish child, let alone a full grown orcess.

"We are people of quality," Thorn said. "She can't take our order with you standing."

Mha stiffened.

The chair might have broken under her weight once, but age had stolen her height and shoulders. Stooped as she was, tall humans could look in her eyes.

Mha's breath shuddered.

Thorn had demanded the labor of sitting in that human chair.

Mha sat. The seat was too narrow, letting her ass hang over either side, and her knees brushed the bottom of the table. She must look ridiculous.

"There you go," Thorn said.

Iris said, "You ladies look lovely I'm glad you came today what delightful outfits you have."

"Why thank you!" Thorn said. "It's a Lanvin. My husband gave it to me on our thirtieth anniversary, and my friend's is..." Thorn frowned. "Who is your dress by, dear?"

That made no sense. A dress didn't go by anything, let alone a person. "Yes, Thorn."

Thorn tsk'd. "What kind of dress are you wearing?"

Mha brushed the leather over her breast. "Orc."

Iris' gaze caught the scars. Her eyes widened. "Prime rib you said?"

"Yes, child. Prime rib with baked potato and this and that."

"We have four six and eight ounce," Iris gasped.

"Oh, four is plenty for me." Thorn smiled. "And you, my dear? How much prime rib would you like for lunch?"

She couldn't demand a leg, could she? No, her rotting guts couldn't eat a whole leg. And *prime rib* wasn't a leg. It had to mean ribs. What kind of ribs would humans eat? Humans ate the best parts. How many of the best cow ribs could she eat?

Mha looked back at Iris. "A pile as big as your head, woman."

Iris swallowed. "I'll get that straight into the kitchen your wine is coming. Bread! There's bread, we bake it!" She retreated with a careful stride, showing more courage than Baywater.

Thorn leaned in and whispered, "I can't remember when I've had this much fun. It feels like forever since I went out and made trouble. Did you catch the look on his face?"

He must be Baywater. He looked like a man who hated orcs. "Yes, Thorn."

Thorn giggled.

The fire in this room wasn't as nice as that in the main mess hall, but the new-laid logs hissed and crackled. The heavy drapes against the back wall shifted as December's breath slipped through the concealed windows. A broad painting opposite the fireplace showed a classic Old World scene, horseback men in red jackets, crops raised as they crossed rich green hills in pursuit of brown-and-white hounds in full cry. To the side, more horsemen hopped down into a dry riverbed, arms raised in excitement. More hounds tore at a fallen orc. In the Old World, orcs without anyone to eat them had another way out.

The Old World made sense. The Army had made sense. Growing old with *that* orc had made sense. Nothing made sense now.

Thorn *nattered*—a useful word, nattered. Nattering meant to speak of things too trivial to speak of. Only humans nattered. The first time Mha had drank *tea* with her, Thorn had said, *oh I'm nattering, ignore me.* Thorn did not give instructions when she *nattered.* She did not require Mha to act, only the labor of her presence.

That orc had cared for Mha all his days. She had appreciated his labor and all he had brought her. Every time *that* orc went to the farmhouse to beg for food, he had listened to Thorn natter. Mha had not known how much work not slashing nattering humans demanded. If she had, she would have thanked him more for that than all the rest.

Through the doorway, Mha had a good view of the Pickle Barrel's bar. Stools lined a long counter so short that a healthy orc could sit on it. When Mha had been in the Army the shelves behind the bar would have been filled with all the different types of alcohol humans loved. Perhaps draught would rupture feeble human throats, but why did they insist on flavoring their whiskey—not to mention that mouse-piss they called ale. Prohibition had emptied the shelves, but surely the Pickle Barrel had a secret hoard. Foolish men had passed that foolish law and promptly ignored it.

She had not tasted draught since before *that* orc died.

Draught was for an orc with a clan, with *worth*. Not Mha. Not a wreck of an orcess whose only labor was ignoring an equally decayed humaness, an orcess who was not even permitted to grease the axle of a wheelchair. Was she supposed to sit and wait for Iris to carry in her food on a platter too big for such a tiny human? Would they steal even that labor from her, in a place that had never had an orc inside its walls?

An orc walked up to the bar.

Mha froze.

No, not an orc.

An abomination. Worse than anything she'd seen in the war, but shaped like an orc.

 19

The frozen mud of the Port of Detroit's parking lot was just as treacherous as ever. The horns and whistles of downtown Detroit were just as chaotic, the surge and fall of countless cars on Jefferson Avenue just as powerful. Nothing had changed, but the whole world felt different. December's breath surged through Uruk's flesh and settled in his bones.

An orc who did not speak orcish. Who moved like a man, but not. Who would not share his line. Who did not *fight* like an orc. The ideas crashed into each other, scattering wreckage across his thoughts.

Uruk's youngest brother, Tara-Tai, had a head always full of too many thoughts. Was this how Tara lived each day? If so, no wonder Tara wanted work as a janitor. He required a labor that demanded much of his mind, if only to herd all the thoughts into order.

"This Blind Pig," Kuru-Norkosh growled. "Where is it."

"We do not go there," Uruk said.

"We follow your orc's word," Kuru said. "Or do you fear what we learn?"

"We follow my orc's word," Uruk said. "Men do not know one orc from another, so we follow the—" his mouth twisted against the next word "—*suit*."

"What orcess would sew such a thing?" Kuru sneered.

"What orcess would *have* such a thing!" Uruk said. "What Lortz fought was no orc!"

Kuru said, "All I see is that the Tai are more debased than I knew!" He grimaced, clutching his oath-marked hand to his chest.

Without the blood oath, Uruk would have slashed Kuru for those words. He concentrated on Kuru's pain-shortened breath and the grimace twisting his face. If the vengeance of Azok-Snaka's magic did not satisfy Uruk, he would have no other satisfaction. Yet. As Kuru straightened, Uruk spoke slowly enough that even a Norkosh could understand. "Azok-Snaka declared that the elves warred on us. This monster is their sorcerous creation. Made to mock us, to tell lies about us. To betray us without understanding us."

Kuru finally hissed, "We must follow your orc's word."

"We will," Uruk said. "Only one man makes suits for an orc. We go to him."

"How do you know this?"

"Because he is proud of it," Uruk said. "Making an orc suit was his greatest victory." He climbed in the passenger side of Kuru's Model T. "Take me to East Detroit."

Kuru bared his teeth. "I am not your driver."

"You demanded to drive," Uruk said. "Drive. Or take me home so I may drive." The passenger seat's tattered leather chilled Uruk's rear, its straw padding poking his canvas pants. "Or break your oath, and free me to find this *thing* on my own. Gratiot Road, north of Nine Mile."

Kuru spat and started the car.

Uruk's visits to the tailor shop had all been at the end of the day, when night flattened all the colors. He had not known that the awning was the bright pink of a salmon's flesh, or that the loopy, frilly swooshes painted on it might be letters twisted beyond recognition. Reading was already so difficult that his sons had stayed in *school* to learn it, why make it harder? Was it a tailor's code? The sun of the shortest day was approaching noon, but bright light shone out through the broad windows, highlighting leather dummies crafted like human torsos and draped in ridiculous human clothes. Even from the street, he saw the crowd within. Humans, mostly women.

The shop was not merely stuffed with senseless human *things*, but the most delicate things. A good fart could break half of them all at once, and a sneeze shatter what remained. Kuru's tight face exposed his impatience and anger. The shop was the most human place Uruk had ever been. Kuru going inside would end with police.

If the police took Kuru, they would take Uruk as well. Uruk's innocence would not matter.

"Around the back," Uruk said.

Festering trash cans and crumbling crates made the dirt-track alley even narrower. December's gusts brought the stink of rot-heated garbage in one breath, the smooth smell of ice in the next. A cat sat on a concrete post and licked its paw, its fur too clean to be a stray and with enough meat on its bones to be worth trapping.

Kuru had not even shut off the engine before Uruk hopped out to pound on the freight door. His first blow shallowly dented the metal and sent a hollow boom echoing down the narrow dirt alley, so he made himself soften the next. It still echoed, but the door didn't crumple.

"A paper man suit. For an orc." Kuru's voice dripped contempt.

Uruk clenched his jaw and rapped a third time.

A muffled voice shouted through the door. Locks clanked. The door swung in a few inches and a short, thin human peered out. "Can I help you?" He blinked. "We don't have any deliveries today."

If Uruk let any of his frustration show, the man would slam the door and phone the police. "I am Uruk-Tai. I look for the tailor—" stupid impossible human names!—"Re-gin-ald."

The man blinked again. Was his vision poor? Perhaps humans with bad eyes helped tailors? "Oh! You're that orc! Just a minute, I'll tell him." The human leaned from the door. "Dad!"

"That orc," Kuru said. "You know him."

Uruk snarled in orcish, "I know *of* him."

"I think you *really* want to come back here." The human's voice was raised as loud as a human could manage without pain. Uruk suddenly saw the tailor echoed in the man's face—darker hair, yes, but the same features pulled back from that sharp nose, skin so pale it might have been washed in vinegar until the veins showed. A son?

Uruk's own fine boys were ten years old, fully orc and old enough to work at the docks with the clan. The *school* thought they could learn to read, though, so they *studied* all day instead. Uruk wanted his boys to have a better life than he did, but the tailor's son made his chest tighten. A proper orc's sons worked with him. As they learned to stand against the world, Uruk should witness their victories—even if those victories were only rising after falling.

Instead of dinner being a celebration of shared challenges, it had become the telling of sagas.

His boys fought to *read*, as no orc had ever done.

Uruk would never understand their war.

Even as he ached to share a war with them, he would gut anyone who blocked their way.

The door swung wide. "Yes, who is—"

Even in the daylight, the tailor Reginald resembled a possum. He blinked and sniffed and peered. His face came to a point in his nose. And, if challenged, he would play dead. Standing together, the other human was clearly his young son.

"Sir?" Reginald said.

Before Reginald could say anything about the suit Sanford had bought for Uruk, Uruk said, "No blood today."

"Er—yes. No blood today."

As if a possum could draw blood—no, even a possum would bite if threatened.

The possum straightened his glasses. "Does sir have a problem with—"

"A second suit," Uruk said. "The second one you made."

"Yes?"

"Who was it for?" Uruk said.

"Mister Sanford said it was for you," Reginald said.

Kuru chortled. "A suit!"

Uruk's hand twitched straight, to slash across Kuru's throat. The blood oath lit fires in the bones of his fingers, making him draw a frustrated breath.

"Is there a problem?" Reginald glanced over his shoulder. "If sir would care to return this evening..."

Uruk forced his hand to relax. Despite the fading flickers of shaman's fire inside his hand, he had to speak softly. Frightened humans called the police. "A second *orc*. Has a suit. Who did you make it for?"

"Oh!" Reginald said.

"A suuuuit," Kuru wheezed in Orcish. "Is it *soft*?"

Fire flared in Uruk's hand again, so fierce that bile rose in his gut and his knees wanted to buckle. He would almost rather have his face scarred for dishonor than listen to Kuru's chortling. He let his knees bend an inch, not to leap, but only to anchor his weight to the ground.

Reginald's white face grew blotches of red. "I made suits only for you."

"Does it have a bright pretty noose so you can hang yourself?" Kuru laughed.

Uruk's own anger made the shaman's fire burn brighter. The need to rip Kuru's head off his shoulders and punt it over the tailor's shop stopped his breath.

Reginald's baby possum stared at Uruk, face tight and watery eyes bright.

Reginald grew pale. "It was all the talk at the Detroit Clothier Association's Christmas dinner last week. It turned out that Mister Wilton was just finishing a suit for an orc, but I had delivered two of mine before he completed his first."

Uruk pushed the anger down. That was an orc's life, swallowing rage at a senseless world that battered orcs every way it could. He sucked a breath through his rage-tightened throat and managed to wheeze, "Another tailor made an orc suit?"

"Go away, orc!" The baby possum thrust himself in front of his father, fists clenched. "I won't let you hurt my dad!"

The boy was maybe two-thirds Reginald's height and had even less muscle. His chin shook. His shoulders quivered. Naked fear shone on his face, but this child still put himself between a full-grown orc and a man?

Just as his own sons would.

His anger with Kuru shattered.

Uruk was bootlegging for his wife, for his sons.

He fought this war for his blood.

No orc had ever won a feud with elves. Elves had money and power. They charmed humans and dwarves even as they refused all the passion that made life worthwhile. Their fancy magic, so full of color and smell and false joy, could create something that mocked an orc while orcish magic merely held blood and bone together.

This feeble human boy could not win against Uruk, just as Uruk could not win against the weakest of Celebrimble's wizards.

But the boy stood, as Uruk stood.

The shaman's fire shattered, leaving Uruk sucking a lungful of air.

Another breath. "You do your father proud." He met the boy's eyes just as he would those of his own boys.

The boy did not look away. Where did he get the strength? Were humans born with courage and lose it somehow? Or was Reginald's woman a warrior?

Kuru still wasted his time laughing, but it washed around Uruk like street slop around a fireplug. Uruk would not let Norkosh foolishness hurt his sons.

If this tiny man could stand against an orc, Uruk could do no less.

Humans needed everything repeated. "No. Blood. Today." Repeated *slowly*. "This other orc with a suit. I must find him."

Reginald raised his chin. "Ah. You want Hudson's."

"Where can I find Tailor Hudsons?"

"No, no." Reginald waved his hands and took the deepest breath his feeble human lungs could manage. "The tailor was Geoffrey Wilton. He works exclusively at Hudson's Department Store, down at Woodward and Grand River. Very exclusively." Reginald let a note of pride enter into his voice. "We discussed how to sew a suit for an orc. Yours will wear *much* better than his."

After all that shaman's fire, how could Uruk's blood run so cold?

Kuru stopped laughing.

Hudson's loomed over Detroit like the Dark Lord Kaiser's tower in the tales of the Great War. Every day Uruk went to the Port of Detroit, he saw its pinnacle looming over other buildings. Orcs were not allowed anywhere near there.

Going to the fabled *de-part-ment-store* would not put Uruk in prison.

It would put him in a grave.

 20

Precariously balanced on an awkward human chair in the Pickle Barrel's private dining room, Mha's heart thudded like the hooves of warhorses. Thorn's nattering dissolved into the crackle of the fire as the flames lit Mha's bones. The bar was in the next room over, but the dining room's walls felt very far away. Her whole awareness focused in on the monster standing at the bar.

That *thing* was not an orc.

Its tusks curved properly but shone too brightly, like a man's teeth. Its purple-green skin gleamed greasily. The scalp reflected a line of light from the Edison lamps. No orc wore shoes tied up with laces, not even thick laces that might have been cut from strips of leather. Above the shoes, giant human-style pants. They had been cut for an orc's muscles, for an orc's knees and waist and ass. They weren't even canvas or burlap, or wool, but some feeble human cloth.

This orc's shirt was a white so bright it would tell anyone who saw it that the wearer had never done real labor, and it had *buttons*. Large buttons made for an orc's hands, but sewn in a tidy row. No orc would wear buttons, not when the fiddly things would slow them down in the morning. Buttons were for men and elves.

So was the fancy paper man jacket it wore over its shirt. Who would wear a jacket that showed off the shirt beneath?

The man Baywater approached the *thing*. "I was not expecting an orc."

It shrugged. "I'm in the business." What was wrong with its voice? "And I can deliver."

Baywater glanced into the private dining room, saw Mha watching him, and quickly looked back. "I don't care if you're a treeman so long as you can deliver without anyone getting hurt. We had trouble last night, and the police here this morning. We can't have that again."

It followed Baywater's gaze and saw Mha. An orc would acknowledge her by flashing a tusk. It nodded at her, like a man.

Shocked, Mha didn't move. Her guts felt liquid. Nothing existed in the world except it and her.

It turned back to Baywater and spread its hands. The talons were even trimmed wrong. Young orcs trimmed their talons, foolishly believing it would keep the police from taking them. This orc's talons were not only trimmed, but polished until they gleamed like his tusks. "I'll tell you what I tell all of my clients. I am a businessman. I depend on repeat business. That means quality product, delivered on time and without drama."

No orc used words like that. They were human words, spoken like a man. That was it! He had no orcish accent.

Baywater said, "That sounds too good to be true."

"I understand your hesitancy," it said. "That's why I offer a discount on first orders. Word is, you need someone who can deliver tonight."

It was like one of the shadows the elven wizards conjured during the war. Something impossible, to terrify the enemy. This shadow cast its own shadow on the carpet, though, so it wasn't wizardry.

Baywater frowned. "All right. I'll give you a chance. But this better go clean, you hear me?" His eyes narrowed. "No trouble at all. If I hear so much as a whisper, if the feds come in, I'm not paying and it's all on you."

"Eminently reasonable."

Two words that an orc would never use, put together? Not even an elf would be this filthy!

"Shall we say midnight?" it said.

"And I want to know who I am dealing with," Baywater said.

It nodded. "My name is Achilles Tai."

Terror flooded Mha's heart.

The Tai clan had claimed her daughter Vara.

Had the clan become—*that*? Was her youngest daughter dependent upon such as that for protection? Was she so dishonored, so lost, so trapped?

Blood surged through Mha's veins, and strength rippled through dried-out muscles stretched over aching bone.

Mha's days as a warrior had ended decades ago. Once a woman was claimed, she no longer saw her mother or father except by accident or alliance. Mha could not seek them out. All custom forbade it.

But if her daughter was lost to such a monster, not even the Greatest Dark would stop her.

21

The first payphone stand Uruk saw had no orcish phone. A phone stand in front of a greengrocer had an orcish phone, but someone had snipped the cord an inch from the phone and stolen the earpiece. An orc would have ripped the cord out. Even Lord Bell fought saboteurs.

They drove back three miles towards Hamtramck before they found a working phone. The phone shed stank and someone had scrawled indecipherable human words all over the walls, but when Uruk picked up the handset and dropped in his quarter he heard the operator. The handset didn't even have that buzz of age. Lord Bell must have recently replaced this one. The wind blew straight into the booth, but Kuru stood so close he blocked most of it.

Sanford answered on the first ring and immediately accepted the call. "Urka-Tai. I have news."

"Uruk-Tai." More words pressed inside Uruk's lips, but he restrained them. Scouts did not always return. Best to let them report before sending them out again. "Speak."

"The request to have your building condemned came through Butzel Law Firm in Detroit." Sanford sounded flatter than Uruk had ever heard, his voice squeezed dry of passion. "It was outside their usual line of work. Their clients are all wealthy families or businesses, however. The richest people in Detroit use Butzel."

Uruk sucked a cold breath through his nose. "Elves."

"Circumstantial," Sanford said. "It is not *proof*. Their client list is confidential. I won't get a better answer."

Uruk waited.

Sanford did not declare that he had finished his report.

Behind Uruk, Kuru shifted impatiently.

The earpiece was very clear. Could Kuru hear Sanford? No matter—the quarter would run out soon. "Is that all you have learned?"

"So far. I'm still tracing rumors about bad liquor, but that's going to take time."

Uruk braced himself for senseless questions. "I have labor that only a human may perform."

"What's going on?" Sanford said.

Uruk spoke slowly and as clearly as he could manage. "There *is* a stranger who sells poisoned liquor. He claims to be of Tai, of my clan. Men think he is an orc, but he is no orc. He moves wrong. He does not speak orcish."

"Okay," Sanford said.

Uruk took a deep breath. "He wears a suit."

Sanford said, "I'll call Reginald."

"Wait!" No, too loud. "I have been to *Reg-in-ald*. He did not make it."

"Huh."

"*Reg-in-ald* declared that it was made by a Mister Wilton, at the great Hudson's tower."

"Ah!" Sanford said. "You want me to go down there and ask him about it. Who it was made for, that sort of thing."

Uruk blinked, unbalanced by Sanford's immediate understanding. "Yes."

"I'll be out the door in five minutes. How do I reach you?"

"We return to the cavern," Kuru's eyes burned into Uruk. "I must report to my clan."

Uruk turned back to the mouthpiece. "The tenement."

Sanford said, "I will knock at the door and say your name."

"I or one of my brothers will answer," Uruk said.

"And mine," Kuru said.

"Anything else?" Sanford said.

"This orc is dangerous," Uruk said. "You are a paper man."

"Don't worry," Sanford said. "If I see an orc in Hudson's, I run. Good work."

Good work? "Go," Uruk swallowed the Orcish *bring back blood*. Sanford would never do such.

Sanford hung up.

The second Uruk hung the earpiece, Kuru said "How do you command a human?"

"With a shaman's patience," Uruk said.

Kuru showed his Lesser Tusks. "By what means do you make a *human* accept your orders?"

The Norkosh had no need to know of the alliance. "That is a Tai matter."

"This whole search is a Tai matter," Kuru said. "A Tai orc that does not speak orcish?"

Uruk hissed. "We will prove this thing is no Tai with its bones."

"And this Zhan-ford," Kuru said.

"Just a man," Uruk said.

"When we show the truth of the Tai," Kuru said, "he can share your fate."

"Attack a man," Uruk said, "and the police will take you. Every orc will lose."

Kuru raised his chin. "Tai killed a child. You *took* our future."

"You want your future taken? Keep being foolish." The oath flashed fire, but shuddered to a halt. How much of Azok-Snaka's strength did each surge demand?

"I stand against Tai lies!" Kuru said.

The need to slash Kuru's face burned all through Uruk, raising an echoing hint of fire from his oath-marked hand. He could not mark Kuru. He could not even knock him into the frozen dirt and give him a harmless choke. He had to *think*. "Can I? Can I lie to you? Have you lied to me?"

Kuru exposed his tusks even further. "I speak only the truth."

"Then lie," Uruk said. "Speak a lie about this war. Does Azok-Snaka's oath bind our tongues as well as our talons?"

"I will not stoop to lying at you. You have been lying since we started!"

Uruk said, "I speak only the truth, while you throw filthy accusations with every breath!"

"If the oath bound lies, every word you speak would set your bones on fire."

"Prove your boast," Uruk said. "Prove it! We are bound by the same oath. Say something you believe to be false. Or do you fear a little pain?"

Kuru's eyes bulged. "Then I lie!" he spat. "You want a lie? I declare that the Tai are innocent of Ragosh's death!"

Uruk's breath stopped. Had he guessed right?

Kuru froze.

Uruk didn't dare inhale.

Kuru doubled over like he'd been headbutted by an angry bull. Even the dim echo of the shaman's fire trickling through the blood oath made Uruk want to clench his fist. Instead, he stepped back as Kuru crumpled to the ground, gasping.

He had guessed right.

The oath bound them to honesty with each other more fiercely than it chained them against violence. Not truth—if the shaman knew the truth, he would have declared it. Uruk's defense of his clan had been honest.

Kuru believed his own words.

Sprawled in the snow, Kuru was beginning to breathe again. His eyes stopped twitching and fixed on Uruk.

"We cannot speak a lie," Uruk said. "I make this promise to you. We will find the poisoner. Whoever they are." He glanced up. "The Sun falls. The Longest Night begins soon. I tell you now, bound by the same oath that chains you. The Tai did not poison your daughter."

Kuru sucked in a full breath and thrust his hands down, wrenching himself to his knees and then his feet. His knees shook with the oath's fire, but he did not fall again. "You do not *know* that," he wheezed. "You *believe* it."

Of course Uruk knew it! Poison was un-orcish. "If we find that a Tai has done this, I shall see him cut away."

Kuru's face twisted. What more could he want?

Everything. He wanted the poisoner slow-roasted alive, the way their fathers' fathers had done to prisoners.

If one of his own boys had been poisoned, Uruk would feel the same.

 22

Mha's mind was too full for thought.

She ate what she was told. "Yes, Thorn." She drank the too-sweet *wine*, tongue straining to catch the feeble burn of alcohol while the rest of her didn't care. "Yes, Thorn." Bite-sized rolls with butter and the thick boneless slab of juicy red cow could not fill the pit of her heart. "Yes, Thorn." Thorn and Baywater lied through their respect chant at the door, then Mha hauled Thorn back to the farm.

The wheelchair rolled easily, but the drivers still blared their horns.

After hours that felt like years, Mha got Thorn back in her house and fled to her sheltering barn. Freed from that senseless labor, she could stop and leash her mind.

Her old stomach bulged with more meat than she had eaten since the war. Its richness sizzled in her blood and made her skull throb. Her hip had stopped aching and started burning, and her back pulsed from the day's comforting labor. Through it all, the memory of that thing calling itself Tai pushed at the inside of her skull.

An orcess did not mourn the daughters taken away by warriors. Raising a daughter who attracted strong warriors was a victory.

But taken by a clan that included such a *thing*?

It would return to the Pickle Barrel at midnight.

Breathe. Breathe, and prepare for war.

She needed weapons.

The board walls had warped with age, leaving slits for December's breath to steal away any heat the feeble Sun might cast. The only new thing was the heap of coal almost as tall as Mha in the corner by the double doors, brought in October to warm her through the winter. An open-top carriage abandoned before Mha was born sat in the back, its rear axle broken and the springs more rust than metal. Two-by-fours leaned against the wall had been left to shrivel. Barrels held scrap wood, chunks of iron, and wadded greasy rags.

Mha inspected the shelves. When she and *that* orc had arrived at the barn, she had searched them for tools useful for hardening the grooms' quarters' in the back. The screwdrivers were corroded beyond use, the pliers snapped.

She had different needs now.

A broken screwdriver could stab. A rusty nail could take an eye. She hefted a human hammer thoughtfully. A corroded hammerhead drove crooked nails but worked just fine against skulls. It was too small for her grip, though. A file with its thin film of protective oil still looked intact—no, did she think she was going to scrape that *thing* to death? She would have died her first day in the Army if she fought with a file!

The curved whetstone would help, if she could find anything to sharpen.

Breathe. Chain the rage until the war begins.

A tin coffee can back in the shadowed shelves had some kind of short rods sticking out of it. Mha pulled it into the light. Galvanized hundred-penny nails, each as long as her hand, meant to hold logs together. She could use them in a spiked club, or she could take the hammer with her to fight. When you nailed a prisoner to a floor, it didn't matter if the nails were crooked.

Maybe one of the two-by-fours could be made into a spear? The ones she could see were twisted and dry-rotted, but perhaps something deeper had survived? A proper orcess could swipe the whole pile aside in one shove, but Mha had to move them one at a time.

Did she really believe her age-sick body could stand against a monster?

This morning, the only enemy she wanted to overcome had been her life. She could not lose tonight's war, though. Not if her daughter was held by a monster.

What would they have done to her?

No. Do not hope for the best. Take this monster. Cut off parts of him until he spoke the truth, then reward him by cutting his throat. If saving her daughter meant journeying to Detroit to kill a dozen more, she would.

Mha tossed another board, more fiercely than she intended, and something toppled out from behind the stack.

A scythe. When it hit the dirt the wooden handle cracked in a spray of dry rot, but the blade itself still had some gleam.

Mha smiled.

The scythe blade had been greased before being hung up one autumn, to preserve the metal through the winter and Michigan's muddy spring until summer summoned it again. Summer had come, but the scythe had been abandoned. A few spots of rust marred the sweep of steel. Nothing Mha couldn't polish out. The blade was sharp enough for grass or corn, but an hour with the whetstone would give it an edge for a warrior.

And Mha had a better handle. A handle worthy of this war.

Back in the grooms' quarters, she lay the blade and whetstone on the table before feeding fresh coal to the cinders in the stove. She would sharpen the blade and attach the handle. She would rest. Not sleep. She could not risk sleeping through her midnight war. She would finish sewing her boots. She would make the handle for the scythe.

That left one weapon, if it still lived.

Smothering a groan, Mha knelt to drag the crate out from beneath the bed. The trophies looked as worn and ragged as she felt: a dried orc hand, talons untrimmed, bitten off at the wrist. Two bronze medals from the US Orc Army, green with age. Beneath them the charms, granted by Army shamans. The feathers belonged to May—useless. Same with September's corn husk and the rune-carved stone from Balabano Bay in Cuba.

Had her age-sick brain made up a memory?

No. The smoke-stained brick on a rope had settled to the bottom.

The shaman had told her that the brick came from the first Detroit. When the old city had been sacrificed to June almost a hundred years ago—over a hundred, now—only the brick chimneys survived. The chimneys endured like orcs.

She hadn't used it since leaving Cuba. A mother's wars demanded different magic—until now, when this mother needed the most primal of magics. Cradling the brick in her fingers, it seemed to tickle her fingers. A lingering echo of the ancient charm? Or a rotting orcess lying to herself?

The stinks of charred wood and burning man-meat surged to overwhelm the coal stove, then faded.

The charm still had life. Not much. Not like she remembered. But life.

A fading charm for a fading orcess.

Mha climbed back to her feet. Her chest heaved and her knees creaked, but they had a moment to catch up as she stripped off her ancient boots and her tunic. Once bare, she hung the brick around her neck and tromped outside.

December's breath hit like an angry bull, plunging into her hide to claw at her liver. The Sun had already begun to sink towards the western trees, lighting her without warmth, but was still high enough to witness her. Before she could catch her own breath, she marched her naked feet into untouched snow.

Mha knelt. The wind had been cold, but the snow burned as it swallowed her legs and thighs and rose over her hips.

On aching knees, Mha bit the base of her thumb talon and pressed the welling blood against the brick. "I choose war," she growled to the Sun-Eater and the Sun alike. "I *take* battle. I *take* the lives of my enemy. And I *take* the Old City into myself."

Was the brick growing warmer?

"As the chimneys of the Old City stood, this orc stands."

Her hand quivered. Fatigue, or charm? No, doubt would ruin the charm.

"Through marrow-burned bones, I *take* victory."

Kneeling on the snow should numb her feet and her knees, but it only burned more fiercely.

"My war!" Mha shouted at the sky. "I declare to the shortest day and the Longest Night, *my* war."

Her cry echoed from the bare trees.

Mha stared at the sky, meeting her gods' gaze and refusing to flinch.

Her rage flooded away, leaving only determination.

Orcish gods never gave. They only took. They had taken even her hopes for death.

But maybe—*maybe*—that monster had offended them. Guessing what would offend gods was a game for shamans and fools, but some filth was so awful that even the Earth could not bring herself to swallow it.

Perhaps they had kept her alive to protect her blood.

23

Only a handful of trucks with worn canvas tents grumbled down the road leading to the tenement, with an occasional Oldsmobile or Buick prowling between them. The blue sky felt fierce and frozen. The Sun, already brushing the western skyline, burned Uruk's tired eyes. With Kuru driving, Uruk could let his mind drift.

Vara would be laboring over tonight's feast with Kovo, trusting Uruk to end the war before the Greatest Dark. She had taken a few dollars from the piles and bought pig, not tripe but sweet muscle and succulent crunchy marrow-bones, planning to bake it all in salt and pepper and bitter olives. They had draught, fernet-branca, a can of grapefruit juice, and a tiny bottle of nutmeg liqueur to make the Longest Dark punch. Oscar and Ivan would be home from *school* by now. Did they even know of the Norkosh war yet, or were they innocently deciding which of the year's sagas to share tonight? No, Daka or Kaba would have spoken to them. They would be standing guard at the stairwells, holding any stray Norkosh out while the older orcs snatched sleep.

Sleep would be good. Delivering booze all night, defending the clan against Norkosh lies, and hunting a false orc across Detroit while dragging Kuru-Norkosh around like a drunk draft horse leashed to his ankle, had left every muscle sore and his skull stuffed with rancid cotton. He wasn't easily exhausted like Grandpa, but he wasn't fifteen either.

If Sanford could track the false orc, Uruk could end the war before dark. After the feast he would tell the saga of making Kuru-Norkosh choke on his lies.

Until then, he would keep his eyes open despite how they felt covered of sand.

A block from the tenement, the Model T slowed.

Uruk opened his mouth to rebuke him.

"Look, you blind Tai," Kuru said. "Look."

For the first time in Uruk's memory, trucks lined the road in front of the tenement. Humans preferred to keep even their vehicles away from orcs. From this far away Uruk couldn't make out any icons on their sides, but the way the sun reflected off the chrome declared their newness.

Disquiet rippled through Uruk's gut. "Roll past."

"Obviously," Kuru said.

Uruk's jaw tightened. Poison. The city declaring the building unworthy. What new attack was this?

The three trucks wore the Detroit blazon on their sides. City trucks. Workmen in city uniforms and wearing metal half-dome hats were removing equipment from the truck beds.

"We have until the end of January," Kuru snarled.

"Why would an enemy stop attacking?" Uruk said. "Park."

Kuru was already turning the wheel to swerve across traffic, prompting an oncoming delivery truck to blare its horn. The Model T's springs groaned as it jolted between two of the trucks onto the frozen mud of the tenement parking lot, and the whole car rocked sickeningly as Kuru stomped the brake.

Uruk was already swinging his feet out onto the ground, letting his coat flap around him. December sent frozen fingers up his shirt, but he ignored them.

He could not run towards the workmen.

He could not bare his tusks.

If Uruk showed any anger at the men violating the tenement grounds, they would summon the police.

Two of the men braced a tripod in the dirt right by the road, arranging it so that they could easily peer into the device at its top. Another pair of men waited beside them, one with another tripod slung across his shoulders. Four more men stood nearby, laboring at nothing but watching Uruk approach.

The largest man raised his chin at Uruk. "Orc."

"Man." Uruk tried to take a deep breath, but quietly. "You are on our land."

"I talked to the other orc," the man said.

"And now you talk to me."

"We are a surveying crew." His words held the firmness that men substituted for courage. "We are here only to measure the lot."

Uruk grunted. They did not *intend* to attack, but how would their measurements be used?

Coming up beside Uruk, Kuru said, "We watch."

The man coughed a laugh and nodded towards the tenement. "All of you are watching."

Uruk glanced back.

He saw his Vara first, near the west entrance. December flapped her coat around her, but she stood firm. She bore a hefty pipe the length of her leg in one hand, her eyes fixed on the men. Uruk's blood burned at how magnificent she looked.

Beside Vara, Kovo, each hand holding a wooden club. Each was smaller than Vara's pipe, but she would still be deadly.

Daka and Kaba stood beside the women. Sunlight glinted off Daka's brass knuckles, while Kaba flexed his fingers and glared at the men. Oscar and Ivan, Uruk's fine boys, stood next.

The Don women of the second floor stood on Vara's other side. They were younger, but held cleavers and clubs. One held a babe in one arm and an axe in the other.

Near the other entrance, the Norkosh women and the clans of the third and fourth floor stood ready to fight.

In front of them all, Azok-Snaka hobbled towards Uruk.

A thread of tension bled out of Uruk. No unarmed man would approach the tenement. "Why do you measure our land?"

The man sighed. "So we know what can be built here."

"This is our home," Kuru said.

"This building has been condemned." Was that a quaver in the man's voice? "You do know that, right? Not even an orc should have to live in this pit."

He condemned their home, while Man Dick's Rancid Fish Speakeasy stood?

Kuru bared his Lesser Tusks. "It is our home."

"We're just doing a job." Yes, that was a quaver in the man's voice. The cowards had sent their biggest man to talk to Uruk. "We have to measure the land."

"We have until the death of January," Uruk said.

"Yes, but—" The man shook his head. "Look, if you interfere with us doing the city's work, we'll have to bring the police."

Kuru hissed.

Maybe Uruk could let Kuru lose his temper. If the police took him—

The oath flashed a warning.

"Or," the man said, "you can let us look. We're walking around outside. Just looking."

Two men propped a ladder against an electrical pole.

"If they are looking at the land," Uruk said, "why climb the pole?"

"We're checking the electricity and water." The man's voice firmed. "Only looking. You still have weeks to vacate."

"We will not vacate at all!" Kuru said.

Uruk would fight for the tenement, as an orc always fought for their cavern. But if they lost, if the wrecking balls came, the Tai would flee and find another shelter.

Uruk blinked.

His clan had money. They could use it to find a place to live. If no orcish tenements had space, Sanford might help them claim a new building. He had said the corporation could even buy them a home.

But without a bootlegger's resources, Uruk's clan would struggle to find a place. They might have to move in with another clan of Tai. Admitting failure. Being forced to offer gifts to their greater clan for protection.

Without those heaps of dollars, Uruk might be as angry as Kuru.

Behind them, Azok-Snaka wheezed, "Kuru-Norkosh."

The shaman had sounded tired and ill this morning, but now his voice had grown hoarse. His pale face gleamed in the afternoon sun, highlighting his scars. Were the lines deeper than this morning? The fur-lined coat had always looked huge, but now it threatened to swallow him. "Hold."

Shame flashed through Uruk.

The only thing blocking the Norkosh from going to open war against the Tai was the blood oath. Azok-Snaka supported that magic with his life. Each time Uruk tested the oath's limits, he stole a share of the shaman's life.

Kuru whirled. In orcish: "They trespass!"

"We must choose our battles," Uruk said. "These men, they only look. Save your anger for the false orc."

"I have enough anger for all our enemies," Kuru sneered.

"Do not fight this battle," Azok-Snaka said. "I gave you labor. These men, they will not hurt us."

Kuru spun to hiss at the workmen, then back to Azok-Snaka, his anger and frustration boiling in his eyes.

"Hold," Azok-Snaka said.

Anything Uruk said would only further anger Kuru.

Kuru trembled.

Spat at the ground.

And spun to Uruk. "We await *your* man."

Uruk gave a nod.

Kuru stomped towards his clan's line.

Azok-Snaka studied Uruk. "I thought I would be dead before you learned silence."

"And you are not yet dead."

Azok-Snaka barked a laugh. "You make progress?"

"A false orc," Uruk said. "It must be a creation of the elves. The man Sanford asks questions in a man store, so that we can track him."

Azok-Snaka raised his watery eyes to the west. "The Sun falls."

The Sun had dropped a sliver in the few minutes Uruk had spoken with the workmen. "It does."

"End your war with the Norkosh soon," Azok-Snaka said.

What could Uruk say? *It is not my war?* The false orc had claimed the name Tai to sell his poison and made it Uruk's war. *Only blood will satisfy the Norkosh?* An irrelevant truth.

If the war carried past sunset, the Greatest Dark would claim Tai as well as Norkosh.

Nearby, a car horn blared.

Uruk turned.

An *elf?*

24

A gleaming bright red Cadillac had stopped on the road in front of Uruk's tenement, all six headlamps gleaming. Black fenders swooped into carpeted running boards. Despite the slush and muck covering the road, the whitewall tires and the wire wheels shone in the sunlight. A delivery truck coming up behind the Cadillac blew its horn and swerved into the left lane, slewing up a line of dirty slush high enough to get halfway up the door.

A pristine car on December's messy roads? Unnatural. Wrong.

Wizardry.

And behind the rolled-down rear window, the elf.

His face was unnaturally slender, the color of burnished bone. Short hair the shade of yellow cotton was brushed straight back from his face. December's wind gusted, but not one hair moved. The shoulders of his suit shimmered against the sunlight.

Uruk had seen this elf before, at a speakeasy down on Cadieux Road. The Tai had held a truckload of elvish holy wine hostage, and Uruk had gone to negotiate a trade for the draught captured by elves. Uruk had forced the elf to negotiate, but he hadn't looked at Uruk, even refusing to soil his tongue by speaking to an orc. The light had been dim enough that Uruk hadn't gotten a good look. Not like this.

Grandpa called elves *forsaken perfection*. Uruk had not really understood until seeing this elf in the light. Life was bruises and cuts. Life was smiles and snarls and groaning on the pot and burning your lips on a warm mug of steaming water because you had worked outside in the cold for too long.

Nothing living looked that immaculate.

A hiss escaped Uruk. An elf should not dare to show himself in sunlight. Not even the pallid light of the shortest day. The affronted Sun should burn him to bone.

Beside Uruk, Azok-Snaka bent and coughed. A wad of brown filth hit the snow and steamed.

One of the workmen turned. "What—oh, it's you, Mister Celebrimble!"

Uruk's blood surged. The lord of the Detroit elves, at the tenement?

The elf accepted the man's fawning with a nod.

Behind Uruk, Kuru growled, "It dares?"

Azok-Snaka raised his left hand, palm towards the elf, fingers twisting against each other. Did the shaman have strength for even the weakest magic?

The workman said, "What can we do for you?"

The elf showed no awareness of Uruk or any other orc. "I am particularly interested in how level the land can be made."

"It's on our list, sir." The man could not grovel more if he put his face to the frozen dirt.

"It certainly is," Celebrimble said.

Uruk itched to throw himself across the fifteen feet separating him from the elf. Reach through that open window and drag him into the sunlight and slash his face until the whole world knew how vile he was. *Police. Prison. Would you leave the clan undefended?* "This is our home!" Uruk snarled.

"You cannot drive us from here!" Kuru bellowed.

Azok-Snaka began an unnerving hum, somehow making two tones at once. His outstretched hand swiveled around. Were those gaunt fingers passing through one another?

The lush aroma of fresh marigolds flooded Uruk's nose.

Elvish magic.

Uruk spun, looking for danger.

The elf's words somehow arrived with the smell, not by Uruk's ears. "This building's electricity and water are unsafe. Turn them off immediately to save lives."

All around Uruk, men stilled. Their faces went blank.

Losing lights was inconvenient, but only a monster would turn off the water.

Don't hurt the workmen. They were innocent victims of elven filth. *Walk quickly between them. Get to the elf's car. Strike.*

Before Uruk could take a second step, Azok-Snaka grunted and thrust his other hand out.

The shaman's bitonal humming swelled and shuddered through the stink of marigolds. The insides of Uruk's nose twitched and buzzed, threatening to rip themselves free and tear a path right up into his brain. Uruk staggered to a stop, pressing his fingers to his face to try to hold the inside of his head together.

Human faces twisted with pain. One of the men groaned and stumbled sideways, balancing himself with a hand against his truck. Kuru gave a snarl, but it trailed off.

For a breathless second, Azok-Snaka stood defiant. The shaman's power stood against the elf's. He was everything an orc shaman should be, glaring eyes and an absolute will that Uruk could never hope to match, pouring out his strength to defend his cavern.

A heartbeat later, a line of blood ran from the shaman's nose.

The marigold stink swallowed the hum.

Azok-Snaka quivered all over, like he'd touched a live electrical line. His jaw dropped.

In Uruk's hand, the blood oath gave one last flare and burst.

Before Azok-Snaka flopped lifeless into the snow, Celebrimble's Cadillac rolled into traffic.

 25

Cold breath flooded back into Uruk, scented with marigolds laced with engine exhaust.

The sun still shone. The hollow sockets of the tenement's blocked-off windows watched without witnessing. Traffic flowed uninterrupted past the tenement, as if an elf and an orc had not just fought a magical battle to the death.

Azok-Snaka's body lay crumpled in on itself, half-buried in the snow. Shouldn't the ground beneath him have cracked, or the winter birds risen in tribute?

An unbalanced world reeled around Uruk's skull. Azok-Snaka had given Uruk his first-breath punch. Grandpa had taught Uruk to fight, but Azok-Snaka had taught him when to *decide* to fight. The tenement's steel support beams were less reliable than the shaman's gristle and bone.

Of course the world had not cracked apart with the shaman's death. Like every orc, Azok-Snaka had failed.

Uruk should gather up the body and haul it to the tenement. Tell Azok-Snaka's orphan to fetch another shaman. Each clan should send one orc to help clean the body. Tonight, every orc should share a saga of how the shaman had guided them. The whole tenement should grieve and celebrate.

Uruk—the Tai—the whole tenement, had no time to mourn the dead.

The city workmen had abandoned their tripods and were collecting wrenches and screwdrivers and unfamiliar tools from the backs of their trucks. One of them said something about *going to blow*, whatever that meant. No, Uruk knew the important meaning. Celebrimble's magic had clouded their minds. If Uruk did nothing, they would block power and water from reaching the tenement. Night-sight would guide the orcs through darkened halls, but without water to drink and cook the building would be uninhabitable.

With the shaman dead, the labor of saving the cavern fell to any orc present.

Attacking a workman would buy a moment, but the other workmen would flee and bring the police and turn off the water. Uruk had to speak against the elven magic, put his skill at the foolish English language to war against a wizard's spell.

With no idea what he was going to say, Uruk started towards the big workman.

Kuru slammed into Uruk's kidneys.

For an endless flash Uruk seemed to hang in the air, pain radiating from the small of his back. The workman's eyes grew with comical slowness, his mouth grinding open as if to shout. Air exploded from Uruk's lungs, leaving him hollow, ribs aching.

He hit the snow face-first, and the world rushed back in on him.

Kuru crashed down on top of Uruk, hands scrabbling at his skull, one knee digging into his spine. "Your fault!" Kuru shrieked in orcish. "You killed us all!"

Uruk thrashed, trying to brace his hands, but the snow gave no traction and only got slipperier the harder he pushed. His hands were somehow sticky—what had he gotten into? His aching chest fought to guzzle air against the pressure of Kuru's knee, and failed.

Somewhere distant, men and orcs shouted.

Kuru thrust a hand towards Uruk's face, trying for a good grip on Uruk's tusks. Uruk tasted blood. Was he bleeding already? Was Kuru? It didn't matter. Uruk jerked his head sideways, snapping at Kuru's outstretched fingers.

Meat crunched.

Kuru howled. The pressure on Uruk's spine eased a fraction.

Uruk rolled rather than pushed, slipping sideways in the snow, dumping Kuru's knee aside and getting his face to the sky. Air gushed into Uruk's lungs as Kuru's rage-maddened face glared down at him.

Uruk had slid the wrong way. Kuru had a knee on each side of Uruk's gut.

A handful of talons slashed at Uruk's face.

Uruk instinctively twisted, trying to get clear, but the snow that had helped him roll betrayed him.

The edges of Kuru's fingers cracked into Uruk's cheekbone.

Hardly any pain. Kuru's talons were trimmed, like any modern orc's. To try to slash Uruk's face, he had to be running on rage and instinct.

Uruk's heart pummeled the inside of his ribs, and his breath came short and sharp and hot. He snatched Kuru's arm before Kuru could bring it back up, wrenching it across his body.

Kuru raised his other hand to strike down.

Uruk scrabbled his feet, trying to get enough traction to bump Kuru with his hips, but the snow turned to ice beneath his heels so he yanked on the arm he held, trying to pull Kuru down close so he could get a tusk in but Kuru wrenched himself sideways so Uruk went with it, shoving the arm straight up and back.

Kuru toppled sideways, one leg still across Uruk.

Uruk spasmed sideways, getting out from under Kuru's leg, snatching the ankle and using that anchor to spin himself around to face his enemy.

Kuru kicked, catching Uruk's thumb.

Pain flashed bright. Uruk's grip broke.

Uruk's head was already spinning and his heart jackhammered all the way up his throat into his tongue. He needed a deep breath, but Kuru was coming in and he wasn't going to get it.

Blood covered Kuru's upraised hands. Was Uruk bleeding? No—without Azok-Snaka feeding the blood oath, the wounds had reopened. No time to think. Kuru lunged and Uruk threw a hand out, fingers extended, trying to catch Kuru's eyes but he slipped sideways and Uruk wound up with an arm over Kuru's shoulder. Uruk grabbed and pulled, clamping himself to his attacker.

Kuru's hands hammered at Uruk's back, but the blows had no strength and Uruk's coat took the edge off.

If Uruk could slide his head down two inches, he could get his teeth into Kuru's throat.

No.

Uruk could do one last thing to honor Azok-Snaka.

Uruk snarled, "You waste your strength!"

"Poisoner!" Kuru spat in Uruk's ear, convulsing against Uruk's grip.

Uruk could not hold this clench for long. "You know the poisoner—is not a real orc!" Bone-skulled Norkosh! "Celebrimble came to taunt us with his face! He would freeze our children!"

"And you brought him on us!" Kuru gasped.

"Elves need no reason to hate us!"

Kuru raised his arm and brought the elbow down between them, trying to lever Uruk's collarbone out of his body. Bone ground on bone. Uruk gasped. Sweat burned his eyes.

The other orcs had moved forward into a rough half-circle around them, snarling and clapping and hissing at Uruk's tiny war. Uruk tried to shout at them to fill every pot with water, but couldn't find the air. Slippery blood sabotaged his grip.

Kuru would be free any second.

Uruk slid his grip up. Kuru laughed, but Uruk smashed the palm of one hand against Kuru's chin and the other on the back of his head, so when Kuru thrashed Uruk could follow, letting his enemy choose a direction and riding with him, rising on his knees so he could crank Kuru's head even further, dragging his whole body after his head. Kuru hissed, fingers clawing at Uruk, then rose on one knee and toppled aside, Uruk's grip tugging him down onto Kuru and letting him wrench Kuru's head so far that the Norkosh plunged face-first into the snow.

Anchoring himself with his grip, Uruk threw a leg across Kuru and settled with his knees solidly in Kuru's ribs. His hands still clenched Kuru's skull.

Kuru screamed.

"You wanted a leader war!" Uruk snarled. "This is it. Move, and I break your neck." He tried to lower his face to hiss in Kuru's ear, but couldn't without releasing Kuru's ribs from his knees. "Your clan's women and children are here, but your orcs are at the slaughterhouse."

"My brothers will slaughter you!" Kuru shrieked.

"Azok-Snaka was right!" Uruk shouted.

Kuru thrashed.

"He gave his life to teach us. Will you listen to the lesson? We *must* ally." Panting, Uruk struggled to raise his voice so that the surrounding orcs could hear. "*We* find the poisoner," Uruk said. "*We* defend the tenement. *We* stand together against the elves, and save our families."

Kuru stilled, but rage burned in his face. "You would have me *trust* you."

"The blood oath bound me to honesty!" Uruk needed to sound calm. He struggled to pull a deep breath. "You proved that yourself. The Tai did not poison your child, but—a child is dead. You must have revenge. You *must*, you must avenge her. Do the elves have the right to ban our draught? Do men? Do elves have the right to kill us for getting it ourselves? Do elves have the right to destroy our cavern?"

Kuru hissed.

"I could kill you now," Uruk said. "I could break your neck. You attacked me. From behind. None would stop me. But we fight an elf! This war demands *every* orc, Norkosh and Tai and any other clan we can raise to this cause!"

"And if I refuse?" Kuru screeched.

"My war!" Uruk shrieked. "*My* war! I will not do an elf's work by killing you!"

Kuru stilled.

"You spread lies of my clan, and *still* I will not kill you!" Uruk steadied his voice, but spoke loudly. "I kill you, and Celebrimble laughs! Ally with me, with my clan, against the enemy orcs were born to fight." He lowered his voice to hiss, "*Elves*."

Kuru glared at Uruk.

I thought I would be dead before you learned silence, Azok-Snaka had said.

Uruk waited.

A long moment later, Kuru said, "Get off me."

"Will you ally?" Uruk said.

Kuru spat. "I speak as a free orc, or not at all!"

Uruk took another breath. Slowly, he eased his aching hands from their death grip on Kuru's skull.

Kuru lay still, chest heaving for air.

Uruk eased his weight off Kuru, then got his feet beneath him and stood. He had only thought his body ached before. Now his aches had bruises.

Kuru waited for Uruk to step away before shambling to his feet.

Uruk tried to slow his panting. Half of the rapidly sinking Sun burned through the trees, plunging towards night.

Kuru panted as hard.

If he attacked, Uruk would have no choice but to kill him.

Kuru said, "If we find a Tai poisoned our child, they belong to the Norkosh."

Uruk nodded. "And any orc, any man, any elf or dwarf or hobble-people who soiled the Tai name pays for it."

Kuru spat, "This is about the cavern. The Tai are arrogant in their labor, but we will stand with them for the cavern."

Uruk said, "The cavern. The Norkosh cower in the dirtiest labor they can find, but the Tai will stand with them."

Uruk held out a hand. The setting sun cast sideways shadows across the fresh blood welling from the cut Azok-Snaka had bitten into his palms.

Kuru spat into the snow, then clasped Uruk's hand. "This war is over. We ally. *Our* war."

The surrounding orcs shouted, raising their weapons. Uruk hauled air into him, willing his head to stop swirling. Oscar and Ivan grinned madly at their father's victory.

Delight in his sons' pride flared in Uruk's marrow.

Out by the road, a siren gave a single whoop.

Police.

 26

Uruk stood in a slender scrap of sunlight near the tenement's muddy lot, watching the workmen load their final tools into their trucks.

Perhaps Uruk could have persuaded the workmen to leave the water on, despite Celebrimble's wizardry. Humans thought that intentions mattered even after they had harmed someone. These men had not *intended* harm, and for once Uruk knew that before they acted. He could have told them that children would thirst.

The six police officers with shotguns did intend harm to any orc who disturbed the workmen.

Uruk would not take a shotgun blast to the belly with no chance of victory.

The tenement had no electricity. No light. No water.

This was no shortest day. By now, Vara should have slid into their bed to wake him and demand his favorite labor. He should be drinking warm water, to ease the chill from his muscles. Bread and porridge with fresh lard to fuel him until the feast of the Greatest Dark. Since the clan had started bootlegging, every meal had fresh lard. This feast should be spectacular.

Instead, he had cold feet and aching legs and a hollow belly.

The war with the Norkosh had ended before the Greatest Dark. Only an hour or so before, but enough. December would not destroy them. The elves had timed their attack as an insult, though, and Uruk knew orcs would not celebrate tonight.

Kuru-Norkosh stood beside him. He had accepted the alliance over death, but Uruk had not demanded leadership. Even with Uruk's talons at his throat, Kuru would not have agreed. A war with two commanders was a thousand times more difficult.

Waiting inside would be warmer, but that would let Kuru meet Sanford first. Men were delicate creatures. Kuru might drive the paper man away before Uruk could question him.

If Sanford was even successful. He was adept at crossing the Canadian border and buying from distilleries, but that was very different than scouting.

Sanford had shown spine with other men. Uruk had to hope it would be enough.

Vara brought him a small loaf of bread, dipped in fresh hot pig juice and wrapped in oilcloth. The taste of what should be tonight's feast warmed his marrow.

She whispered in his ear, *Two pots of water*. Enough for a couple careful days.

A howl from the side of the tenement announced that one of the brawling children too young for school had lost a round of Ice Pants. Shrieks declared their vengeance. Not long before, Uruk had watched his two boys play their games in snow and mud and rain and, sometimes, on green grass under a softer Sun. The days had been simpler then. Haul freight for money, nights with Vara, help his boys grow strong so they could bear the world's burdens when Uruk no longer could.

If Sanford took too long, they would have to go to the Blind Pig and interrogate a human who couldn't tell an orc from an orphan.

December cast a swirl of loose snow into his face as he ate the last bite of bread, a few flakes blowing straight up his nose. By the time he cleared it, a bright blue Dodge four-door flat-top with gleaming black wheel guards that shrieked of wealth was turning into the tenement's dirt lot.

Uruk fought to keep the energy-wasting surge of tension from his spine. Sanford, at last? Or someone turning around in an empty lot?

The car stopped.

The door opened.

Uruk recognized Sanford's plush overcoat and heavy knitted cap.

Kuru was already stomping forward.

Uruk trotted forward. Not too fast—he mustn't scare the paper man.

Kuru sped up.

Uruk would not run. Kuru would shout loud enough to scare a human, but would not attack.

Sanford's eyes fixed on Kuru. His face tightened, but he did not move his feet.

"Man!" Kuru snarled. "What do you know?"

Sanford flinched, but didn't look away from Kuru. He also held silence—not from the shock of an orc's bellow, but with a jaw thrust of refusal. Was the paper man learning how to behave from Uruk?

Uruk let his lips draw back in a small smile, letting his Lesser Tusks show. "Zhan-ford."

Sanford nodded at Uruk.

Uruk braced himself to correct Sanford's pronunciation of his name.

Instead, Sanford only said, "I learned some interesting things."

Kuru snarled, "You will not ignore me!"

Sanford quivered. He turned to Kuru and said, "I do not know you, orc. I intend no disrespect to you or your clan, but why should I share private business with you?"

Uruk's mouth dropped open.

The words were wrong. That foolish human insistence on meaningless *intentions*. He had expected Sanford to flee or cry. Instead, he'd done the correct thing in the worst possible way.

The man had more strength than Uruk expected.

Defending the alliance against another orc was simple, though. Would Sanford defy a man, or an elf? Was he really a partner Uruk could rely on?

"Kuru-Norkosh!" Uruk snarled in Orcish. "He does not know you. You do not know him. He speaks to me."

Kuru said, "I will hear his words."

Allies did not mean *trust*. "Zhan-ford," Uruk said. "This is Kuru-Norkosh. We have allied to defend the tenement."

"Huh." Sanford studied Kuru. "He's very angry." His voice shook less than Uruk expected. Where had the paper man found the courage?

Uruk said, "His brother's daughter died of poison draught last night."

Sanford winced. "Mister Orc. I'm sorry for your loss. We will find the people responsible."

More human noises, saying the childishly obvious—and *mister*? Before Kuru could bellow Uruk said, "Zhan-ford! Speak of Hudson's."

Sanford nodded at Uruk. "I found Wilton, and asked about a suit for an orc."

"And?" Uruk said.

"Wilton said that it had been a special case, for a special customer." Sanford gave half a smile. "I asked how special an orc had to be to get Wilton's attention, and he said it wasn't the orc. It was the elf who brought him in."

Uruk's blood surged.

"This orc called the elf *father*," Sanford said.

Revulsion twisted Uruk's bowels. An elf would not look at an orc. Orcs would look at elves, if only to aim their talons at their throats. No elf would buy an orc a *suit*. No elf would offer a dying orc the mercy of a slit throat.

Kuru said in orcish, "How can even a man say such a thing! He has to be lying."

"He does not know us well enough to lie," Uruk hissed.

Kuru spat. "We must find this—*thing*."

Uruk's breath eased out. "Elves live in Grosse Pointe."

Kuru tried to spit again, but nothing came out. "Can your man learn more?"

Letting Kuru order Uruk's conversation with Sanford tasted bad, but at least Kuru had stopped accusing the Tai with every breath. Uruk turned to Sanford. The paper man stood a few yards away, leaning against the trunk of his expensive Dodge as he studied the traffic. Was he so unconcerned? "Zhan-ford!"

"Yes?"

"We must know more," Uruk said.

"I know more," Sanford said. "I was interrupted."

Human arrogance felt almost comforting. "Go on."

"No more interruptions," Kuru said. "Speak it all."

Sanford's voice was tight. "The elf was Celebrimble."

Uruk hissed between his teeth.

Kuru tried to spit again.

Sanford said, "Celebrimble told Wilton to not say anything, but when I flat-out asked him, he wanted to brag. He did refuse to tell me anything other than he had finished three more suits."

"Then we go to the elf's home," Kuru said.

"Madness," Uruk said.

"Excuse me," Sanford said.

"We must be smart," Kuru said.

"There is no smart way," Uruk said.

"Excuse me!" Sanford shouted.

Uruk pivoted back to Sanford. "What?"

Sanford's voice held the quiet of command. "I was told there would be no more interruptions."

Kuru coughed in frustration.

Uruk had sent Sanford to scout, and then not let him finish reporting? He needed to do better. "Tell us all. Say when you are done."

Sanford nodded. "I bribed a delivery clerk. Five dollars got me where the suits were delivered to. The orc has his own home. The address is 2502 Iroquois, in Indian Village. His name is Achilles Tai."

Tai? Uruk had half expected that, but hearing it made his blood burn. And what sort of name was Achilles?

Uruk could see Kuru decide to not throw more accusations. Good.

Sanford fell silent.

Uruk looked at Sanford.

"That's it," Sanford said. "Done."

Uruk echoed Sanford's own words back to him. "Good work, paper man." His humorless grin might split his face.

 27

Traffic thickened as the Sun dropped and the human workday raced towards its end, but Sanford's bright blue Dodge flat-top was easy to see amidst the countless black Ford Model Ts. Every one cast thin plumes of blue-gray smoke and clattered and rattled down the four lanes of Mount Elliott Road, but hundreds of them combined into a haze that numbed the tongue and ears.

Uruk felt comfortable behind the wheel of the clan's Model T, despite the crush of traffic. It clattered more than any of the cars around them, and the rust-scarred body declared to anyone with eyes that it belonged to orcs, but newer cars left space all around him. Men assumed orcs drove poorly. If Uruk had a car built to an orc's size, rather than a human car with the seat pushed back a vital foot, he could be an even safer driver. The clan had saved dimes for months to buy this fourth-hand Model T, and Uruk would not damage that treasure.

If it was damaged today, he could reach beneath a floorboard and pull out enough to buy a replacement. Maybe even a brand-new car?

No, they had more money than that. Uruk could buy new coats *and* new cars for himself and all his brothers and their women. What would driving a new car be like? Un-orcish, yes, but was owning a new car un-orcish because it was wrong, or only because no orc had ever been able to afford such?

Sanford had discussed this *corporation*. It also sounded un-orcish, but having so much money was un-orcish. Hiring more orcs? Bringing more and more liquor across the river until the money overflowed the apartment and spilled down the tenement stairs? Wiping his ass with dollar bills and insulating the walls with twenties? Some of the bills were *hundreds!*

If Uruk rejected Sanford's corporation plan, he would have to make his own.

Perhaps his brother Tara would have ideas. He worked for Lord Dodge as a janitor. Uruk had learned the hard way to trust Tara.

Kuru sat in the passenger seat, jaw set, glowering over the Model T's doors at the other cars and the passing buildings and the lights sparking against the coming dark without seeing any of it. Let his heart consume him for the ride and burn out some of that anger. The surging, ebbing roar of traffic and the gusts of wind through gaps between door and roof made talking quietly impossible, and they should not shout of their war. The silence would be welcome.

What would it be like to drive a car with *windows* on top of the doors, blocking out the exhaust and the cold? It couldn't be a Model T, an orc needed a place to put his elbows. Sanford's Dodge cost more than an orc made in months, but Uruk wouldn't fit behind that steering wheel either.

Orcs struggled through a world built too small for their bones, and were punished when they tripped and shattered something that shouldn't have been built so fragile.

The blue Dodge swung into the left turn lane, behind a long line of black cars. This must be the Warren Avenue that Sanford spoke of.

The Tai clan, and their whole tenement, were under threat. They knew the address of the false orc, but turning that into knowledge required getting Sanford to use his gazetteer and decipher the white-on-black letters of the street signs. The future of the clan depended on a human reading for them.

Forget the money. The clan's true power would come from his sons learning to read. The paper man had been a better ally than Uruk had expected, but the clan must be able to stand on its own. If December thought they relied too much on Sanford, she would take him.

An elf respected a man enough to look at him, but would still kill him.

The light turned green. The line of cars inched forward, as if they could slip through the column of oncoming traffic.

Uruk kept his front bumper as close to the rear of Sanford's big Dodge as he dared. Warren Avenue led to Iroquois Street, but without Sanford to read the street signs Uruk would be lost. Humans who saw an orc driving unescorted through their neighborhoods would call the police, and the police would sweep away the clan's fortune as easily as wiping away a sneeze.

The police were everywhere in Detroit. Even this intersection still had a uniformed police officer in a heavy knit cap standing on a pillar in the center of the intersection to operate the traffic light. He raised a hand to stop the oncoming traffic, and with a squeal of his whistle waved for the line of cars to turn left.

Kuru grunted. He was not so buried in his heart that he did not know what was coming.

Sanford's Dodge had just started to accelerate into its turn when the officer raised a hand at Uruk and blew his whistle once, hard, stepping on the lever to change the light to yellow.

As always. Uruk braked.

Sanford's car swung left, finishing its turn, quickly becoming invisible across the four lanes of traffic filling Warren Avenue.

Kuru huffed, but said nothing.

Sanford would notice they were missing and pull over until they could catch up. But Uruk had to wonder... if an orc drove a new car, would an officer even realize who drove it?

One day, he would find out.

28

Uruk had driven down Jefferson Avenue, past the mansions that loomed over Lake Saint Clair. He had visited Sanford's home, a box in a field of boxes. He had seen human tenements, tall buildings stuffed with rows of windows that stank of boiled cabbage and tortured potatoes. Iroquois Avenue was entirely different.

Five or six homes like Sanford's could fit in any one of these homes. Fields of knee-deep snow surrounded each, wide enough that another ridiculously huge house could be built between them. Humans often claimed their homes by painting them different colors, or planting trees in different spots, or even growing different shrubs between the front door and the road, but these homes were different in their bones. One with a pointed roof where each side sloped almost to the ground sat next to a stone citadel, complete with a three-story tower as if they wanted to be a Dark Lord but had failed. The citadel's windows were too large to defend, so it wasn't a real castle. A house made of circles, and another of triangles? Red bricks that might have been stacked by a two-year-old just learning to not chew on other people's feet, but somehow holding together into walls? Lights behind curtained windows cast squares and circles and even triangles of colored light. In front of some, the snow had been trampled. Men had stacked two or three balls of snow the size of Uruk's belly and stuck sticks in the sides. One had a fancy corncob pipe stuffed into the uppermost ball, with a scarf wrapped beneath it.

Did men raise snow sacrifices, as orcs did before the Winter Melt?

Sanford stopped in front of a two-story cube of dull gray brick. Too many windows covered the front, and shorter wings on either side bore still more. The wings had flat roofs ringed by iron railings surrounding tarp-wrapped lumps that hinted at furniture. Did the man who owned this home spend time on the rooftops? An iron gate blocked off the smooth concrete driveway that ran to a garage in the rear. Not a one-car garage, or even a carriage house for two cars. It had two sets of broad double doors—a four car garage? How many people lived in this block of brick? It was large enough to shelter a dozen men and their families.

Not an elf's home. Not nearly grand enough.

Perhaps the fancy homes on this street were where Lord Dodge and the Lord Mayor and all the other human lords lived. Why would one of them allow an orc, even a false orc, to live here?

That's why they had the large garage. They needed a place to keep the orc.

Uruk stopped the car. Kuru climbed out, quickly but without the haste of rage. A red shape was coming up the road behind them—was that a car? A *red* car? Uruk waited to open his door, letting it pass. The red car's engine was longer than his entire Model T, with sweeping fenders that curved back to a tiny shelter that might hold two small men. The driver stared at Uruk with a curled lip, noticed Sanford, and relaxed.

Uruk stilled a snarl. If Uruk showed his feelings, Sanford's presence would not protect him. Instead, he clamped his jaw and stomped up to Sanford.

Sanford nodded. "The last time you knocked on a door, it didn't go well. I think I should do the talking."

That had been Sanford's door. Was Sanford saying that he would call the police again? No, the policeman and the red car had left Uruk feeling weirdly helpless. "You lead the knock," Uruk said.

In orcish, Kuru said, "You do not lead me."

"He speaks true." Uruk let a Lesser Tusk show. "Or can you make a strange human speak to you?"

Kuru grunted.

Uruk took one step for every two of Sanford's, swallowing his frustration. The paper man could do what an orc could not. If Sanford was strong, he would not need Uruk.

The stoop stretched ten feet from the front door, roomy enough for Sanford to ring the bell and Uruk and even Kuru to stand behind him without crowding. Uruk stilled his hands and adopted the flat face orcs wore around men.

The door opened. "Yes?"

The man wore the strangest suit Uruk had ever seen. A jacket of pure black, with broad lapels folded back to expose lining of softer black and a brilliant white shirt. A broad band of intricately stitched black circled his waist, making a stark boundary above the black pants. His bleach-white *tie* didn't dangle from his neck like a noose, but was bound in a neat bow against his throat. The collar was so high and stiff it must cut into the bottom of the man's chin, but he showed no discomfort. Sanford's suit, even Uruk's awful suit, moved with him. This man's suit looked only binding.

"Good evening," Sanford said. "My name is Trevor, and I have business with Achilles Tai."

Another false name? Why would Sanford keep doing that?

The man's gaze flicked between Sanford, Kuru, and Uruk. "Master Tai is not at home this evening. If you have business, you should phone his office and make an appointment."

Master Tai? Why would a man call an orc that?

"I fear my business is rather urgent," Sanford said.

"It might be urgent to you, sir, but not to Master Tai." The man started to swing the door shut. "Call his office and request an—"

Uruk flung an arm over Sanford's head before the door could close. It bounced back, leaving the man glaring in outrage.

"Urka—" Sanford started, then leaped aside as Uruk stormed in.

The man raised his hands, palms out. "How dare you!"

Uruk took two steps and snatched the man's lapel. The day's bottled anger bubbled up inside him, screeching like an overheated boiler, but he made sure his fingers caught cloth instead of ribs.

The man gulped.

Kuru followed a heartbeat later.

"Damn it," Sanford muttered, then shut the door behind him. "Don't hurt him."

"This feeble *thing* is not worth hurting." The man's suit was a repulsively soft cloth that constantly threatened to slip or shred in his grip. The texture made his stomach shudder, but he firmly held both his grip and his horror.

Kuru swore in orcish.

Uruk raised his gaze from the terrified man, and caught a greater shock.

He had seen many rooms, in many buildings. The warehouses at the Port of Detroit had high ceilings so cargo could be stacked into towers tall enough that only a crane could pluck the uppermost crates. The tenement had been built for men, decades before, and Uruk could not stand straight in his own room. Visiting a city office to pay the fee for the clan's Model T, he had to bend his knees and narrow his shoulders just to get through the door.

For the first time in his life, he was in a home not built for men.

The couch was much like one a man would use, covered with soft red fabric and resting on six wooden legs. Each leg was as big around as Uruk's bicep. The cushions were as thick as Uruk's thigh. And it was too high for a man to sit on, with blocky arms to cradle a weight no human skeleton could support.

Two chairs, too large and sturdy for men.

A table tall enough that Uruk could sit at it and eat comfortably.

The false orc did not live *with* men.

This house was built for an orc.

29

The grooms' quarters was too cramped for bone-melding, but Mha made it work. Bone-melding should be done beneath the open sky. It should be done at a roaring fire built up from entire trees torn from the soil and the bones of slain enemies, witnessed by the clan. She had a tiny stove heated until it gleamed in her night-sight even through the sunlight drifting through the high narrow windows.

And all the orcs she knew witnessed from gleaming eye sockets.

She had feared she had forgotten the rites, but her ragged voice recalled the words and her age-bent hands remembered the motions, the gestures, the twist of bone against bone until they caught one another and bound harder than iron. The comforting smells of scorched bone and burned blood and viscous sweat filled the air.

That orc's thighbones were not long enough, so she added the shin bones. The smaller calf bones went on the side, to give the shaft a sharper shape so her feeble hands wouldn't slip. Not that a properly bone-melded shaft could slip in its maker's grip. The kneecaps, worn to smoothness by decades of joyful life, nestled together perfectly on the bottom as a base.

The bone shaft, melded end-to-end, stood almost as tall as her. The exact correct height. It had no choice but to be correct. *That* orc had fought for her his entire life.

You couldn't meld metal to bone, so Mha used a precious strip of *that* orc's leather to bind the scythe blade to the thinner end. The leather knew it belonged to the bone, and the bone to the leather. A dot of her blood and a murmur of gratitude reminded them of their duty to one another.

Mha's tongue was parched to leather, her back ached from the day's labor, and her hip felt like it had been nailed into her, but she had a usable weapon.

She stood as straight as she could, one hand wrapped loosely around the shaft. It settled perfectly into her grip, a good sign. She rested the base on the warped wood planks of the floor, took a breath, and relaxed her fingers.

The shaft stood, nestled against her palm.

She opened her grip, fingers still loosely curled.

The shaft did not slip.

Mha completely flattened her hand.

Any other tool would have fallen, but this shaft stuck to her palm.

She switched hands. The shaft let go of the one hand and clung to the other.

Mha bared her tusks in delight. Her hands *had* remembered. The melded bones knew they belonged to her. A cannonball to the gut could not make her drop this weapon. So long as she touched the shaft constantly for the next day to let the charm settle, it would remember her for more years than she had left.

And holding a real weapon for the first time in decades sent a shiver of delight down her spine. She felt like a proper orc again.

One final task.

After the stifling air filling the groom's quarters, leaving the barn felt like plunging into icewater. The sweat on her face instantly chilled, and

December's breath whipped up under her coat to wash away her labor's warmth. A deep breath brought clear air to scour smoke and scorched bone from her lungs, sending a surge of dizziness through her. The new boots cradled her feet in warmth. She leaned on the scythe for a breath, then another, until her head steadied. Standing over a fire fitting bones together did not look like wearying labor, but bone-melding demanded strength.

Mha didn't dare hope she had enough strength left for tonight's war. Hope existed so the gods could take it. During the Spanish-American War, though, she had more than once reached what she thought was the end of her strength and found herself fighting on. She had to find that within her again.

The decision to endure had always carried her further than foolish hope ever could.

The walk up to the farmhouse was longer than she remembered. Her guts gurgled with the remnants of the feast. Was she so feeble that *eating cow* sapped her strength?

Scythe in hand, she gently opened the door and slipped inside. "Thorn, I am here."

"Mantis?" From her voice, Thorn must have been in the parlor. "What's wrong? I'm coming!"

Mha used the cool, porous bone staff to give her the balance to bend and wipe the snow off her new boots. An orc's boots accumulated mud and blood, but she wanted to keep these boots pristine as long as she could. When they got soiled, it should be with blood.

Thorn tottered in the kitchen, balanced on her twin sticks. "What's wrong?" She narrowed her eyes, peering through the thick glasses perched on the tip of her nose at the scythe. "Uh... Mantis?"

"Mha n'Tass," Mha said. "I go to war."

Thorn blinked. "What happened? If there's more trouble, we can call the sheriff."

Why? A lord's authorities gave orders. Mha was not a scout, to be reporting in. "If I do not return to make *tea* tomorrow, know that I have fallen."

"Hold on," Thorn said. "Is this about this morning?"

This morning had started her war, but only as the dawn started the day. "I accepted the labor of aiding you. While I breathe, I will not abandon you."

"Hold on a minute. You're my friend. Tell me what's going on. You've been here for years without trouble." Thorn's face tightened. "Who threatened you? I'll set them straight, never you mind!"

Thorn had declared this morning that she and Mha would face any enemies. Mha had dismissed her words as human pride. What could she do, prod an intruder with a cane? Thorn could not help in this war.

But if Thorn summoned the sheriff, Mha's war would end before it began. The sheriff would order her to stand down. She would refuse to obey, like a foolish youngster who had just drained her first bottle of draught, and the sheriff would kill her. "It is an orcish matter."

Thorn's eyes flicked to the scythe. "I didn't know we had any other orcs around here."

"We do not."

"Listen," Thorn said. "Sit down. Tell me about this. We'll figure it out together."

The Sun still shone through the trees. Hours until midnight, until she violated all custom and fought a war during the Greatest Dark.

And Mha's throbbing hip would thank her for a moment of rest, even on the low wooden bench.

Mha sat.

Thorn spidered into her chair. "Put the scythe down and tell me about it."

"I cannot release the bones until sundown tomorrow," Mha said.

Thorn visibly decided not to ask or argue. "Tell me. Who threatened you? Whatever it is, we'll deal with it together."

How had Thorn not understood that this war was orcish? Humans could be especially thick-skulled.

No. This was like back in the Army. Mha had given her labor to a human. Humans always insisted on dictating *how* labor was done, even when an orc knew better.

An orc did not chase after their daughters taken by another clan. It was enough to raise strong orcesses that other clans coveted, to share the sagas of their marriage wars. That was the end of a daughter's saga and the beginning of a woman's.

Humans didn't care about such matters, though.

Forced to expose herself, Mha bared her lone remaining Lesser Tusk. "My youngest daughter might be in danger."

Thorn stilled.

Mha watched. Humans couldn't listen, but—had Thorn truly heard her? Her age-bent spine felt a chain of tension.

Thorn finally said, "The sheriff will do nothing."

The chain loosened.

Mha breathed. "No."

Thorn said, "How can I help?"

As if the old humaness could join her in the battle! Mha closed her eyes to hide her frustration. Her eyes relaxed, but the exhausted burn in her sockets somehow flared. "Know that I have not abandoned you."

Thorn made a clucking noise. "I'm sure there's more." She shook her head. "And here I asked you to wheel me to the Pickle Barrel today! Mantis, I am so sorry."

"I gave you my labor." Mha could keep her eyes closed for another breath. No longer. No matter how good they felt. No, they didn't feel good, only less achy, but that was as close to *good* as Mha could expect today.

"My boy is a pain in my heart sometimes," Thorn said. "Out there in his fancy New York bank job, never coming home. But if he was in trouble, I'd be on the first train out there. That's what a mother does. I applaud you for it."

Thorn knew nothing of raising orcs. A human babe didn't even have birth-tusks to pry milk from its mother's breast. Somehow, though, Mha could imagine Thorn clattering through a crowded boxcar, jabbing and crowing until someone gave her a place to sit. She might not fit blades to her sticks, but she would intimidate humans until they cowered and surrendered, the way humans fought when they did not have proper wars. It was enough for her to say, "Yes, Thorn."

"When do you go? Where? Do you need a ride? I can call Miss Brown."

Mha could only imagine cramming herself in the tiny housekeeper's Model T, her body stuffed in sideways and her scythe hanging out the side. "Tonight," Mha said. "I walk."

"My dear, you are exhausted. You're not walking any distance, not in this cold."

"It must be done. I will do it."

Thorn said, "This is the coldest December I've seen, you'll freeze in a mile!"

"It is not even a mile."

Thorn stilled. "You saw something at the Pickle Barrel. That orc egg, the bootlegger."

Egg? Orcs did not come from eggs, and if they did the abomination was long hatched. And Thorn had been facing away from the bar, how did she know? Did those thick glasses let Thorn see behind her? "Yes."

"When did he say he was returning?"

Thorn had trouble understanding Mha, but had picked up that discussion? Mha swallowed her irritation. The word *midnight* was simple enough for a human. "Midnight."

"Seven hours," Thorn said. "You have time to rest. I'll see you get hot food in your belly before you go."

Mha shook her head. "No rest."

Thorn's gaze sharpened. "My dear, you are too tired to stay awake until midnight. And you need to be razor sharp if you're going to talk to that orc."

Talk. Yes, Mha would talk to the abomination. After she nailed it to a floor. Shame fought her tongue, but if she did not satisfy Thorn the humaness would make her war even more difficult. "If I go to sleep, I might not wake up in time."

Thorn leaned back in her chair. "That's easy enough. You nap here. I'll wake you up in plenty of time."

Mha jerked her eyes open. Trust Thorn to protect her daughter? "I must stay awake."

"My dear," Thorn said. "I understand worrying about your child. I *do*. But you can't do everything alone. You must have a few hours of sleep."

No. In the Army, Mha had remained awake for three days at a time.

But she was no longer that orcess.

The muscles around her spine throbbed, and the bones between clattered every time she moved. Her sore hip had a hot coal embedded in it. Even her ears ached. How could ears hurt without even a stick in them?

Shame made her head sag. She could sleep in the barn, or while lurking in wait for the abomination, but her rotting body would sleep. "I must leave three hours before midnight." The words tasted of failure.

"Get there early," Thorn said. "Good, good. Watch and wait, that's the way." Thorn had not fought in war. Had her husband taught her that? "I'll wake you at eight o'clock. That'll give you time to eat. I'll make some nice soup to warm you."

Soup? Mha had smelled human soup. She might choke it down, but not before a war. "Not soup."

"My soup is—" Thorn stilled herself. "Then what?"

A human would not make orcish porridge. Even if Mha felt like explaining, Thorn would insist upon *doctoring it up*.

"If you must—oatmeal."

"Oatmeal?" Thorn frowned. "That's hardly fit for you."

"Oatmeal."

"All right then," Thorn said. "Oatmeal it is."

"Plain." Humans sugared everything.

Thorn made a face. "Let's get you in the guest room so you can have a nice rest."

Mha straightened. Sleep in a strange place? "I can sleep in my bed."

"It will be dark, dear," Thorn said, "and the barn is full of junk. What if I fall on the way to wake you?"

Mha grimaced. "Your guest room."

The bed was far too soft, draped in enough blanket to smother an orc.

But sprawled on the wooden floor, boots off and fingers cradling bone, Mha was asleep before her third breath.

 30

A home built for an orc?

Uruk felt like he'd taken a sledgehammer to the gut. His skin shuddered against his muscles and his toes curled so tight inside his steel-toed boots that his talons scratched against the metal.

The ceilings were high enough for Uruk to stand straight, the walls covered with intricately patterned gold-and-white paper. A true orc could not live here—one sneeze would ruin the paper.

But directly in front of the window sat a fancy chair too broad and solid for a man, with sturdy legs that wouldn't quiver beneath the most restless orc. Despite the fresh polish, the shadows of old scratches from bare orc feet lingered in the floor tile. Where a man like Sanford had a low table in front of his couch, this house had a man's dinner table. Next to the orc-sized couch, it looked like a low table. Another chair was built for a man. The couch and both chairs were covered in identical rich red fabric.

And the space! An orc in a human room had to huddle into himself to fit down the halls or between a table and its chair. If Uruk sat in that chair, he could lean back and set his feet on the edge of the table—or sit up straight, put a mug of draught on the table, and easily reach it.

An orc room.

"Un-orcish." Kuru whispered.

Was it, though? An orc home should not have glittery paper on the walls. But why shouldn't an orc home have a tile floor that resisted scratches from toe talons? Why shouldn't it have a ceiling high enough to stand straight, a light in that ceiling placed so an orc's skull wouldn't shatter the bulb with a wrong step, a table high enough to sit at, a comfortable chair?

An orc had only what he fought for. Had this Achilles fought for that chair, those ceilings?

The false orc didn't matter. Was *Uruk* willing to fight to take the same?

Uruk's father had labored his entire life, and while the world owed an orc nothing, if the clan had money and Uruk was willing to fight to take it, why shouldn't worn-out Grandpa have a comfortable chair instead of the tiny old human thing he squeezed his saggy ass into every day? Shouldn't his Vara have a comfortable chair and warm clothes and a stove that didn't fight her every day?

The place even smelled of orc, intermingled with roasting meat and candle wax and—was that *perfume*?

Uruk's bile surged. Men wore perfume. Not orcs.

The building was orcish.

Some of the contents, not.

He had almost forgotten the man in the constricting black suit. "Unhand me!" the man sneered. "Trevor, control your orcs!"

"Ah." Sanford shook his head, making sure the door was firmly closed behind them, then slouched against it. "You misunderstand the nature of our relationship. The orc holding you is my partner."

So long as my clan remains useful, Uruk thought.

The black-suited man's sneer grew broader. "You partner with an orc?"

"And you are an orc's butler," Sanford said.

"Master Tai is no ordinary orc." No man should sound so patronizing while being dangled on his toes, but if Uruk shook the man he might break.

"Zhan-ford," Uruk said. "*Butler?*"

"Head of the house," Sanford said. "This man supervises the cook and maids and any other staff. He takes Achilles' orders—oh, pardon me, that's an assumption." He raised his eyebrows. "Achilles Tai owns this home, does he not?"

The butler said, "He does."

None but an orc would have orc-sized furniture, but the words still shocked Uruk.

"He will be very angry," the butler said. "So will the police."

Kuru spoke before Uruk could. "Why?"

"Because you criminals have invaded his home!" The butler hung limp in Uruk's grip, as if he could not be troubled to struggle. The fabric of his suit jacket repelled Uruk, making his hand itch to slip free, but he tightened his grip instead.

"No," Kuru said. "Why would the police care what happened in an orc's home?"

"The police defend all citizens," the butler said.

Laughter exploded from Uruk's gut. "Police do not protect orcs."

Kuru's laughter echoed Uruk's own. "The only thing police do with orcs is send us to prison."

"Or shoot us," Uruk said.

Sanford let their laughs fade to chuckles before saying, "Sir, my partner finds your claim not credible. This puts me in an uncomfortable position. I *do* hate seeing blood."

Uruk snorted. Sanford turned green at the faintest hint of violence.

"So," Sanford said. "I'm going to search the house. I'm sure your employer has a study. Perhaps I will discover a diary, or appointment book, that will tell me where I can find Achilles." He spread his hands. "Meanwhile, my partner and his friend will ask you where they can find him. And... any other questions that come to mind."

He'd taken charge without asking, again! But the division of labor was obvious.

Interrogating a man was like heaping water, but he would try. Uruk let his Greater Tusks show.

Kuru grunted.

The butler's face turned pale. "Wait! That's what you want?"

"Yes," Uruk growled.

"Why didn't you say?" the butler said.

"You told us to make an appointment and tried to shut the door." Sanford looked at Uruk. "A few screams will make the rest of the staff hide until we're gone. But not too loud, please. We don't want to alarm the neighbors."

Did Sanford mean that? Humans spoke badly, and a human would never tell an orc to hurt a man. But what else could he mean?

Kuru smiled.

"Wait!" the butler gasped. "I'll tell you! I'll tell you!"

Uruk shook the butler's coat, making his head flop around. "Declaring that you will speak is not speaking."

"His father!" the butler choked. "He's visiting his father! Dinner!"

His father? Was this Achilles truly spending the day not just with an elf, but with *the* elf? Perhaps the magic sustaining him needed renewing? Or

Celebrimble wanted his groundskeepers' shovels polished? That would explain it.

The butler's jacket ripped free. The man's heels touched the ground, but the rest of him followed too quickly and he wound up sprawled on his side at Uruk's feet.

Kuru took two quick steps to loom on the butler's other side. "When will he return?"

The butler's wide eyes mirrored the O of his mouth. "I don't know."

"We can wait," Sanford said. "With you."

"He's going to work afterwards," the butler said.

Work? No orc worked on the Longest Night. "And where is work?" Uruk said.

The butler licked his lips. "He runs a warehouse. In Hamtramck. Makes deliveries."

The man answered too quickly. Would the *head of the house* surrender knowledge so easily? Surely a man who led others knew how to hold secrets!

"Deliveries." Kuru dropped to a knee to snarl straight into the butler's face. "And what does he *deliver*?"

The butler's voice was so thin Uruk could barely hear. "Master Tai does not confide in me."

Perhaps this butler surrendered so easily because he recognized that a false orc deserved no loyalty.

Sanford said, "And do you have an address for this warehouse?"

"Joseph Campau and Casmere," the butler wheezed.

Uruk's back tightened. Half a mile from his tenement? His hands straightened, all on their own. Kuru's growl became nearly constant, an engine of anger ready to charge.

"Indeed," Sanford said. "I fear, sir, that we require independent verification. Can you direct me to Achilles' study? Perhaps some papers therein that would verify your claim?"

"Down the hall," the butler said. "On his desk. He keeps bills, on his desk!"

"Uraka-Tai." Sanford erupted in a cough.

Surprisingly closer, but still not correct. "Uruk-Tai."

Sanford pounded weakly on his chest as if to clear the cough. "Please don't rip off his fingers until I've had a chance to check."

Uruk had never ripped off anyone's fingers, man or orc. He nodded and focused on the butler. "Man. This false orc you serve."

"He *is* an orc," the butler said.

Kuru glared around the room. "No orc would live like this."

Would they? Or was it that orcs never had? Fart away the perfume and use the hair on his ass to scrape off the wallpaper, and it might be comfortable.

The butler glanced between Uruk and Kuru. "He is the finest of orcs. Even Celebrimble says so."

Uruk's feet twitched, but he stopped before he kicked the man. Kuru hissed and drew his hand back to strike, but Uruk snarled "No!" in orcish.

"This thing is no orc," Kuru answered.

"This *man* knows nothing of orcs," Uruk said. "He cannot declare the finest of us. And a dead man will bring the police for us."

Kuru hissed.

Uruk switched back to English. "Tell me of this—this, one you serve."

"He is a good person," the butler said. "Good to the staff. A straight dealer with his business partners. Literate. Reads every night."

"Reads?" Kuru said.

Uruk's blood hummed. His boys were learning to *read*. If they could. If any orc could. They might fail. A false orc that could read did not mean that a true orc could learn. But still—

"Every night," the butler said. "When there's a new *Black Mask*, the staff knows to leave him undisturbed."

The false orc wore black masks? How could your enemies know you threatened them if they couldn't see your face?

"More," Uruk said. "Speak more."

"His valet cares for his clothes but he won't let him help him dress."

No orc would need help dressing. "More."

"Crispy bacon every meal." The butler's eyes flickered back and forth. "He works late and sleeps late."

Of course the false orc slept late. Bootleggers worked at night. And bacon every meal? Uruk had tasted bacon on his wedding morning, to prove to Vara that he could defend a family. What would it be like to have that precious treat every day? "More."

Sanford reappeared. "It seems he spoke the truth. There's an electrical bill with a Hamtramck address."

The butler closed his eyes and breathed deeply.

"So," Sanford said. "Mister butler. The question is, what to do with you?"

"I won't tell anyone," the butler said. "Just let me go, and I'll keep my mouth shut."

Sanford gave a tiny nod. "And tell me—does your master hold grudges?"
The butler blinked. "What?"

"Does he forgive betrayal?" Sanford nodded at Uruk. "I've been working with my partner some time now, and I can assure you—an orc might tolerate many things, but never betrayal. Like you, telling us where to find him."

The butler swallowed. "You made me!"

"Made you?" Sanford laughed and turned to Uruk. "What did you do? You tore his jacket, right? That was it?"

"I asked questions," Uruk said.

Kuru said, "He answered them."

"And now you declare you'll not say anything if we let you go," Sanford said. "Telling your boss we were here? That's a betrayal." He looked at Uruk. "What was it your brother said, the first time we met? You cook a man with apple and fennel?"

Uruk had heard the recipe from Grandpa as a child, but nobody in modern America cooked anyone. "Yes." The thought of eating this scrawny servant of a false orc made him queasy. The only thing Uruk could take from this *butler* would be weakness.

"I won't tell," the butler said. "I won't, I swear."

"You won't tell," Sanford said. "And if you do?" He shrugged. "Your boss will know you betrayed him. An orc does not forgive. Does he keep apples in the house?"

The butler grew even more pale.

Sanford looked to Uruk. "Anything else?"

They knew where to find the false orc. If he evaded them, they could return to this horrible house. "No."

Sanford glanced at Kuru.

Kuru gritted his teeth, but shook his head.

Sanford opened the door. "Then we shall leave you to your day, sir. Speak if you must, but remember the apples."

"Wait," Uruk said.

The butler's eyes got big.

"You betrayed your lord to us." The man's weakness would also drive him to betray Uruk, as if one betrayal could cancel out another. They needed the butler to hold his silence. One sure way was to kill a helpless man who had not even tried to fight, a thought that repelled Uruk even more than the disgusting fabric of the butler's suit. "He will kill you. If you speak of us to him, you betray us. We will return and kill you."

For the man to choose to hold his silence, the man needed a path forward.

Uruk dug in the pocket of his canvas pants and withdrew his handful of folding money. Two months ago, it would have been a fortune. "Here." He peeled off one twenty-dollar bill after another, dropping them by the butler's face. "You must flee. Take your belongings and flee." Four bills, five. "Go where your betrayal is unknown, and serve a man." Six bills. Enough. "No orc needs a *butler*."

Better to pay that feeble man a fortune than kill him.

But Uruk's fluttering guts hinted that soon, he would have no choice.

 31

The Sun had surrendered to twilight. A thin sliver of the shrinking Moon followed an arm's length behind. Uruk's eyes ached even in the dimness. December's chill was already freezing the road slush and turning Uruk's breath to steam. Shadows had started swallowing the wealthy houses lining the street, but curtained lights shone through their chaotic windows.

Uruk filled his lungs. The air was cleaner here—not as pure as further north in Clinton Township, but the stink of traffic was less and a sharp hint of the icy Detroit River made it crisp and rich. December sank into his chest with his breath, claiming her due sacrifice of warmth, but as Uruk exhaled she also took the lingering taint of the false orc's awful perfume.

"We cannot strike at an elven mansion," Kuru said in orcish.

"No orc is that foolish," Uruk said.

Sanford stopped on the sidewalk, turning to Uruk. "This orc—*false* orc. We need to know who's in charge of him. Who he sold to. He won't want to tell us."

It would be a fight, and Sanford would only hinder them. "Tonight is not paper man work."

"What does it matter, who he sold to?" Kuru said.

Sanford looked Kuru in the eye. "They need to be warned that their booze is poisoned."

"Anyone who bought booze from this *thing* should expect death," Kuru said.

"He claimed Tai," Uruk said. "Deaths would be blamed on my clan."

Kuru growled. "We will ask questions before we kill him."

"Joseph Campau and Casmere," Sanford said. "I'll be... one block south of there? What time will you start?"

Uruk needed a nap and a meal. "Moonset?" The moon would set a few hours after the sun.

Kuru said, "Moonset will do."

"Moonset? When is—" Sanford shook his head and looked up. "Never mind. I'll be there for a couple hours, or until things go very bad. If you need me, come get me."

In a fight, when the paper man wasn't vomiting in fear he mewled in panic. Sanford already understood his weakness, so Uruk said only, "No blood tonight."

Sanford said, "Between you and I, never."

Foolishness. Everything ended in blood.

"Wait," Kuru said.

Sanford paused.

"He is mine," Uruk said.

"Men love elves," Kuru said. "Why do you fight one?"

"I said, he is mine!" Uruk said.

"Men do not ally with orcs," Kuru said.

"I will answer that," Sanford said.

Uruk said, "Kuru-Norkosh and I are allied." Sanford understood nothing. "He insults the Tai by questioning me."

Sanford met Uruk's gaze. "We have no time to fight each other. And if you must fight, it cannot be here. I will answer him so he stops insulting you, and you can demand your apology elsewhere."

Apology? Senseless human thing! But the men who lived here would already be peering through their windows and reaching for their luxurious private phones. Uruk made himself nod.

Sanford faced Kuru. "I was inconvenient, so one of Celebrimble's wizards cursed my wife. She nearly died." He bent his head towards Uruk. "If he hadn't known enough to recognize their magic, she would be dead." His voice picked up a nearly orcish passion, outlandish on his tiny body. "I do *not* forget. And I will *never* forgive."

Uruk bared his Lesser Tusks in a tiny smile. Shared gain was good, but even a Norkosh could understand a shared enemy.

Another breath, and Kuru grunted.

Sanford nodded. "I'll watch you get in your car and drive off, so nobody calls the police on you."

Kuru grunted. "No blood tonight." Turning away, he said in orcish, "If you speak of violence to a man, the police will take you. If a man speaks it for you, they do not?"

The alliance was a Tai matter, but Kuru had seen him working with Sanford. He would not be put off. "Not yet."

"But you must obey him," Kuru sneered.

"Only when it makes sense," Uruk said. "We both war against the elves. And tonight, he leaves everything with me."

"Men always leave war to orcs," Kuru said.

Uruk grunted agreement, climbing behind the driver's seat. "He is useless in war, but he found our next battle."

Kuru slammed his door behind him. "The Longest Night is no time for war."

"It is not." Uruk began the complicated procedure to start the Model T. "But war with elves? The Longest Night might be the only time we can win."

Kuru grunted. "Tonight."

"This false orc will not be alone," Uruk said. "Bootlegging is heavy labor. We need more than the two of us."

"My brothers bring their women and children to feast tonight," Kuru said.

"As do mine." Uruk put the car into gear and started back towards Vernor Avenue.

Kuru said, "Moonset."

"Moonset."

Kuru's voice picked up a sharp note. "That home. This creature is not an orc. I claim its life for the Norkosh, as payment for our lost child."

"He masquerades as Tai," Uruk said. "*We* must have him."

"His blood is ours by right!"

Uruk thought quickly. "I challenge you for him."

"How?" Kuru snapped. "How do you divide a life owed?"

"We take him. We learn what we must. And then…"

"Who kills him?" Kuru snapped.

"We take turns," Uruk said. "Making cuts. Breaking bones. As we choose."

Kuru sneered. "You'll slash his throat."

"I said, I challenge you," Uruk said. "Whoever makes the last cut, the cut that kills this false orc? They lose."

Kuru stopped.

"The Tai can make him last for hours that way." A gap opened in the traffic on Vernor Avenue, and Uruk tapped the accelerator to swing into the flow. December's cold, heavy with the stink of exhaust, rushed past his head. "Can the Norkosh?"

"Cuts, and breaks, and fire," Kuru said. "Fire will stop him from bleeding out too soon."

Uruk bared his tusks. "Agreed. The winner has their choice of prize."

"Last cut loses," Kuru said. "Done."

Uruk nodded. The false orc's skull would make a fine porridge bowl.

 32

Thin white clouds skittered across the black sky, veiling and unveiling the brightest stars. December had drawn her winds high, leaving the dark street still and icy and unwelcoming. The scattered streetlights along Joseph Campau Street shone over the shops and factories, softening the Longest Night's engulfing darkness and filling the air with the sparkle of tiny flakes drifting down from above.

A stolen nap hadn't erased Uruk's exhaustion, but that and a warm meal of porridge with extra lard and pissing enough to drown a dwarf had granted him the strength to grind through it. He kept his fists pulled up inside his coat sleeves to hold a little heat, but December caressed his fingers just as she brushed his bare cheeks and crept beneath his coat collar. His coat swung with every step, weighted with the orc-scale revolver and two sets of brass knuckles, giving December freedom to reach up from below and deepen her claims on his warmth.

The Longest Night was for the clan. Arguments should be settled with feats of strength. The year's treasures should be shared, along with the sagas of struggles to remind the clan of what they accomplished together. The lost should be remembered, and celebrated, and left to the departing year. Every year since they were born, Uruk would wrestle both his sons at once. Two years before, Oscar and Ivan had finally pinned him down and left his heart bursting with pride. Last year, he had had to take one at a time, pinning each after excellent struggles.

In a few more years, they would pin him.

He hated the false orc for stealing this precious night.

Now ten years old, tall for their age but not yet their full growth, his boys— no, not boys. They had stood through their draught challenge. Uruk's *sons*, his young orc warriors, the legacy of his family and his clan and all he had worked for, followed Uruk into war.

An orc should not hope. And Uruk could not hold his grown sons back from a war against the clan, even if their future was more precious than his own. They would fight well.

Uruk's brother Tara walked beside them, barely taller than either but fuller in his chest. His labor as a janitor did not make him strong, but did keep his overbusy head out of trouble. Uruk's other brothers, sturdy Daka and hulking Kaba, followed. Kaba's coat bulged with the stolen elf-enchanted Tommy gun. No orc could tell if the weapon itself was enchanted, or only the bullets, so they had saved it against a desperate need. Like tonight.

If the clan had to war on the Longest Night, Uruk could not ask for better.

Except for the Norkosh.

Kuru-Norkosh stomped along beside Uruk, eyes glittering in the dark. His coat was more worn than Uruk's, his hat threadbare. The only outward sign of Kuru's caged anger was the way each breath snorted out a cloud of steam.

Four Norkosh brothers trailed behind Kuru.

Two lines. One followed Uruk. The other Kuru.

The Norkosh fought alongside the Tai, but not *with*.

The Longest Night should be full of cheer and laughter and boasting of the clan's triumphs, not anger at accusations and rage for the dead.

Almost invisible on the dark side street, the two lines of warriors approached the false orc's warehouse, a two-story building of sturdy cold-eating brick. Leaking warmth outlined a roll-up garage door and the smaller rectangle of a human door in Uruk's night-sight. A corner streetlight spilled a harsh white glare that hid more than it exposed, but the shadows it cast revealed two men, bundled against the cold, shifting their feet on either side of the man-door.

Men, standing frozen guard on the Longest Night?

Whatever lay within had to be precious.

Uruk paused. Kuru took two more steps, just to show he wasn't following Uruk's lead, and turned to face him. "We take the guards."

"They will raise an alarm," Uruk said.

Kuru shrugged. "Two of my brothers will circle around the back of the building where the men cannot see, then attack around the corner. We will batter them down before a man can panic."

"And face a locked door?" Uruk said. "We need them to open it."

"We take their keys."

"And if they have no keys?" Uruk said. "What if they must shout a password through the door?"

"Then we beat it from them," Kuru said.

It could work. It could fail. "Even the smallest of my brothers can make the men open the door for us without raising the alarm."

"You boast."

"Tara-Tai!" Uruk hissed, voice just above a whisper. "Make the guards open the door. Kuru, once Tara-Tai has finished the hard part, your brothers can silently take the guards."

"You do not command here," Kuru snarled.

"I prove my boasts," Uruk said. "Can you?"

Kuru drew breath threw his nose. "We can."

"Tara-Tai," Uruk said. "Go."

Tara studied the guards for half a breath. Had Uruk chosen poorly? Would Tara's thoughts cripple his feet?

Tara pulled off his flat cap and held it to Uruk. "Guard this until I claim it."

Uruk let out a breath he hadn't realized he was holding.

Tara trudged towards the streetlight and the shadowed guards.

Uruk opened his mouth to tell Kuru to act, but he was already muttering orders. Two Norkosh took off into the darkness.

Approaching the guards, Tara said, "No blood tonight."

Uruk barely heard the guard's soft human voice from this distance. "Orc."

Tara's bare head steamed in night-sight. "I seek labor." He stood only a few inches taller than the guards. Uruk could not imagine a less threatening orc to send in.

A guard grunted, but a car rattling down Joseph Campau drowned his feeble words.

"I am a fully trained janitor," Tara said. "I know the Four Degreasers and the Three Solvents."

"So does my wife," a guard said, "but I won't let her work here."

Cold struck Uruk's Lesser Tusks. Tension had made him expose them. He deliberately pulled his mouth closed. Tara would succeed, or not.

"I can sweep every shred of metal and speck of dust from a floor," Tara said.

"We'll just stomp all over it again."

"I can clean toilets until they are white again," Tara said.

The other guard brayed like a donkey. "He's got you there, Joe."

A truck grumbling down the main road swallowed all sound.

"Hey Dick," the first man called through the door. "Let's see if the boss wants another pig."

Pig. The man would pay for the slur—but, a second man named Dick? Why would one man call another a dick? Was Dick a title of respect? Or maybe his was bigger than Uruk's pinky? Perhaps he wanted all to know he preferred men to women?

A heartbeat later, the door transformed from an outline of warmth into a rectangle.

Uruk's marrow thrummed with Tara's success.

Instantly, two orcs flung themselves out of the darkness. One of the men started to shout, but was cut off as an orc crushed him into the snow. The best way to fight a man was to crash into him, knock him to the ground and crush the air out of him until he stopped fighting.

Tara threw himself through the open doorway and out of sight.

Kuru was already running, so Uruk darted forward.

Tara flung an unconscious man into the street and met them with a finger across his lips.

Kuru paused at the doorway, blocking Uruk's way, and bared his tusks. "No boast," he growled.

Uruk nodded at Kuru, then at Tara. "No boast."

Kuru nodded a grudging acknowledgement.

They entered the warehouse.

 33

Uruk had seen bonded liquor warehouses in Windsor, with crates of whiskey and beer and wine stacked to the ceiling awaiting transport out of Canada.

The false orc's warehouse shamed it.

Racks of closely spaced shelves stood two stories high, each stuffed with case after case of Canadian Club. The aisle ran to the warehouse's back wall, where oak barrels big enough to make Uruk reach for a winch sheltered more whiskey. A dangling light bulb cast deep shadows that hinted at more rows of shelves, more stacks of booze. Selling all this whiskey would make so much money that Uruk could tear up every floorboard on his clan's part of the tenement and still not have enough space to hide it all.

Uruk drew a deep breath. An alcohol tang saturated the air, over bitter notes of truck exhaust and bleach. It wasn't exactly warm, but the building had captured the shortest day's meager heat and wouldn't easily surrender it.

Somewhere behind the shelves, bottles clanged. Men shouted. The cheerful, senseless chatter of men performing labor that rightfully belonged to orcs. A rough-voiced man shouted *careful with that*, but without heat.

Uruk unknotted his hands, letting his knuckles creak as December eased her grip. His talons ached from the cold, but he fumbled in his pocket for brass knuckles. The braided ones, this time. The spikes drew blood, but the braids broke bone.

Behind him, Daka-Tai pulled the door shut and slid the bolt home. His face was calm, blank, betraying neither fear nor excitement. Good.

Next to him, though, Kaba-Tai's eyes flickered nervously from side to side. Kaba was always the biggest orc in any group. His size had robbed him of the chance to develop his courage, and tonight demanded courage. Tara might be the smallest of them, but he had faced the guards without a flinch and reclaimed his warm cap from Uruk without a hint of bragging.

Kuru stood by Uruk, gaze dancing to assess everything. A Norkosh orc had gone to the end of the aisle and peered around the corner. Another Norkosh had fit his head between two crates on the shelf, trying to peek into the next aisle.

Daka looked to Uruk, raising his eyebrows.

If Uruk did not act, Kuru would seize command. Uruk glanced towards the far end of the aisle, near the closed garage doors. The sound seemed to be coming from that direction.

The Norkosh peering through the shelves waved a hand, pulled his face back, and pointed between the crates.

Uruk picked another gap between crates and peered into the darkness. The back of a stack of crates. The same with the next.

In the third gap, though, Uruk had a slice of vision.

A canvas-tented truck, parked. A dozen men in a workman's fancy clothes heaved crates of whiskey from a pallet into the back of the truck. Another pallet of what looked like crates of wine bottles stood ready to load.

"Careful doesn't mean sandbag," the supervisor shouted.

Uruk froze.

The supervisor was an orc.

Except he wasn't.

He had the build of an orc, heavy through the chest. He wore a suit, though, and even from this distance Uruk could see it was wrong. The fabric was that disgusting flimsy stuff men made their clothes out of, and it hugged the false orc's shoulders too tightly. It had been cut to go around an orc, but not to fit the way an orc moved. It would bind a true orc. The purple-green skin of its face *gleamed*. Some humans used grease to make their skin shine like that. Had this orc been greased?

The false orc raised a hand. "Mister Reterstorf! If you break that case, it comes out of your pay!"

The voice had the depth of an orc voice, and the roughness. No orc spoke like that, though. No orc knew English well enough to speak so smoothly. And that name, unpronounceable to any orcish throat?

The false orc's raised hand showed off its talons. Every American orc trimmed their talons to square the sharp ends, but this *thing* had gone further. Its talons were filed to bluntness, and then filed thin. It had nails, not talons.

It was pretending to be a man.

Uruk refused to believe that the world might have two false orcs like this. It had to be Achilles.

"Sorry, Mister Tai," the bumbling loader said.

Achilles smiled, showing un-orcishly bright white teeth and his Lesser Tusks. "Better, Mister Reterstorf. Docking your pay would not please me."

No man would accept such a reprimand from an orc.

Achilles stepped towards the whiskey, studying the crates.

He wore *shoes*. No orc could wear shoes. Their feet were too wide. Even trimmed talons would wear away the toes in days. But this creature wore low-topped shoes of gleaming leather, too wide for a man and bound with fragile leather strings knotted at the top.

Uruk tore his gaze away before his guts completely rebelled.

Rows of shelves on the other side, supporting yet more booze. A fortune in alcohol. An office like a tiny shack.

In front of the office, an elf.

She sat at a table, studying a heavy leatherbound book. One upraised hand held a crystal wine flute, half-full of a sparkling liquid so transparent that it shattered the stark lighting into tiny rainbows. Mirovar. The elvish holy wine. She might have been sitting alone in the room, for all the attention she paid to anyone.

"A brand-new client tonight," Achilles bellowed. "We must prove we can reliably deliver, on time, without any trouble. Miss Earwin can't leave until we're loaded. I'm sure none of us want to delay her any longer than necessary."

Uruk stepped back, the urge to vomit fighting sudden shrieking rage.

Ten feet away, Kuru had stepped back from his peephole. His face mirrored Uruk's disgust.

Uruk concentrated on his steps. Even humans busy with labor would hear him stomping back to Kuru.

Before Uruk could speak, Kuru whispered, "We take him alive."

Uruk's marrow shrieked that Achilles had claimed Tai and needed to die before he shamed the clan any further. Those thinned nails, those clothes, everything about it debased *all* orcs.

But they had an agreement.

He forced himself to draw a slow breath. "He dies, but *slowly*."

Kuru nodded. "The last cut loses. Did you hear the name Earwin?"

Rage for his clan's defilement burned in Uruk's blood. He didn't trust himself to speak without screaming, so he nodded.

Kuru said, "Celebrimble's oldest daughter. Second only to him."

Next to them Tara whispered, "How do you know that?"

"Men at the slaughterhouse," Kuru said. "They speak of how they would take her."

Uruk felt grateful when Tara shook his head, giving him a moment to recover.

"Men are fools," Tara said. "She would destroy them."

"Men are fools," Kuru said. "They obey a false orc."

"The elf," Uruk said. The echo of the oath's fire gave his voice a quiver. He took another breath to firm it. "We need her answers."

Kuru nodded. "We take her alive."

Uruk said, "And we must not be seen until we can strike." His voice was almost steady, the oath-fire only a memory.

Kuru looked to his shortest brother. "Shurka! You saw where the power came in?"

Uruk had not thought to look, but bony Shurka-Norkosh nodded. "Middle of the back wall."

"Go outside. Kill it," Kuru hissed. His gaze met Uruk's. "We attack at darkness. Prepare."

Uruk paused. The Tai did not follow the Norkosh.

But they could follow darkness.

 34

"It's time."

The last time something prodded Mha's bare foot, it had been her two-year-old firstborn with the war-staff she'd brought back from Cuba. For a heartbeat Mha was twenty-three years old.

No, the ground was too hard. It must be rock. She was fifteen, sleeping on an outcropping on the southern side of the Sierra de Los Organos, rising before dawn for the march on Havana. Today she would meet *that* orc. Her bayonet would take an enemy's throat as *that* orc's blade took a kidney, and they would argue for hours over the kill, battlefield or no, except *that* orc would raise his rifle and snarl *behind you*. When any other orc would have fired, *that* orc would offer the respect of letting her kill those who dared attack her.

Mha instantly knew that she would fight for *that* orc. She would take *that* orc, own *that* orc, make *that* orc *my* orc.

A precious day, today. One she would remember all her days.

No. The ground was too clean. Not ground, floor.

This was not a good day.

Mha creaked her eyes open.

One hand held bone. Walls the blue of a summer sky. The air stank of boiled green things with a note of flowers. Not elvish magic, real flowers, but dried like humans used. A human space?

She lifted her head, and forty years plunged onto her shoulders.

Another poke at her bare foot. "You awake?"

"Thorn." Her mouth tasted like something else had died in it. "I wake."

"Eight o'clock sharp," Thorn said.

Mha wiped crust from her eyes with her free hand.

Thorn was not an easy human to labor for. She demanded senseless un-orcish tasks, like eating *muffins*, that frustrated Mha beyond all sense. But Thorn had declared she would wake Mha at eight, and had not failed.

Mha needed to remember that.

"Your oatmeal is ready," Thorn said.

Mha dragged her new boots onto her feet and followed Thorn into the kitchen.

The two-gallon pot sat on the stove. How had Thorn gotten the pot up there? Mha should have moved it for her, but her feeble body had demanded sleep instead.

On the table, two bowls. A tiny one at Thorn's place, and one the size of Thorn's head at Mha's bench. A small dish of sugar sat next to Thorn's, but the oatmeal's heady aroma carried no hint of sweetness.

What had Mha done differently, that Thorn had listened? Could she do it again?

"Sit, sit," Thorn said. "I've never had oatmeal for dinner, but—why not? Nothing wrong with it. Especially after that lunch."

The oatmeal wasn't as delicious as the *prime rib* earlier today, and Thorn had cooked it far too long, but it soothed Mha's aching mouth and warmed her gullet. She was eating far too much today, but she would need the strength and the heat. Thorn spooned only a morsel into her dish, coating it with a horrific amount of sugar, but obviously enjoyed her tiny bites.

Not a proper feast for the Greatest Dark. Thorn would not understand Mha's struggles of the last year. She would not offer proper toasts or recognition. Even if Mha set aside that her children should have eaten her before she rotted this much, the Greatest Dark was not a time for war.

"Is that enough?" Thorn said. "I've never made so much oatmeal before, but I saw how much you ate at lunch and wanted to be sure you wouldn't leave hungry."

"Enough." If Mha ate a second saucepan, she would be too full to fight. "Yes."

"I have to talk to you." Thorn pushed her empty bowl away. "About two things, really."

Mha paused, her spoon halfway to her lips.

"You're going to talk to that orc we saw," Thorn said.

They would talk, after they fought. "Yes, Thorn."

"And he's going to fight you. My Bristol told me that's how orcs argue."

Not in that order. "Yes, Thorn."

Thorn inhaled deeply through her nose and plucked something from a pocket. "This helped keep my Bristol safe in the war." From her fingers, a tiny bronze medallion dangled on a feeble chain. "A Saint Christopher medal. I want you to have it."

Mha stiffened. That tiny bit of metal kept Lieutenant Harrison safe? How? When Lieutenant Harrison had been attacked, Mha and that orc had killed for him!

"You were sent to protect my man," Thorn said. "This reminded God that Bristol needed him, and God sent you as His hand."

Mha blinked. No human god had—

No, it was a charm. A human charm.

Perhaps it had drawn Mha's attention at the critical instant, allowing her to perform her labor. Shamen spoke of such charms. Mha relaxed.

But would a human charm work for an orc?

It didn't matter.

The nap, the charm—Thorn was offering alliance in this war. A weak ally, true, but even a war-orc needed sleep and food. But what labor did the charm need? She had needed to claim the chimney brick in sunlight. "How do I take it?"

"I think it will fit around your wrist," Thorn said.

That simple? How could a human shaman make such a charm? Mha would never know. No human shaman would speak of such to Mha.

The cool metal chain went twice around her wrist, leaving only an inch free once she thrust it through itself, the tiny medal dangling. The medal had no sense of presence. Would a human charm work for an orc? Did it still live?

Mha needed every weapon. She would wear the charm.

"Perfect," Thorn said. Did she sense the charm as Mha could not?

Mha scraped the last bit of oatmeal from her bowl.

"One other thing," Thorn said slowly.

Mha swallowed and waited.

"The sheriff said that orcs don't like us to use your names," Thorn said. He had said that. Mha waited.

"I can't just call you *orc*, though," Thorn said.

Of course she could.

"That's not right," Thorn said. "You're not just any random orc, you're my friend. But every time I say your name, you say it too."

She seemed to expect an answer. "Yes, Thorn."

Thorn blinked, twice. Was that a tear? How could acknowledging her words cause pain? "But you don't really have a job, either," Thorn said. "You're here—we take care of each other."

Did Thorn deny that Mha labored for her? "I lift things for you."

"You do!" Thorn reached out as if to pat Mha's arm, but changed her mind. "And I do the baking. But that's not a job with a name, I mean."

True. Nobody, not even Mha, thought *orc who lifts small things* was worthy of a title.

"The world has no place for two old ladies like us," Thorn said.

True. "Yes, Thorn."

"The only thing I ask is that you be here, so we can help each other out. I've got to call you something. So, what if we say your job is to be my... Mantis?"

Mha stopped.

The world had no name for her labor. The world had not thought what she did for Thorn labor worthy of anyone, until November and the Sun had given it to her. If an orc ever heard it, they would not tie the word *Mantis* to *Mha n'Tass*—they sounded nothing alike.

Acceptable.

"Yes. I am your Mantis."

Thorn's face split in a grin so broad, she might have just ended a marrow feud with a hammer and hundred-penny nails. "My Mantis."

It was Thorn's idea, why was she repeating it? Did she think Mha was not listening? "Yes, Thorn."

"You're all done?" Thorn peered into Mantis' bowl. "Go and teach that sharp orc to not mess with the likes of us, then come back and tell me all about it."

Mha stood. The few hours of sleep had eased the burning in her eyes and the ache in her back, and the oatmeal in her belly promised warmth as she waited. With the scythe in her hand, she felt as ready to fight as an ancient orcess could be. She gave Thorn a nod. Thorn claimed to be her friend. Mha had no idea how a rotting orcess and an equally decayed humaness could fight a common enemy, but Thorn had woken her on time and fed her and offered the respect of no longer trying to say her name, all in the first hours of the Greatest Dark. It was a start.

As Mha started for the door Thorn said, "I'll make muffins to celebrate."

35

Lurking at the end of the aisle at the forefront of two clans of orcs, ready to charge onto the warehouse's main floor when the lights failed, Uruk checked his weapons.

A revolver, with six .75-caliber bullets. He left it in his coat pocket. Firing in darkness was foolishness.

The braid-faced brass knuckles chilled his knuckles, his palm supporting the leather-wrapped grip. He had to remember to override his instincts and punch, not slash.

Uruk narrowed his eyes and closed his breath, sucking his anger into his center.

Two months ago, Uruk would not have dreamed of attacking a human work gang. Elves had not taken another clan of Tai bootleggers and seized their draught. Uruk's clan had not killed an elf wizard. They had not hijacked a load of mirovar and exchanged it for stolen draught. They had not learned to smuggle whiskey and draught across the Detroit River or forged an alliance with a paper man. Celebrimble the elf had not given the tale to the human broadsheets, making the Tai known to the whole of Detroit and declaring war against the clan.

Uruk-Tai had been content with his labor and his growing family. Hungry for more, yes, but knowing no orc would ever have it.

The elves had raised a false orc against the clan. They even had an elf—Earwin, Celebrimble's oldest spawn—supervising it!

The elves had started this war.

Tonight, Uruk's clan would end it.

They could even claim the contents of the warehouse as trophies. No—where would they put it? Perhaps Sanford was right. The Tai needed their own warehouse.

But first: take the orc and the elf. Alive.

He could do this. He was an orc. War flowed in his blood.

And without this war, without the false orc, he would not have seen a home built for orcs. The memory burned. A ceiling tall enough to stretch his hands overhead. Chairs built for orcish bones and tables that did not need to be crouched over.

Beside Uruk, Kaba breathed too quickly. Tara laid a hand on his bicep and squeezed.

Uruk hoped that Kaba would gain confidence from winning this fight.

Eleven orcs against a dozen men, one false orc, and an elf? They should win.

But Lortz-Tai had said that the false orc fought *wrong*. Young Lortz had little experience, but even so he should not have been beaten so badly. Uruk needed to strike the false orc before any others.

Unless the elf Earwin was a wizard. No. Foolishness—why would a wizard hang around a bootlegger's warehouse? Even for an elf, she looked too young to be a wizard.

The garage door rattled open, drawn upward by a motorized chain, admitting December's frozen breath in a shroud of steam.

Uruk tensed. "If your orc doesn't bring us dark—" he hissed.

"He will," Kuru hissed back.

The warehouse plunged into darkness.

Men shouted in anger and confusion.

Uruk charged.

The switch from light to dark gave his night-sight no time to settle in. The hood of the truck still glared from the engine's lingering heat, but the truck's body was a vague shadow. The warehouse walls were invisible, the closest shelves mere pale rectangles. The men's bare faces were pale ovals above dim haze where their clothing hoarded their warmth. One man had opened his shirt, exposing a bright triangle over his heart. The elf was a weaker shadow, her face tinted to blue. Grandpa was right—elves even burned cool. She was already rising.

But in middle—the false orc, blazing with heat just like a real orc. The warmth of his body made the suit jacket glow and his pants burn. His bare head shone like a beacon. Night-sight hid the disgusting gleaming skin or how his talons were filed to un-orcish thinness.

Take him first.

The false orc shouted, "Stand and fight, men! Stand and fight!"

In Uruk's path a man turned on his feet, head wrenching this way and that like he would see light if he only looked in the right direction. Uruk slipped around him, his thigh hitting something—a table? A cart? No way to tell in the dark, bouncing off it and stumbling forward. His night-sight was steadying, outlining the truck's canvas top and sketching an empty pallet on the floor. Two more men stood against the back of the truck, an arm's reach out of Uruk's path.

A dozen men without sight, against nearly as many orcs? The orcs had to win.

Light blossomed overhead. Uruk grimaced, night-sight shattered.

A diffuse cloud spilled through the rafters, sparkling with blue and orange, stinking of orchids. Directly beneath it Earwin stood, one hand raised, concentration written in the tightness of her mouth and the narrowness of her eyes.

The elf was a wizard.

"There they are!" Achilles again. "Fight, men!"

Uruk burned to crush the false orc's throat so he wouldn't have to hear that nearly *man* voice again.

No time to fear. Or rage. Only time to fight.

One of the men by Uruk's path raised a fist, gleaming with spiked brass knuckles. The other fumbled in his pocket. If Uruk charged the false orc, they would take his back.

He swerved, leather-soled boots slapping the smooth concrete, raising his own fists. The first man swung his brass knuckles, but Uruk got his long arm inside the man's reach just before they hit, crashing straight into the man and smashing him up against the truck bed. The man coughed out his air, and Uruk felt something inside the man break.

Uruk let himself bounce back, letting the man sag to the floor, but a fierce flare of pain in his side made him stumble.

Knives. The other man, a knife in each hand. Each eight, nine inches long. One shone with Uruk's own blood. The man held each blade point-down from his fists, backwards from the way Uruk always held a knife when he was cutting something, but his stance and the way he held his arms told Uruk that the man had reason for doing that. A man didn't need a nine-inch blade to fight a man. Fighting an orc, though, that extra length would give a skilled man reach and depth.

The man had *talons*. And the way Uruk's side burned testified that he knew how to use them.

The knife-bearer grinned. "Let's see what you've got, little orc."

Little? Uruk was bigger than him.

A whiskey bottle sailed past Uruk to crash into the man's forehead.

The man wobbled, raising his hands to his face.

Uruk threw himself forward, fist swinging. His brass knuckles struck the man's chin. Bone crunched.

The knives were already whirling, but Uruk threw himself sideways. One blade caught in his coat, slicing through the heavy wool, but it missed his meat.

A gun fired. Was he hit? No. Not yet.

An orc bellowed in rage.

But nobody stood between Uruk and the false orc.

Achilles wasn't just smiling, he was grinning. Both his Greater and Lesser Tusks were out, mingled anger and joy dancing in his eyes. He had his hands up, but his fingers were outstretched and a little bit bent, thumbs tucked against the others.

Young Lortz-Tai had said that the false orc had fought wrong.

Fighting men, orcs charged and crushed. Fighting another orc you closed in, clutched, slashed with talons and tusks, rolled on the ground and put a knee in the gut and a thumb to the eye. The way the false orc held his hands out said he didn't want Uruk to seize him, but the smile on his face disagreed.

What was *fighting wrong*, anyway? A fight had no rules.

Uruk charged.

The false orc shifted to the side, drawing his knee up into his gut so fast that Uruk could barely see. Almost instantly, that foot crashed straight out. Not like a regular kick, but an unnatural sideways stomp.

That heel plunged into Uruk's gut, knocking the air out of him and sending him whirling backwards. His lungs strained to draw breath as his feet tried to get ahead of him, slow him—one foot, that's all he needed, one true foot planted firmly would stop him cold but he couldn't get it out fast enough because a table was in his way and Uruk smashed into it, through it, tumbling down in a rain of splinters and shards and bouncing his skull on the concrete.

Even after Uruk's body stopped, his head whirled. His gut ached and his lungs didn't want to draw breath. The false orc's shoes hid orc-sized feet, and he'd struck with orc strength.

Get up. Grandpa's voice, or the memory of it. *The ground is for the dead.*

He still couldn't breathe, but jerked himself up to his butt. Could he inhale? Not yet. Plant a hand on the cold, pebbly concrete.

Achilles watched.

A gun went off. A man screamed.

Focusing his strength, Uruk heaved himself to a knee. His lungs strained, and strained, and ripped free, letting him draw a giant whooping chilly breath of booze-flavored air. The room steadied around him.

Kaba-Tai charged in, wielding a chair like a club.

Uruk got one foot on the ground.

Achilles stood, hands still raised but open. A feeble defense against such a huge orc, but the throbbing in Uruk's gut said neither he nor Kaba could see Achilles' true defense.

Kaba swung.

Achilles ducked and spun all at once, his feet seeming to leave the ground as he flowed into the space beside Kaba, his arms reaching and tangling the larger orc's, circling Kaba and Kaba somehow circling him, then Kaba crashing face-first into the concrete floor as Achilles twirled out of reach.

Quicker than a fart, and Kaba lay still.

Uruk heaved himself to his feet. "False orc," he hissed in orcish. "Liar. You are no Tai. You are no orc!"

"Sorry, friend." Achilles seized Kaba's discarded chair and spun. It flew through the air, cracking square against Uruk's gut right on top of the kick. New pain flared, distracting Uruk long enough for Achilles to dart sideways, fleeing behind the truck's shelter. No orc would be so cowardly.

The elvish wizard-light quivered. Shivered.

Two Norkosh had gone for Earwin. Both writhed on their feet, mouths clamped open in silent screams. Groaning and broken men lay on the ground everywhere while orcs moved among them. Kuru-Norkosh was running for Uruk.

No sign of the elf wizard. Had she fled? Her light flickered—no, it didn't, it was a shadow, Earwin glided overhead like she'd taken an impossible leap but no leap shuddered and juked like that.

More wizardry.

All the tales spoke of wizards calling lightning, but her unsteadiness spoke of strain. Earwin was young, and so was her magic.

Uruk snatched Kaba's abandoned chair. His bruised guts complained as he heaved the flimsy thing skyward. Even with perfect aim, he wouldn't hit. A wizard would swoop out of the way, or call lightning, or shatter the chair to dust, but maybe it would distract her long enough for him to draw his revolver—

The chair hit Earwin's legs.

Uruk froze, shocked.

The chair fell, back shattering against the hard cold floor.

Earwin wobbled.

Plunged.

Uruk threw himself forward, shambling all-out to cross the few feet of ground, and got himself beneath Earwin a split second before she hit. She was too light, too soft, stinking of flowers and honey and cedar and a sweet spiciness that Uruk had never smelled before but his marrow shrieked at what could only be the filthy stench of elf.

A truck engine started.

Earwin lashed out an arm, catching Uruk upside the ear. Uruk snatched at her—no, that was a leg, an arm, a softness no good to hold. Hair—close!

Earwin screeched strange words. The beginning of a spell?

Uruk's hand found her neck.

A small squeeze.

Earwin's voice cut off with a gulp. Uruk's arms had her squeezed up against him so tightly that she couldn't move, her arms twisted further than a man could stand, her soft face with its bulging eyes and skin the color of lard so close to Uruk's mouth that he could have bent his chin and tapped her with a Greater Tusk.

The skin of her neck felt repulsive in his hand. Smooth. Soft. Like a slug, but dry.

Uruk whispered, "One spell, one twitch, and you die."

The lips quivered.

Uruk tightened his grip a hair. Her pulse hammered against his thumb. "I said—one twitch, you die!"

Killing her would be easier than letting her live.

Uruk had been raised hating elves. Elves hated orcs, after all. Elves hated the joys orcs lived with, the way orcs celebrated and mourned and fought. An elf would not look at an orc, would not admit that orcs even existed. Wasn't that enough reason to hate them?

But holding this elf at his mercy, Uruk suddenly understood just how awful elves were. Their skin. The sweet stench of their breath. The way their eyes shone. Everything about Earwin repelled his breath and marrow and gut. His hand itched to squeeze, to pop her skull off her spine and toss each piece away, so far apart that when he was done pissing on her body, he'd need to fasten his pants back up for the hike to her head so he could finish the job.

No. If Uruk killed her, it would be because he decided that she needed to die. Not because she was un-orcish.

The wizard-light flickered out.

Uruk barely caught himself from reflexively squeezing.

The truck lights went on.

In his arms, Earwin twitched.

Uruk saw only the taillights. Orcs shouted. An orc struck metal, hard, and snarled, stumbling between the taillight and Uruk.

Uruk quivered. He was at the back of the truck, he could leap and—

All he had to do was drop the wizard. Who would burn him to bone and ash.

Uruk steadied his grip on her repulsive hide.

The booze-laden truck lurched forward, shot out the open garage door, and disappeared into the dark.

36

Uruk's night-sight settled in enough to make out the battlefield.

Kaba-Tai stood, but his nose was a spot of burning heat. He must have broken it when Achilles threw him at the floor. His face was a mask of cooling blood. Daka mopped Kaba's face with a man's coat.

Tara, limping, was helping one of the Norkosh drag wounded men into a row. Another Norkosh cradled his broken arm.

Seeing Oscar and Ivan alive warmed his heart, even though they grinned like children. If Uruk had fought in such a war at their age, he would have done the same. They would do him proud.

Men lay scattered all over the warehouse floor. Most lay still. Two—no, three—clutched wounds and hissed or cried or gasped.

Uruk had fought men before. When they'd hijacked a load of elvish mirovar, a wizard had knocked him unconscious. The clan had survived a midnight gunfight on Lake Saint Clair by being more brutal than the attackers. But this was the first time he'd fought men with his own hands. The man he'd crushed against the truck lay still, the warmth of the blood trickling from his mouth visible against his cooling skin. The man who'd stabbed Uruk's side still breathed, but lay unmoving.

Despite the burn in his spleen, Uruk felt satisfied.

Human buildings were flimsy, their laws ridiculous, their contempt for orcs obvious in every breath. Humans built delicate walls and cracked sidewalks, then punished any orc who tripped and broke either. Orcs had to squeeze themselves down to fit into a world built for men. There was no answer to any of that. Orcs endured.

These men, though? They worked with—no, *for*—a liar who had declared war on orcs. They had raised arms against the Tai clan. They had poisoned a child. They deserved to be crushed. The broken bodies sent satisfaction deep into Uruk's bones. For once, he had answered the world's indifference. These men had paid for allying with a false orc.

A false orc who had vanished.

Uruk's marrow seethed. So close!

Kuru staggered up. "You did not take him!"

Uruk turned, exposing the nearly weightless Earwin tangled in his arms. "I have the wizard hostage."

Kuru grunted. "Two of my brothers leapt for the truck as it left. One lost his grip when they turned onto the main road. The other has not yet returned."

Uruk grunted. "May he bring back blood."

Earwin's neck shuddered in his grip.

Uruk said in English, "I said, do not move!"

The trembling grew fiercer, her pulse thrumming in her throat so fiercely he felt it in his fingers. She had surrendered to terror, pinching her lips and eyes tight shut.

Squeeze. End this. Instead Uruk said, "I do not want—" no, he couldn't say that, he very much wanted her dead if for no better reason so that he could stop *touching* that awful soft skin. "You can live through tonight. No wizarding. No fighting. Stay still, and silent, and live."

Earwin only squeezed her face tighter, like she couldn't bear hearing his voice. Uruk had offered all possible patience.

The fading excitement made the wound in his side burn more fiercely. His canvas shirt felt sticky and warm. "Oscar! Ivan! Stand watch outside. Let us know if anyone approaches. Kaba! Tara! To me!"

Tara-Tai was first to him. Uruk's youngest brother might be the smallest and weakest and most thoughtful of them, but the grin on his face declared he was no less an orc. "Four men live."

Uruk grunted. "Let others deal with them. Can you see my wound?"

Tara glanced down Uruk's body. "No."

He must not be bleeding too quickly if it hadn't soaked through his coat. "Under my left elbow. Don't touch the elf."

Kaba tromped up. "Uruk!" His mouth was tight and his nose leaked blood down his chin, but his fierce eyes glittered even in night-sight.

"Zhan-ford," Uruk said. "He can talk to men. There are papers here that he can read. We must know where the false orc went." Frustration sharpened his shoulders. "And we have to find a way to follow!"

"I can run for the Model T," Kaba said.

"It would take only two of us," Uruk said. "That orc—" Pain flared in his side, pushing his breath out of him. "The false orc. He fought like no orc I have ever seen. Two cannot take him."

"Four," a Norkosh kneeling over an unconscious man said. "We go."

"Even four might not be enough." The words tasted bitter. Uruk's next words did not want to come out his throat. December knew, though. On the Longest Night, there was no hiding from December. "Kaba and I. He put us down like we were children. We need all of us." The admission made his stomach burn.

"Steal a truck from the *produce distributor*?" Kaba said, using English for the un-orcish words.

Only a block away. "Guarded," Uruk said. "They will call the police."

Wounded or not, four orcs or only himself, he would follow the false orc. Uruk would lose, but he would go. An orc did not cower, but Uruk chose to face a different pain and looked down.

Tara had Uruk's coat pulled open, but was looking up at Uruk with a strange expression. He wasn't angry. He wasn't choking fear. He wasn't hungry, or lust-ridden. Was that—yes, Tara's thoughts were overflowing his brain and leaking out his eyes and his mouth. Tara had fought well, but those troublesome thoughts had claimed him. "Tara! My wound!"

Tara blinked. "A slash. Not deep. Get Daka to bind your side." He stood. "I have a way to follow Achilles. All of us."

Uruk blinked. "What is this?"

Tara shook his head. "I will return in ten minutes. Learn where we have to go."

"You do not lead our clan!" Uruk said.

Tara bared his Lesser Tusks. "What I do, I do for the clan. Or must I remind you?"

Once, Uruk had distrusted Tara. Uruk had been wrong. Tara's thoughts might be numerous, but they could be trusted. "Go, then. Do you pass Zhan-ford on your way?"

Tara shook his head, but was already turning and running.

Uruk would bind his own wound. "Daka! Fetch Zhan-ford. Kaba!" Uruk switched to English. "Take the prisoner. If she moves. If she speaks. If she breathes wrong. Break her neck."

The elf shuddered even more fiercely, but was smart enough to not protest.

Kuru looked over from where he was speaking with one of his brothers, but said nothing as Kaba claimed Earwin. Kaba settled her carefully in the crook of one arm, then slipped his hand alongside Uruk's to claim the elf's throat. His face quivered in disgust when he touched her, but Kaba mastered himself and claimed the prisoner. Did she breathe more easily? No, she should. Uruk had crushed her against himself, while Kaba cradled her like he might a child.

A child he planned to choke.

Tara had spoken truly. His wound was long, but lacked the stink of leaking bowels. A tiny thread of relief wove through him, and he bent to seize the knife-fighter's jacket. "Kuru-Norkosh!"

Kuru looked up from stacking corpses. "What, Tai?" Readiness for battle thrummed in his voice.

Uruk breathed deeply against the pain in his side. "We must learn where the false orc went." With a single pull, he tore a strip off the bottom of the knife-fighter's fancy jacket. "Our man will look at the papers, if we can find light."

"Shurka fixes the lights now," Kuru said.

An orc who understood *electricity*? Uruk did not have time to be amazed. "We must ask these men as well."

"And how do we follow him?" Kuru snarled.

"Tara-Tai returns with transport." What had Tara thought up now? Uruk tore another strip of cloth and began binding his wounds. "We have ten minutes. You will—" Uruk paused. He did not command, and did not have time to fight. "These men loaded the draught that killed a Norkosh child. And we need answers."

Kuru turned to a man lying on the ground.

A slow smile split his face.

 37

A gap in the icy clouds exposed the stars of the Greater Cleaver, then scrubbed it away. A sign from December that blood would be spilled tonight, but forgotten. Like everything else.

December had fully claimed Mha n'Tass, sapping every scrap of warmth but the flicker of life in her marrow. Snow lingered on her worn coat and over the thighs of her orc-leather tunic. She'd cut a length of burlap from her old dress to wrap her head, both concealing her hideous hair and slowing December's gnawing at her skull. December still might claim her ears or her fingers, but the best part about being so old was that she didn't have to save anything for later.

A pit squirmed into a snowdrift behind the Pickle Barrel sheltered her from any drunken men who might stagger out of the building, unless their eyes were sharp enough to catch light reflecting off her narrowed eyes. Each exhalation warmed the snow just below her nose until it had softened and shrunk into ice.

Her last war had been dust and sand and mud. Snow was not that different. Both gave her a place to lurk and watch and wait.

Her new boots, though? The boots cradled her feet the way she'd held her babes to her breast. Lined with rags, they held warmth. They supported her the way *that* orc always had. Proper orcish boots, boots that knew she had to be here.

Orcs had only what they could take. Her daughter had been taken in orcish custom.

If that monstrous orc's clan held her daughter, Mha would take her back.

Only five cars remained in the Pickle Barrel's parking lot. Would the abomination wait until everyone had left to carry out his business? Or might he appear now?

No way to know. She would lie here and let the cold swallow her aching back and legs.

She could not move to warm herself. Instead, she deliberately tensed and relaxed each muscle, one at a time, exactly as she had in Cuba. It wouldn't make her warm, or flexible. But it would be enough to let those limbs move when the abomination appeared.

Her daughter needed her.

Yes, *her* daughter. Mha claimed that daughter. She would fight for that daughter.

If this Achilles Tai returned as he claimed, she would violate all custom to learn what happened to her eldest daughter—even if it meant she never left the Greatest Dark.

Her heart thrilled to have an enemy worth dying for.

 38

Two Norkosh built a fire of scrap wood in a soot-crusted barrel. The blaze promised to throw heat eventually, despite the chill seeping through the warehouse. With any luck, both clans would be gone before it grew healthy coals.

The electric lights returned, illuminating the sprawling warehouse stuffed with expensive bootleg booze. Was Sanford right? Could the clan really have a place like this, overflowing with everything they needed to become wealthy and powerful?

Was the paper man's *corporation* an escape?

Oscar and Ivan were on watch. Kaba held Earwin prisoner. Tara had obeyed his thoughts and gone to fetch transportation. Uruk finished bandaging the annoyingly bloody but shallow slash over his spleen. Strips of cloth torn from a dead man's clothes made poor dressings, but he had nothing else.

Any breath now, Daka would return with Sanford. Seeing blood made the paper man even weaker. Would seeing the dead cripple him?

Uruk swallowed bile. "Kuru-Norkosh."

Kuru stood idle with two of his brothers, satisfaction on his face. "Uruk-Tai."

"My man has no marrow for blood. I want him to read the papers." Uruk could not command, so he made a statement. "Seeing the dead will distract him."

Kuru had studied Uruk's face for two breaths before saying, "The Norkosh choose to grant this Tai request."

Uruk had not asked for aid, he had declared the consequences!

No, they were allies. He had to let the Norkosh have that minor boast.

The last corpse had barely disappeared behind the box of an office when Daka led Sanford in, wrapped in a giant furry coat that looked warmer than all the Tai coats together. "Uraka!" He coughed. "Are you all right?"

Less wrong, but still wrong. "Uruk-Tai." Uruk waved a hand to the broad table in front of the tiny shed that served as the warehouse office. "The false orc escaped with a load of whiskey. We must know where he will take it. There is paper."

Sanford nodded, shaking fresh snowfall from his shoulders. "It is in the interest of the corporation that we get a place like this."

They might need a warehouse to store all the money, but why would Sanford think to bring it up now?

"I'll see what I can find." Turning to the office, Sanford's face picked up a greenish cast.

What had upset the paper man now? The corpses were hidden behind the office, leaving only two—no, three—blood trails. Kaba held Earwin on his one arm, his other hand at her throat but not even choking her. The four prisoners sat or lay on the concrete near the fire. Shurka-Norkosh gripped the healthiest man by his arms from behind, making him face the fire. In English, Kuru said, "Not hot enough yet" and thrust the business end of a monkey wrench back into the flames.

Sanford's voice sounded weak. "Maybe ask the people?"

Uruk said, "I will not take the prisoners from the Norkosh." Five Norkosh and three Tai? A fool's fight, for nothing.

Sanford said, "Do you mind if I ask them?"

Had Uruk been unclear? No, this was more human stupidity. "The human prisoners belong to the Norkosh." There. That should be simple enough.

Sanford nodded and swallowed.

Kuru worked the monkey wrench in the flames. The fire was still all light and very little heat, but the heavy pine smoke raised a few cinders. The man pinned by Shurka-Norkosh babbled something meaningless.

Sanford took a deep breath and took two steps toward Kuru. "Excuse me, mister orc?"

Mister orc again?

Every orc, even Daka and Kaba, turned to Sanford.

The prisoner grew even more pale.

Kuru looked to Uruk and said in orcish, "Does he mock us?"

Uruk said, "No. He knows nothing of orcs."

Still holding the wrench in the fire, Kuru looked at Sanford. "Man."

Sanford said, "Maybe I could ask him a couple questions?"

"I'll talk," the prisoner babbled. "I'll talk!"

Kuru studied Sanford. "Uruk-Tai tells me that you will read the papers for us." He stirred the fire with the wrench. "If you do not find what we need quickly enough, *I* ask questions."

Uruk expected Sanford to look back to Uruk for support. An orc could not cover up another orc's weakness, let alone a man's! Instead, Sanford only said, "I better start then," and scurried to the paper-strewn table.

Kaba said in English, "No."

Did Kaba object to Sanford reading the papers? Or how Kuru dealt with his prisoners? No, his attention was on his own prisoner. Had the elf moved? Earwin sat even straighter on Kaba's arm, with Kaba's hand at her throat, but she had opened her eyes to glare at the table.

Uruk followed her gaze. "Zhan-ford! That leather book. It belonged to this wizard."

Sanford jerked his hands back from the table. "Wizard? You have a wizard? *Prisoner?* A wizard, prisoner?"

"We can always kill her later," Uruk said.

Sanford shook his head and muttered something Uruk couldn't make out, then started sorting through papers.

Kuru turned the wrench. "Hot enough to boil spit. Not enough to boil eyeballs."

Sanford flipped even faster through the papers.

Why did Kuru threatening their enemies make Sanford work more quickly? Was it only blood Sanford disliked, or would a hot wrench to a prisoner's face distress him? He must hate blood even more than he loved paper.

Sanford thrust a sheet of paper into the air. "Got it!"

Uruk had not expected such quick results. "What have you learned?"

"This paper says—" Sanford stopped. His eyes narrowed.

"What?" Uruk said.

Sanford pointed at the prisoner. "You."

"He is ours," Kuru growled.

Sanford hoisted the paper. "You said you'd answer questions. If you tell us where that truck was going, I will ask them not to hurt you."

"He is ours!" Kuru said.

"Pickle Barrel!" the man shouted. "The whole truckload for the man at the Pickle Barrel!"

Pickle barrel? Uruk had unloaded southbound freighters stuffed with barrels of pickles fresh from fabled Pinconning. How would anyone deliver whiskey to a barrel of pickles? No, some insane human must have named their speakeasy that.

Uruk would *never* understand humans.

Sanford's smile looked more suited to a family dinner than an interrogation. "That's fine." He turned to Uruk. "The paper agrees."

"You had no right to question him!" Kuru snarled.

"If I said what the paper said first," Sanford said, "we could not have asked him for verification. So I keep my word. Mister orc, please don't hurt him."

Kuru bared his Greater Tusks. "He is mine."

Sanford shrugged. "I asked."

"You bastard!" the pinned prisoner shouted.

Kuru's eyes narrowed. "You do not demand."

Sanford said, "Orcs have very definite ideas about who is in charge. I said I would ask. I fulfilled my word."

The prisoner shrieked obscenities.

Sanford coughed. "Uraka-Tai." He coughed again, harder.

No man could speak an orcish name, but the man still fought for it. Uruk almost respected that kind of foolish stubbornness. "*Uruk*-Tai."

Sanford nodded. "I would say..." He took a deep breath. "Most men want one thing more than they want anything else."

Uruk laughed. "Who knows what men want?"

"At a time like this?" Sanford tipped his head towards the swearing prisoner. "They want to go home. This man will promise you anything, do anything, if it means he gets to leave here alive and go home."

Kuru bared his Lesser Tusks. "Coward."

Sanford nodded. "Yes."

"He fought us," Uruk said.

"He did," Sanford said. "And you have a choice. A man who knows that if he fights your clan, he dies? He will fight to the death."

"As he should," Uruk said.

"But!" Sanford said. "If they know that they face the Tai? And that if they drop their weapons and surrender, they will live?" He shook his head. "Almost everyone will run."

"Nonsense," Kuru said.

Uruk frowned at Kuru. "Zhan-ford has never lied to me."

"You defend this man?" Kuru said.

"He uses his knowledge to do what an orc cannot, to both our benefit." One day, his boys would *read*. They would have less need of the paper man.

"These men gave our child poisoned draught!" Kuru shrieked.

"Did they know it was poisoned?" Sanford said.

Humans and their *intent* foolishness! "What does that knowledge matter?"

Sanford closed his eyes and drew a breath. "It really doesn't to you, does it?"

Uruk said, "Only impact matters." The world changed by what an orc did, not by what they dreamed.

Lashing out against those who had soiled the name Tai had satisfied Uruk all the way down to his marrow. Hearing the survivors scream would be still more satisfying.

But Tara would return any moment, with his mysterious transport. "Zhan-ford. Can you guide us to this Pickle Barrel?"

"I have the address," Sanford said. "Out on Sixteen Mile Road. I'll look it up in my gazetteer."

Uruk nodded. In orcish he said, "The prisoners are yours." Obvious, but he had to acknowledge it.

Kuru grunted.

Uruk paused. "They obeyed the false orc."

Kuru stared at Uruk. "Do not tell me you want *mercy*?" He had to use English for the strange word.

"No," Uruk said. "If we had time, if their screams would not draw police, I would tell you to make them live for days." Grandpa had spoken of how to make a man survive days of torture, but Uruk had never heard of a modern orc even trying. He suspected Grandpa was only repeating what his father or father's father had told him. "But we have no time. We have the knowledge we need. Your choice is to gut them quick, or to let the world know they are shameful every day they choose to live."

Kuru's face didn't move.

To Sanford, Uruk said, "Get your gazetteer. Tell us where to go. We will face this false orc in front of his customer."

Kuru said, "The dead feel no pain." An old orcish saying.

Sanford glanced at Kuru, eyebrows bent in confusion. Did he expect them to discuss orcish matters in English?

Uruk nodded. "The dead feel no pain." Kuru would let the prisoners live. Even men could not fail to understand a scar-covered face.

Outside, a large engine growled.

Police? No, they would have brought bullhorns and shouted. Perhaps Tara-Tai? Had it already been ten minutes? Time flew while you were scaring men.

The roar settled. It wasn't a truck engine. Something bigger.

A door slammed. Orcish feet thudded on concrete. Oscar emerged from behind the wall of shelves to hit the button that opened the garage door.

Uruk could not make sense of what rolled into the warehouse. It had tires. It had a beast of an engine. A halo of fresh-falling snow swirled in around it. It had no windshield. No body.

"In the name of God." Sanford's mouth dropped open.

Even Kuru stopped turning his monkey wrench to stare.

The engine clanked into neutral.

Tara climbed out from behind the wheel and raised heavy brass-rimmed goggles from his eyes. "Our transport."

 39

It was a car. But not a kind of car Uruk had ever seen before.

Glancing over the unfamiliar shapes, his eyes caught on the front tires. They were half again the height of those on a Model T, and twice as wide. Heavy rough-surfaced knobs circled their treads.

The tires were attached to an axle that looked like it might belong on one of the giant industrial trucks.

Between the front tires, an engine big enough to fit a small cargo ship. Exhaust pipes the size of Uruk's biceps that swept towards the rear of the frame. Uruk had never seen a car with its frame exposed like this. No seats. No side panels. No trunk. Only an engine on a bare frame, a transmission big enough to conceal a hog, a rear differential the size of a barrel buzzing naked between two rear tires as huge as the front.

The motor idled like an angry bull in an outhouse, hinting that it might go berserk at the wrong word, that it could trample them and devour their carcasses at a whim. It did not belong in this warehouse. It did not fit.

Yet, it felt bizarrely right.

Sanford let out a laugh. "It's not an Oldsmobile, it's an *Orcsmobile!*"

Yes! Uruk let out his own bellow of laughter. It did not fit here exactly as Uruk did not fit. The shelves, the furniture, everything was for people too small and feeble to pick up a sow. This was an orc car. Complete enough to run and nothing more, not even a floor over the frame, but built to orc scale.

Tara reached behind the wheel. The engine died with a reluctant grumble. Tara's grin threatened to split his skull in half.

"Tara-Tai." Uruk forced himself to draw a breath. "What have you *done?*"

"I have started to build a car for orcs." Tara's voice dripped pride, but Uruk found himself too stunned to rebuke him.

"How?" Kuru demanded. "How have you done this?"

"Bomlin the dwarf has declared a debt to me," Tara said. "He teaches me to choose the parts. To put them together. We got it running only last night."

"And you said nothing?" Uruk demanded.

Tara's face grew serious. "I would not boast of unfinished labor. But tonight—" He glared at Kuru. "On the Longest Night, we war with elves. We need transport, and have none. There are no seats. I drive on an orange crate strapped to the frame. If you would fight this false orc, you must tie yourselves to the frame and hang on tight."

"You want us to ride that?" Kuru said.

Tara raised an eyebrow. "My brothers will ride."

Uruk fought his own smile, while Kuru hissed. Tara had not quite called Kuru a coward. "We will ride!"

"No!" Kaba shouted.

Uruk whirled.

Earwin had shifted on Kaba's arm as if to slide out. Her face bulged from Kaba's fingers wrapped around her neck.

Had the Orcsmobile distracted Kaba again? Had he failed to guard the prisoner? "Kaba!" He'd caught her in time, but still.

"I hold her," Kaba said.

"See that you do." Uruk turned back to Tara. "This… no orc has done such a thing."

Tara bared his Lesser Tusks. "*This* orc has."

A Norkosh understood electricity. His boys were learning to read. "This orc has," Uruk said.

"We cannot all fit," Kuru said.

It was true. The frame was huge, but eleven orcs would overflow it.

Tara nodded. "Oscar and Ivan, and the two weakest of yours, run for the Model Ts and follow. The rest of us?" He lowered the goggles over his eyes. "Hold on. Tight."

Oscar let out a small hiss of disappointment.

"No!" Uruk said to Oscar. "You and your brother are the smallest of us. Drive the Model T." He had to fight down the tiny thread of relief that his sons would not be riding this incomplete, dangerous, utterly orcish vehicle.

If anything, adding a floor and seats would make it *less* orcish.

To Tara he murmured, "Well done."

Tara grinned. "Not yet."

Sanford came in bearing a duffel bag over one shoulder, and clutching a flat paper book as wide as his scrawny chest and as mysterious as Earwin's leather-bound grimoire. The bag shifted every time he flipped a page, forcing him to shove it back. Watching him flip and shove, flip and shove, shot frustration through Uruk's determination. Sanford was a valuable ally, but why did he have to be so *feeble*?

"Here!" Sanford said. "Terror, you're driving?"

Tara had accepted that name for his janitor job. "Yes."

Sanford frowned. "There are direct routes, along the mile roads. That way's going to get complicated, though. Lots of weaving around. The simpler way might be faster."

Uruk choked his impatience. Sanford would spend more time deciding on the fastest route than they would lose by choosing the slowest. "If you were to drive it, what would you do?"

"Gratiot," Sanford said instantly.

"Then Gratiot," Uruk said.

"Have you seen the Groesbeck Highway build-out?" Sanford said to Tara.

The big road being built a mile west of Gratiot. "He has," Uruk said.

"Yes," Tara said.

"Take Gratiot up to Sixteen Mile," Sanford said. "Turn left. West. Sixteen Mile and Groesbeck, on the northeast corner."

"You will not guide us?" Uruk said.

"You want to get there quickly," Sanford said. "You want to confront Achilles in front of his buyer, you said?"

Uruk grunted. Sanford had listened.

Sanford pointed a finger at the Orcsmobile. "That *thing* is either going to break every racing record getting you there, or it will explode and kill each and every one of you."

Tara laughed.

Better dead in a wreck than dead by an elf's hand.

"My new top-of-the-line Dodge can't keep up," Sanford said. "I'll follow as best I can." Uruk started to speak, but Sanford held up a hand. "One last thing. For you."

Uruk paused.

"You face this enemy in front of a human," Sanford said.

Uruk knew that. Sanford knew that. Why say it again? "Yes."

"Your fight is in front of a man." Sanford tightened his face. "A man who can call on the police. Who might have other men there, with weapons."

"You speak what all know," Uruk said.

"You must command the same respect Achilles does," Sanford said.

"We will prove respect on his meat!" Uruk said.

"You fight not just this orc!" Sanford yelled.

Uruk leaned back in surprise. When had Sanford's balls grown large enough to shout into Uruk's face?

"Even if you defeat this orc, the man could destroy you!" Sanford said. "He could destroy us, you and me and my wife, and I will not permit that. You must demand respect before you open your mouth. You must *show* that you are at least as respectable as the false orc."

Foreknowledge tightened Uruk's throat.

Sanford heaved the bag off his shoulder and held it out. "Tonight. This war. If no other time." The weight made his arm tremble. "Wear the suit."

Uruk's heart thrummed, his Greater Tusks creeping out.

"Tonight," Sanford said, "you told Kou—" he coughed "—the other orc that I never lied to you? I would not waste that trust."

So like a paper man, to use Uruk's own words against him!

"Tonight," Sanford said, "the suit *matters*."

Uruk drew a shuddering breath, then snatched the bag out of Sanford's hand.

Kuru snickered. "We need time with the prisoners."

Seeing the Norkosh mark the men would upset Sanford. "Go," Uruk said. "We will pass you."

"Or not," Tara said.

Kaba said, "And what of this one?"

Uruk studied the elf. Her terrified quivering had eased, but her huge eyes were fixed on Uruk's face. In English he said, "We will bind your mouth and your limbs. I am sure that when the men recover, they will free you."

Kaba started in surprise, but held his grip.

"Recover?" Sanford said.

"I said go!" Uruk snarled. "This is not paper man business. They will live. With all their fingers and eyes and even their dicks. Be content."

Sanford paled, then scurried for the door.

Earwin seemed to have stopped breathing. Her gaze did not flicker from Uruk.

"We do not desire war with you," Uruk said. "If we kill you, other elves will come. But the next time you or yours think to raise a hand against us, remember—we could have killed you."

"Foolishness," Kuru said.

Uruk snarled, "My prisoner! Mine!"

"You are a fool," Kuru said.

"Killing her gains only the pleasure of her death," Uruk said. "Perhaps that is enough for a Norkosh, but not for us."

Kuru shook his head and turned to his brothers. "On the face," he said in English. "Not too deep. Four or five cuts each."

Earwin's eyes shouldn't have been able to open wider, but they did.

"Remember," Uruk said. "Next time, you die. You, and anyone you raise against us. We will burn your homes. We will—" What were some of the things Grandpa said in his stories? "We will cook your children and use your *books* to wipe our asses!"

Earwin shuddered, closing her eyes.

"Or you can leave us alone." Uruk raised his voice. "Gather ropes! We ride!"

 40

Uruk balanced his butt on a crosspiece of the Orcsmobile's frame, letting its chill soak into his ass. The soles of his boots rested against the next crosspiece forward. A loop of heavy hemp rope lashed in a sailor's knot around the weld of crosspiece and frame on either side served as loose reins. Another rope tied his long coat up around his waist.

Beneath him, the sleeping driveshaft.

Bracing his legs would keep Uruk from falling forward. The rope would keep him from tipping backwards, and help balance him when cornering. He had a solid six inches between his ass and the driveshaft, and another ten or twelve to the warehouse floor.

Kaba sat in the front, next to Tara, with Sanford's shameful duffel bag tied between them. Kuru and Daka flanked Uruk in the middle. The last two Norkosh sat in the rear to weigh down the drive wheels, with their knees over the axle. More weight back there would give the drive wheels better traction, but any orc that straddled the rear differential would get his balls ground off.

Uruk would never tell anyone how glad he felt he'd sent his boys to fetch the Model T. Riding this beast was a challenge worthy of an orc, but anyone who lost their grip on the Orcsmobile might lose their life. Likewise, Kuru had sent the Norkosh with the broken arm and his smallest brother for their car.

Uruk dared hope that the Model Ts would arrive too late for the fight. His fine boys had fought this battle well, but this false orc was impossibly dangerous.

Tied on his orange crate, Tara glared over his shoulder and said, "This is *my* auto. Mine! *I* drive. While you ride, I lead and you obey."

Obey his younger brother? What orders could Tara give? The wind would drown his voice. Uruk contented himself with a grunt.

Kuru said, "The Norkosh do not surrender leadership!"

"Then walk," Tara said. "All who ride must obey until they stand again."

Kuru bared his Greater Tusks.

"That's the rule of the road," another Norkosh said. "The driver commands."

"He does not make our decisions!" Kuru said.

Tara said, "Here are my orders. We go to this Pickle Barrel, as fast as we can, to face our enemies. We stop only when the road declares we must. If you weaken and fall, we do not return for you. This car has never been on such a long trip. If I declare that something must be done to keep us moving, you will do it. I do all in my power to get us there, and you do all in your power to support that. If you cannot agree to that, find another way."

Kuru glared at Tara's back, then at Uruk.

"This engine does not start until you agree," Tara said. "Or you get off."

"The Norkosh agree!" Kuru's mouth twisted. "Get us there so that we can fight the real war."

Tara's only answer was to turn the key.

The engine growled to life.

The crosspieces vibrated angrily, making Uruk's butt slide forward an inch. He tightened his legs to recenter himself, pushing himself back so he had to clutch the reins. Next to him, Daka snarled.

Tara raised his voice above the noise. "All ready?"

Uruk joined in the grunts of acknowledgement.

The chassis thunked as Tara put the transmission in gear.

Beneath Uruk, the driveshaft slowly turned. The six inches between the slowly torquing metal and his dick suddenly felt far too short. Uruk wrapped the reins around his hands more tightly. He tightened his legs to brace himself more firmly. His bandaged side ached. One boot slipped, the heel forcefully smacking the warehouse's concrete floor.

Uruk swallowed. If the car had moved more than an inch—

No. Worrying about what *could* happen was foolish. He would arrive at the Pickle Barrel alive, or his brother's magnificent nightmare would spindle him to death and trample his remains. All Uruk needed to do was endure, and hold on with all his strength.

But not so much strength that he pushed his feet into slipping again.

The brakes eased.

The concrete below began drifting past.

The combination of whirling driveshaft and the moving concrete bewildered Uruk's eyes. He raised his gaze, but couldn't see over Kaba's shoulders. He'd claimed the most dangerous place, right over the whirling driveshaft, not realizing it would make him almost blind.

Vibrating, the Orcsmobile backed through the warehouse doors and into the night.

His weight pulled to the side as Tara turned the car from the warehouse doors onto the side street. His butt wanted to slide over the crosspiece, making him reflexively clench those useless muscles, but he shifted his weight on the heavy hemp rope instead.

The rope scratched his palms. Uruk's hands had hardened from years at the docks. Had a few weeks of bootlegging stolen that toughness?

The car stopped.

Tara shouted, "And now—forward!"

Uruk took a deep breath.

The jolt pushed him backwards, but pulling on the reins a little more fiercely than he braced his feet held him in place. He felt rather than heard Kuru's huff of effort, and smiled.

Then December slapped Uruk's face. The night had been cold, but the car's motion let her breath shoot up the sleeves of his coat straight up into his armpits. Was the car moving that fast already? No, looking to the side showed that Tara couldn't be going over ten miles an hour. How cold would it be out on the main road when Tara could get up to thirty miles an hour, or Gratiot's impossible fifty?

And Tara was going *away* from Joseph Campau? Yes, he had command, but—why? They had to get to a mile road and over to Gratiot, not cut through innumerable side streets with all their tiny homes and orcish tenements and garages and businesses.

Fresh flakes of snow struck Uruk's face. December, discouraging them.

The asphalt slid by too quickly below, but glancing at the houses showed he couldn't be going above a run. What was Tara thinking? Uruk hated staring at nothing but another orc's back. Why had his biggest brother claimed a spot directly in front of him? Icy air shooting up the sleeves of his coat kept his frustration from boiling into anger.

The car glided to a stop. A crossroads.

Tara shouted, "Adjust your grips! What doesn't work? Fix it. We go again in five breaths. A couple more stops until Mound Road and we really hold on."

Uruk's frustration eased. They could move on Mound Road. And no orc knew how to ride a beast like this.

Kuru was looping his reins around the cuffs of his coat and then his hands. Uruk hated to offer the Norkosh satisfaction, but did the same.

After two more stops, Uruk had almost adjusted to the constant vibration and the splintery rope digging into his hands. His butt was icy, but his coat kept a core of warmth around his vitals.

Tara shouted, "Mound Road. We ride!"

The motor surged.

The crosspiece shook more fiercely than anything Uruk had ever felt. His hands tightened on the reins even as his ass bounced once, twice, three times and the road flashed past so quickly that Uruk couldn't make out any details and the driveshaft whirled into a frenzy and the transmission's clatter rose up his spine, delivered through the frame and not his ears.

Ice hit his face. No, not ice. Snow. Snow, at Orcsmobile speeds.

Something stabbed his thigh. Had the driveshaft broken? No, if that happened he would already be dead. A pebble, perhaps? Was he bleeding? Uruk wasn't going to let go of the reins to check. Maybe it had torn his canvas pants. Bleeding might kill him slow, but losing his grip would shred him instantly.

Cascades of snow rose on either side, thrown up by the giant knobby tires.

The whole car bounced. Uruk's butt left the crosspiece and crashed back down. Pothole, maybe? How fast were they going?

To their right, a Model T came into view and fell backwards.

They were passing traffic? Uruk had never dared pass traffic before. The police would stop him and seize the Model T—

A fierce grin split his face.

The police could not stop them. Not during the Greatest Dark. Not in the Orcsmobile.

All he had to do was endure the noise pounding his skull and keep the reins in his hands and the thrown-up snow building up on his butt and legs and December's constant attack on every scrap of exposed skin.

And keep reminding himself that the deadly driveshaft was a solid six inches below him. So long as the most important part of his pants remained whole, there was no way his dick could get wrapped around it.

Another flung pebble stabbed his thigh. Maybe tearing his pants, too.

Uruk clenched his jaw and held on.

As the Orcsmobile spun onto McNichols, scattering the headlights of lesser cars around it, though, Uruk couldn't help laughing. "This!" he shouted at Kuru. "*This* will be a saga our children's children retell at every Greatest Dark!"

Kuru stared at him for a breath, blinking ice from his eyes.

Then the whole carload of orcs, Tai and Norkosh alike, split the night with their laughter.

This madness was everything America should be.

 41

By the time the Orcsmobile left the luxurious four lanes of Gratiot Avenue and swung onto Sixteen Mile, December held Uruk in frozen misery. The inches of dirty road snow crusted on the bottom of his pants provided no protection against the debris the tires kicked up. His eyes felt like spears of ice sunken into his frozen face, and he didn't dare wipe away the ice and snow that had pummeled him.

Fortunately, his hands had frozen around the reins. Ice crusted into his ass had attached him to the frame's crosspiece. So long as Tara didn't drive into a ditch, the Orcsmobile wouldn't kill Uruk. December had claimed that privilege.

Engine fumes filled his nose. The Orcsmobile had no muffler, no exhaust, and spewed its noxious breath right next to the driver. The wind blew everything straight up Uruk's snout, lightening his head and revolting his guts.

The only warmth he had was beneath the bandaged wound on his side. It pulsed at every pothole.

Uruk had never endured more than this.

He was barely aware of the car slowing. It had slowed many times, at stop signs and traffic lights.

It stopped, again.

But this time, the engine cut off.

The sudden silence and stillness struck like a hammer to the head. His ears rang. The ice plastered over his pants swayed, while layers of bruises proclaimed the crosspiece's triumph against his ass. He was so cold, maybe his dick *had* fallen out and gotten tangled in the driveshaft. He wouldn't know.

Into the silence Tara said, "We are there. So is the truck."

All that, and Achilles had outraced them? Uruk was too frozen to find outrage.

"The truck is still warm," Tara said.

Achilles had not been here long, then. Good.

"Stand, and I no longer lead," Tara said.

Behind Uruk, an orc groaned.

With Kuru on one side and Daka on the other, Uruk had been comparatively sheltered. Had this trip been more than *any* orc could endure?

With focused will, Uruk uncurled one finger at a time from around the reins. His arm was pure ice. Dragging the rope from around his coat cuffs sent nails into his fingers and palms so fiercely he had to hiss, but free hands let him batter petrified snow from his face.

Something round and warm touched his lips. No, not warm, merely less icy than him. "Drink," Kaba said.

Draught splashed across his tongue. Uruk downed one mouthful, two, three before Kaba pulled the bottle away. He ached to snatch the bottle and drain the rest, but his arms were little more than clubs. The draught felt like hot metal burning down his throat, shattering every layer of ice and restoring life to his tortured meat until it struck his gut and exploded everywhere.

Another dozen breaths and his legs had enough feeling to let him drag his feet off their crosspiece. They hit the ground like dead weight, but more nails were throbbing in his toes and heels.

Next to him, Kuru coughed. The Norkosh was regaining life.

Uruk focused on his frozen fingers. They moved as he commanded, but slowly. Red lines around his hands showed where the splintery hemp rope had scraped away skin. He flexed both hands twice, then fisted them and pulled them into his coat sleeves. They would thaw, eventually.

Next to him, Daka groaned and toppled onto the ground.

Standing felt impossible.

Uruk did it anyway.

Blinking cleared the snow, and the draught had sent lines of heat into his eyes. They still ached, but he could once again see.

Even in night-sight, this place was dark.

The Orcsmobile sat in ankle-deep snow. The sky was impossibly black, without Moon or stars or even clouds.

The two lanes of Sixteen Mile Road were an even colder line of asphalt and ice. The ugly shapes of plows and tractors and other strange vehicles surrounded them. Beyond them, the irregular clawing shadows had to be trees.

Perhaps two hundred yards behind, a low building cast glowing warmth.

Uruk worked his mouth and nodded towards the building. "You know that is it?"

Tara said, "It is the only living building here. The construction crews tore the others down."

Kuru said, "You drove past it?"

Tara said, "Kaba and I were right up against the engine, and we were cold. You needed draught before you could fight. The engine is still loud, so I drove past so they would hear our engine leave."

"Well done," Uruk said. The draught softened as it sank into his limbs, its heat fading as agonizing feeling returned to his battered flesh. "Draught. You have more?"

Tara stiffened. "Yes—but." He pointed.

Ice-crusted Daka lay unmoving on the ground.

Uruk's heart clenched.

One of the two Norkosh riding over the axle had fallen backwards. The other still balanced on the end of the frame, the reins in his hands. Both bore three times the ice as Uruk or Kuru.

"Shurka!" Kuru struggled to stand. "Gushbaz!"

Uruk tottered to Daka. His brother still breathed, but the right side of his body looked like an ice floe ready to float down the Detroit River.

Kuru knelt by his brothers. "They breathe. Lucky for you, *car leader*."

"We knew this was dangerous," Tara said.

"And the eldest of the Tai sat sheltered in the middle of us." Kuru bared his Greater Tusks. "*Ally.*"

"You did not volunteer to have your balls scrape the driveshaft," Uruk said.

Kuru hissed, but turned back to his brothers. "They must have heat."

"The engine," Kaba said. "It's still warm." He started towards Daka.

"No," Uruk said. They had to hold the alliance.. "I have Daka. You help the Norkosh. Who is most cold?"

"They are both ice," Kuru snarled.

"The smallest, then. In the middle. Daka's warm side to him, your other brother on the other side." Uruk's neck almost worked. "Tara. How much draught do you have?"

"One more bottle," Tara said.

Uruk nodded. "Share it even. The engine's warmth, out of the wind, draught. It is all that can be done."

Kuru stared at Uruk. What more could the Norkosh ask for?

Finally Kuru nodded. "No more can be done."

Shifting Daka and the two near-frozen Norkosh to the sheltered side of the engine hurt, but the motion knocked the ice from Uruk's joints. By the time they knocked the worst of the ice off them, propped them in place, and split the draught between the three, Uruk's muscles stopped shrieking and merely moaned.

Four stood. Tara, small but full of thought. Kaba, large but placid. Kuru, bound to his anger over a child's death. And Uruk, injured.

Against a viciously lethal false orc spawned by elves to destroy the Tai.

Uruk tried to spit, but his mouth was too dry. "We need every advantage now."

Kaba tugged the enchanted Tommy gun from beneath his coat.

Kuru studied Uruk, then drew an orc-scale four-gauge shotgun from inside his coat. The barrel had been cut off just above the stock.

Tara revealed a narrow knife. It looked familiar. Was it the weapon that had wounded Uruk?

Uruk had his revolver and his brass knuckles, but they walked into a human space.

Sanford's voice: *I would not waste that trust.*

Bile burning in his gut, he reached for the loathsome duffel.

42

A canvas-topped truck backed into the rear doors of the Pickle Barrel.

Mha n'Tass began counting fifty slow breaths.

The snow pit had slumped to hug her body, her slowly leaking heat cooking it to crust. Despite the cold, sweat trickled down her spine and in her armpits. Her ceaseless flexing of every muscle had kept her ready to move, and icy crust was warmer than snow. The ancient brick charm hung around her neck. Her bone-handled scythe lay on the snow next to her, cloaked by an inch of fresh fall everywhere but where her hand cradled it. Breathing in through her nose filled her with December's chill, but instincts thirty years idle compelled her to breathe out through her mouth and down into the snow. Breath was warm. The best way to avoid enemy night-sight was spreading your warmth into the world. Don't exhale a plume—exhale into loose sand, or snow, or underwater.

The last time Mha had waited to strike, the heat of the Cuban sand had threatened to broil the marrow in her bones. *That* orc had been with her. She might have moved for herself, but she would not risk drawing sniper fire towards *him*. They had ravished each other after the battle, so eager that they'd accidentally tipped a captured mess wagon. Sergeant Morgol had waited for them to finish before telling them to right the wagon and search it for fennel.

Better to think of the chill sinking into her marrow, not the one permanently ruling her heart. December's cold had eased the ache in her hip, but new pains stabbed her knees and shoulders.

They would pass.

Fifty breaths. Enough time for the monstrous orc to meet the human and lower his guard. Let them start unloading that truck. Wait for his hands to be full.

Slash a blade across his belly. Expose the bowels, don't puncture them. Enough of a gash to cripple the monster, but let him speak. Discover the truth of the Tai clan. If he knew of her Vara, take the truck. Find her daughter. *Take* her.

If the abomination knew nothing, destroy him.

Thirty breaths. Flex the feet. Break the crust.

A low car growled down the road, slowing as it approached the Pickle Barrel.

The car looked wrong. The engine glowed too brightly, as if it ran without a cowl, but nobody would be that wasteful. December would ruin a bare engine. The body was strangely lit and too long and low.

It rolled into the dark construction site two hundred yards further up, and stopped.

Her old eyes needed a moment to sort out the half-frozen orcs tumbling from the—cart? A motorized wagon, maybe? The way they beat ice and snow from their bodies told her their vehicle had affronted December. Did they come for the monster? Or were they his allies?

The three most frozen orcs were abandoned by the wagon's engine. Another four broke into a loose run along the road, heading for the Pickle Barrel. Lingering body heat gleamed from long arms.

Mha flexed her left foot, breaking the snow crusted around her. Then the knee. The hip.

Forget the count. When the four orcs entered, she would follow.

Mha flexed her ice-frosted fist, freeing her frozen talons.

 43

The Greatest Dark, yet anger burned. A false orc had soiled the reputation of the Tai.

His brother Daka had nearly frozen to death on the journey here, making him angrier.

Sanford had persuaded him to wear the suit, feeding his fury.

But worst of all? What made rage seethe in his marrow?

The suit was *comfortable*.

The plush wool hugged his form without binding his motion. The heavy socks cradled his feet in the gleaming boots. The wool pants held his heat in a way canvas or burlap never did, and the suspenders gave them a strange sense of solidity. An orc had to tightly tie his pants, or give up on pants and wear overalls, but the suspenders combined the liberty of pants and the security of overalls.

The wool shirt with the orc-sized brass buttons was so white it gleamed in the dark, but the jacket smothered the color and held his heat.

Strangest of all?

The hat.

A human *fe-do-ra*, with a curved brim and a band around the crown, in a pleasantly scratchy felt that smelled faintly of rabbit. It left his ears bare, but it trapped as much warmth over his bare scalp as his treasured flat cap.

Wrapping his beaten ass and cut flank and road-debris-battered thighs in comfort felt wrong.

Kuru had laughed with his eyes, but held silence. Good. Uruk would have hated breaking the alliance by strangling Kuru.

He could learn to *like* wearing the suit, and he hated it. Suits represented men, and men dismissed and discarded orcs every day.

Except for the underwear. It was both un-orcish and uncomfortable, the way it hugged everything up tight. How could anyone know which way was up if nothing hung down?

And then the overcoat. The cloth had to be an inch thick, every bit of it an unfamiliar wool. Uruk had chosen the cloth from a bin of ragged scraps, but the tailor had done something to make it outright plush without offending his orcish senses.

A coat, over a coat, over a shirt? Ridiculous. The combination might be warm enough to thaw him even without the draught. Uruk draped the coat over Daka and the Norkosh.

Kuru said, "You trust this Zhan-ford."

"We share a goal," Uruk said.

"Not that," Kuru said. "You would not wear that thing unless you *trusted* him. You believe that he will not betray you."

Uruk paused. "Who else would read?"

"Not the point!" Kuru said. "His scouting brought us here. You dress like a man because he demanded it."

"He did not demand," Uruk said.

Kuru said, "He said he would not waste your trust, and used that to demand without demanding."

Uruk had thought the same.

Kuru leaned in. "And you are in the habit of obeying him."

"He must lead when we talk to men," Uruk said.

"He claims to hate elves," Kuru said. "He claims a human marrow feud with them."

"I saw their curse," Uruk said.

"Listen!" Kuru said. "You made me listen to you, *ally*. Now you listen to me."

They had no time for this! But Uruk did not lead this war, and Kuru would not move until he spoke. "I listen." Uruk bared his Lesser Tusks. "Ally."

"Men never choose orcs over elves," Kuru said. "Never! Men are fickle. Soft. All men are prey to elven magic, but even more to elven persuasion. An elf's voice is a charm, softening the hardest man's will to the elf's wishes!"

"Every orc knows this," Uruk said.

"But you are in the habit of obeying him," Kuru said. "I would be a poor ally if I did not remind you. Zhan-ford will betray you."

Sanford claimed to be Uruk's partner. Their alliance had brought wealth to them both.

But how deeply could a human hate? An orc hated down to their marrow, but men fell for elves exactly as Kuru said. Sanford had developed strength and proven his value, but he was still a paper man. Could Celebrimble persuade him to betray them?

Of course he could. That's what humans did for elves.

Sanford claimed to be a partner. Uruk had doubted the strength of that partnership before Kuru had even spoken. Men *used* orcs. "I will... consider Sanford's ideas before acting on them."

Kuru studied his face, then gave a nod. "Let's go."

Approaching the Pickle Barrel was not a matter of stealth. The only choice that didn't involve breaking through yards and yards of waist-high drifts was to run down the road, up the drive, and to the building. Draught had loosened Uruk's muscles, but none of the orcs could manage anything over a slow trot. December had come within a few breaths of claiming them, and would not easily surrender her grip.

Uruk's muscles loosened by the time they got to the parking lot, but the treacherous crushed snow made them all slow to a walk.

Around the rear, where the false orc's truck was backed up to open double doors, light washed out of the doors and around the truck. Uruk blinked.

His heart was beating too hard. Past deeds rose to remind him that no orc simply *made* war, they lived it. The clan had hijacked a load of sacred elvish wine. When a boatload of armed men came to set their bullet-riddled corpses adrift in Lake Saint Clair, his clan had sunk them instead. He and his brothers—and yes, the oath-bound Norkosh—had vanquished the warehouse workers. War flowed in an orc's veins. The brass knuckles on his left hand and the revolver in his right should soothe him, not send lines of tension all the way up his arms and into his spine.

A proper orc would not be afraid.

This fear was the suit's doing.

Kuru and Uruk reached the truck side by side, but Uruk was a little quicker and able to slip into the gap between truck and door one step ahead of Kuru. Kuru hissed, but too faintly to be heard more than five feet away.

Around the truck, and inside.

The man standing by the doors leading further in had to be the barkeep.

The false orc stood by him, a stack of whiskey crates on his two-wheel dolly.

Perhaps orcs could not trust men, but men needed to trust orcs.

"Stop!" Uruk switched to English. "The booze is poisoned!"

 44

Mha's eyes were old and cold, but not too decrepit or frozen to see true.

The four orcs tromped around the back of the building with all the stealth of angry bears who'd eaten too much bad meat and wanted to get out of smelling range of their cave before crapping their bowels out. She'd just started to rise when extra light flickered out by the road.

No car. No buildings. Not even a lantern.

Only light, flashing and sparkling and disappearing. And was that a faint scent of lilac? In December?

Mha froze.

Elf magic.

Mha would die to kill the monster orc.

But the thought of killing an elf made her want to *live*.

 45

The Pickle Barrel's back room was a space for the kind of labor orcs did, built to exclude orcs.

The brick floor was swept, the paint fresh, the recessed electric lights mercilessly exposing every flaw. Stacked wooden boxes held jars with brightly colored labels depicting different vegetables. Did this speakeasy serve food? A heap of hardwood firewood cured in the corner by the doors leading deeper inside. The air was heavy with the scents of cooking fat and roast meat and baked bread. An orc could lift crates, but these were sized for human arms. The firewood, cut to human lengths. Even the ceiling was a little too low for orcs.

The man standing by those doors looked soft. His gut was soft, his arms were soft, his face had never known pain. He stared at Uruk, at Kuru, at Kaba and Tara, mouth hanging open.

Achilles stood with his hands on a dolly loaded with crates of whiskey. In this better light, his suit wasn't as solid as Uruk's. The cloth was thinner. Uruk would have to touch it to be sure, but he felt sure the fabric was the disgusting human wool the tailor had first offered Uruk. The foolish shoes were shaped like they should fit a man, wide enough for an orc foot but with far too much toe. It looked as if someone had taken a suit for a man and made it bigger so an orc could wear it, without paying any attention to how an orc moved or sat.

Achilles snarled, baring his Lesser Tusks. "I thought I taught you better."

Kuru said in English, "He brings poison. His draught killed my brother's daughter."

Uruk, in orcish: "And you claim the name of Tai." Uruk's hands trembled with fury. "You are ours."

Achilles smiled. "Sorry, friend, I don't speak that gabble."

Playing Last Cut Loses on his hide would improve the world.

"And you!" Achilles said to Kuru. "How dare you impugn the honor of another orc?"

"You are no orc," Uruk said.

"Whatever this is," the barkeep said to Uruk, "take it outside before I call the cops."

"The police do not help speakeasies," Kuru sneered.

"You heard me," the barkeep said. "Out!"

"The booze is poisoned!" Kuru said. "And we are owed this orc's hide as payment."

The barkeep's eyes never left Uruk. "Last warning."

"You are buying bootleg whiskey," Uruk said. "The police will not help you." The same thing Kuru had said, but men refused to hear.

This time, the barkeep grimaced.

Uruk's fingers straightened in frustration. The barkeep listened to the suit. Sanford had spoken the truth.

Kuru said, "An orc would face us for the death of a child."

"I most certainly am an orc," Achilles said. "When my parents died, Celebrimble himself adopted me."

Tara coughed.

Kuru bellowed laughter. "Make your lies believable!"

Uruk's brain flew.

Was Celebrimble so twisted that he would raise an orc for his own amusement? Teach him to wear expensive clothes? To trim his talons and do whatever it was that men did to whiten their teeth? Elves lived for centuries. The life of an orc was nothing next to that. A fifty-year prank?

"Mister Baywater," Achilles said, "I assure you that the whiskey is not poisoned."

That smooth, un-orcish voice made Uruk's guts clench anew.

Baywater looked from Achilles to Uruk.

"An orc is dead," Uruk snarled. "Men have fallen ill. And this false orc is at the center of it all."

Achilles rolled his eyes. What did that mean? Uruk had seen men do the same, but never an orc. "My business is new," Achilles said, "but I use my father's contacts to procure the finest whiskey and wine this side of the Detroit River."

"I said no trouble," Baywater said to Achilles. "This looks like trouble."

"It's trouble," Kuru growled.

"All trouble," Uruk said. "Blood tonight."

Achilles reached into the uppermost crate on his dolly and pulled out a tiny fifth of Canadian Club. "Permit me to demonstrate."

Uruk gave a feral smile. He had done the same only a night ago. The difference was, Uruk's whiskey had been good. Let the false orc sicken himself.

Achilles twisted off the cap and raised the bottle to his lips.

From the double doors leading further into the speakeasy, a high-pitched voice murmured, "Stop."

 46

In the bright light of the speakeasy's back room, Uruk had the clearest view of an elf any living orc ever suffered.

Celebrimble stood just inside the double doors, looking relaxed and perfect. His suit looked even softer than Achilles'. A noose of the brightest blue Uruk had ever seen stood out against his white shirt, marked by a sparkling clear gem the size of Uruk's thumb. A diamond? It had to be a diamond. An elf would have nothing less.

If the elf had a woman, she had never held him.

An orc seized life. An elf lived above it.

"Father," Achilles said.

Uruk swung his revolver up. "You do not call that thing your *father!*"

Beside him, Kuru aimed his sawed-off shotgun square at Achilles' head.

Kaba tucked the Tommy gun into his shoulder, eyes and barrel alike fixed on Celebrimble.

Achilles stepped to the side so he could see both Uruk and the elf. "Why should I not? My parents died when I was barely born. Other orcs left me to die."

As they should. A clan that could not keep itself alive should not have children. An orphan endured, or it did not.

"Celebrimble took me in," Achilles snarled. "He had me fed. Sent me to school. And now he's given me the backing to build my own business."

Uruk thumbed the hammer back, keeping the barrel trained on Achilles.

Achilles didn't flinch. He was at least that much of an orc.

Uruk said, "Elves crush orcs. They do not—*raise* them."

"And yet," Achilles said, "he legally adopted me. I have a sister and two brothers."

"Yet you claim the clan Tai!" Uruk said.

Uruk glimpsed motion behind Celebrimble. Earwin, peering out from behind her father.

His stomach clenched in fury. He had been so un-orcish as to let an elf live, and she returned to attack him?

His hand tightened on the trigger.

The revolver hammer fell.

The stink of sickly-sweet flowers flooded Uruk's nose and the air itself turned heavy. Elvish magic pinned Uruk's breath in his mouth, air like tar sticking to his tongue and cheeks and teeth. His eyes bulged. He tried to step forward, but thick air pinned him in place.

The revolver hammer sagged against the cartridge with a nearly silent *clink*.

Uruk tried to snarl, but the air in his lungs refused to move.

"I apologize for this disturbance." Celebrimble's eyes never left the barkeep.

"I am managing this situation," Achilles said. No orc could sound that calm.

Uruk squeezed his chest, hard as he could. A thin line of air trickled out of him. His heart thundered in his ears.

Neither Kuru nor Kaba moved.

Straining as hard as he could, Uruk couldn't pull more air in. The edges of his vision began to soften. Fiery sweat burned on his back.

"You are special, my—*son*." Eyes never left the barkeep. "You are the greatest of orcs."

Uruk would not die like this. He would not.

The tarry feeling eased. Uruk sucked in a whooping breath, hearing the other orcs do the same.

"I got to you young enough," Celebrimble said. "Other orcs? They must be broken before they can be remade."

Remade? Uruk fought to yank the revolver towards Celebrimble, the thickened air making every inch its own war.

Unable to move, but able to breathe?

Celebrimble wanted him alive.

Did he think to make Uruk into something like Achilles?

Baywater said, "Listen up, all of you. I want this circus out of my place. Right now. I asked for a no-drama delivery, and this is anything but."

Kuru wheezed, "They would poison you."

Achilles glanced at Kuru, then raised his bottle. "I assure you, this whiskey is top quality."

Uruk focused everything in dragging the revolver through the air. Gritting teeth or baring tusks would have wasted his strength. Maybe the thick air wouldn't let him fire, but he needed to be ready to seize any chance.

Celebrimble said, "Earwin. The barkeep."

Earwin somehow grew even more pale, but raised a hand. Her face twisted in concentration.

Baywater's eyes unfocused. He wobbled on his feet, barely staying upright as his mouth fell open.

"Better, child," Celebrimble said. "You improve."

Earwin's concentration didn't flicker from Baywater, but she murmured, "Thank you, Father."

Trapped.

Two elven wizards.

The human witness, befuddled.

Mingled rage and terror made Uruk want to scream, but his lungs couldn't breathe that hard.

Orcs always lost. When they fought elves, they lost hard.

Broken. Remade.

When Uruk got that chance, should he shoot the elf or himself?

47

If Mha's drill instructor had seen these feeble youngsters, she would have spent two hours excoriating their clans, their blood, their marrow, and their brains before wetting her throat and bellowing at them for another hour about their privates.

On her stomach beneath the truck, peering out from behind the tires, she could see everything important in the storage room. Faces meant nothing. Feet and hips and the bottom of the spine told you everything. If you saw those, you knew the fighter's stance. The stance said what limbs would strike fast and which would hit hard.

The young Tai orcs had outrage, but no ability to fight for it. They faced the elf straight-on, giving him their whole bodies as targets. With their weight flat on their feet, how did they expect to move?

The only orc who stood properly, who had any idea how to use his body as a weapon, was the abomination.

She could *smell* the elves, all arrogance and filthy flowers. One real wizard, powerful enough to summon the Swamp Air even in December. If he had skill he would have summoned Lightning Kudzu or the Vile Bowel, so he had strength but no precision. Nothing was more easily bewildered than a human man but the second wizard, the elf child, struggled to befuddle the barkeep. She was generations from learning real power.

The smallest orc, the one in the back, in the janitor's coveralls? He had cracked open a scabbed knuckle. Good. He had rubbed the blood on his thumb. Also good. He thrust the thumb against the Swamp Air, good. Then he feebly wheezed out the most useless shaman's phrases Mha had ever heard, things he had heard and remembered but not understood. It would be easier to fly yourself to Cuba on a pillar of your own farts than sacrifice to August in the Greatest Dark.

How were these children still alive?

But the orc with the little revolver had declared he spoke for the Tai. Young and stupid like all of them, yes—but every young orc was an idiot. They thought laboring for barely enough money to feed their family taught them about hardship, and loss, and the raw futility of an orc's life. It wasn't until your own body failed, when everyone who you had ever known had fallen, when your children wouldn't eat you and you couldn't even persuade a sheriff to shoot you, that an orc could begin to understand what it meant to endure.

Stupid. But orcish stupidity.

If her Vara belonged to such as him, she could accept it.

When his own children were gone, he would learn the rest.

He even looked a little familiar—although after all these lonely years, her age-sick brain would recognize anyone with tusks as a long dead brother.

And if she had to choose between an abomination who claimed an elf as his father, or a handful of idiots?

She'd pick the idiots, every time.

Mha drew the scythe up beside her and dragged her wrist across the freshly honed edge. Thumb blood got attention, but wrist blood was better. Blood from an open wrist meant *commitment*. Especially blood enough to smear across the length of the blade.

As long as her wrist bled, the scythe would slice through magic. Most magic.

You could see the edge of Swamp Air, if you knew how to look. Shiny, secretive elven magic offended the world. In Cuba, sand had itched itself away from the edge. In December's Detroit, a single stray flake of snow that had drifted in around the truck hung suspended in air inches from the back of the truck, unable to melt or move or merge with its kin.

The elf offended December.

"All that I am," she whispered, inching the scythe blade towards the edge. "All of every war, mine and my mothers' and my mothers' mothers. Let us fight as orcs should."

There.

With all her strength, she thrust the scythe into the Swamp Air and screamed. "My war! *My* war!"

 48

Air gushed into Uruk's lungs.

He didn't stop to breathe, or to wonder at the creaking scream from behind, but slapped one hand against the revolver's hammer even as he swung the weapon towards Celebrimble and squeezed the trigger.

Kuru shrieked. His four-gauge sawed-off blasted a split second later, drowning the echo of Uruk's shot.

Tara had thrown himself to the side—fleeing? No, he had the stolen knife out and was bringing himself in line with Achilles. The false orc (adopted? No, impossible, elvish trickery, had to be) was going to kick Uruk's little brother in half, but Tara held the knife point-down with confidence so Uruk focused on Celebrimble.

Baywater shrieked and threw himself back against the wall.

Tiny glowing dots hung in the air in front of Celebrimble. The elf had his head cocked to the side and his eyebrows raised. One of the dots was bigger than the others—Uruk's bullet. The others were shotgun balls.

Behind Celebrimble, Earwin lay on the floor. Uruk glimpsed blood.

Had Celebrimble stopped bullets meant for him, but let his own daughter be struck? Even a *human* would step in front of a bullet meant for their child!

The thing behind Uruk shrieked again, but he didn't dare look away.

Kuru-Norkosh shoved another round into his shotgun. "He can't stop all the bullets!"

Something shambled past Uruk, making him jump in surprise.

He had never seen an orc that old. Orcess? She wore a long tunic, had to be an orcess. His own father had a few strands of hair, but this ancient had a whole head of tough strands tied back with a leather band. The tunic was scarred and scratched leather with a pale blue symbol stained in the back, an orcish skull surrounded by human letters.

No, not stained.

Tattooed.

Grandpa had spoken of the days after his mother had died, how his father had smoked her meat and used her bones for tools and even saved her hide as a blanket to warm the children at night.

This orcess *wore* her mate.

She lurched like one leg was four inches shorter than the other. A blade as long as Uruk's arm flashed in front of her, on the end of a brownish-white handle of orcish thighbones. Nobody practiced bone-melding today, not when you could get wood or metal for pennies, but this ancient orc had melded two thighbones end-to-end and fixed a scythe blade to the end.

She had not yet struck, but bright red blood coated the blade.

On a rope tied around her hips four orc skulls shifted and clattered, their polish gleaming in the harsh light.

A war-orc straight out of Grandpa's old stories, risen from the dead to face an elf?

No time to think, or to wonder, or even to admire.

Uruk shouted his own cry and cocked the revolver again.

49

The children were wise enough to let Mha pass to the front.

Or not foolish enough to get in her way.

The day had left her feeling like she was no longer an orc. Now, she was orc incarnate. *That* orc's thighbones hugged her hands, releasing her when she twirled the blade and guiding itself back to her grip. Her life's blood trickled from her wrist, feeding the blood on the blade edge as she scythed through the elf's Bullet Wall and crashed down to split his skull, his spine, and his asshole in one blow.

The filthy little elf stepped to the side.

Mha hissed and swept the blade to the side, hoping to catch his leg, but he spoke a word that hurt Mha's ears.

For a heartbeat, her skull felt too tight.

The storeroom churned around her.

The floor was no longer brick, but dirt buried in a foot of filthy fresh ash. The greasy air stank of burned wood and scorched flesh, so heavy she could taste it. The clouds were low and black and putrid with smoke. The ache that ruled her hip spread throughout her body, every joint creaking and groaning, her ribs shuddering against each other, the mortar holding her together crumbling.

Mortar?

Her body was brick, and mortar, and ash, standing defiant in a scorched landscape.

She was a ruined chimney in burned-out Detroit a century ago. A chimney with a scythe of bone, facing an elf.

The brick charm had given her its strength.

The elf's magic surged, and a brick toppled off the top of her stack.

"Foul beast!" the elf shrieked.

If she squinted, she could see the elf. Almost as tall as her, strong and angry, his perfect face an insult to every orc that had ever lost anything—let alone an orcess who had lost everything.

More bricks fell.

The elf gritted his teeth.

Mha bared her tusks. "I know wizards," she hissed, swinging the scythe.

The elf leaped back, almost gracelessly.

Mha thrust the scythe. "A wizard who lives through their first five wars is dangerous."

The elf spat something.

More bricks fell. The chimney was crumbling. The weight of the elf's spell bore down on her shoulders. It would crush her. Soon.

But fear was for orcs who would live.

And in her grip, *that* orc's bones hugging her hands to the end.

Mha said, "How many wars have you fought, little wizard?"

"Disease!" the elf screamed. "Mistake!"

The weight on her grew. That crunching feeling in her spine—was that brick or bone?

"Not enough," Mha grinned. "Not nearly enough."

 50

The war-orc's bone-handled scythe swirled everywhere. If Uruk fired his revolver, the blade would split his bullet before it hit the elf.

The storeroom was too small for this fight. Achilles faced Tara, but his smile was gone. Blood ran down his legs. How had little Tara managed to stab the false orc in both legs, multiple times? No, no time for that. Earwin lay sprawled on the ground behind Celebrimble. Gunsmoke and blood and spilled whiskey filled the air.

Kaba fired the enchanted Tommy gun.

A hole appeared in Celebrimble's fancy coat, but the elf did not even stagger.

Uruk cursed. The Tommy gun's magic was gone, or Celebrimble had made himself immune to it. Kaba had stolen the weapon from the elves. The elves knew how it worked.

The war-orc's blade filled the air, but no matter where she swung, somehow Celebrimble danced out of her path. A thick haze surrounded his upraised hands, flowing from him towards her face. Whatever magic it was, it drained the healthy purple from her skin.

She would be dead soon.

Kuru waved the shotgun barrel as if trying to find a clear path. If Uruk couldn't get a .75 slug through the fight, the sawed-off shotgun wouldn't hit anyone but the war-orc.

Kaba shifted his feet as if thinking of charging forward, raised the Tommy gun, and shook himself. "Die!"

Tara shouted in pain. Was he hurt? No, no time!

Screams would not work. The elf's shoes moved so fast as he danced around the blade, he almost shimmered—

"Kaba!" Uruk said in orcish. "The Tommy gun!"

"It doesn't work on him!" Kaba spat.

"Give it to me!" Uruk said, reaching out.

Kuru said, "We blast him together!"

"Not the elf!" Uruk said.

"Who would you fight?" Kuru shrieked.

"His shoes," Uruk said.

Kuru blinked.

Uruk wrenched the Tommy gun to his shoulder and aimed low. "Unbalance him. Bad ground, he will trip. Give her a chance to plant that blade."

Kuru grinned and hoisted the shotgun.

No way to track the elf's footsteps. He moved too fast. Uruk picked a spot on the floor right by his feet and waited.

A fancy shoe flashed into the sights.

Uruk pulled the trigger. Too late—Celebrimble had already moved away.

A heartbeat later, Kuru fired.

Two bricks shattered into dust, but the elf still wasn't there.

"Both of us," Uruk said, still in orcish. "Right in front of the bricks you destroyed. When he steps there, fill the space with lead. Ruin his footing."

Kuru hurriedly shoved another round into the four-gauge.

The Tommy gun was almost too small to fit against Uruk's shoulder, but he squeezed his arms in so he could hold the trigger and peer down the sight at the brick.

The war-orc was too pale. Celebrimble's magic would crush her in a breath. Uruk itched to fire, even if it couldn't work, and suddenly understood why Azok-Snaka worked so hard to teach orcs patience. "Hold..."

Celebrimble's foot flashed through his sights.

Uruk squeezed the trigger.

Simultaneous shots shattered the air.

Celebrimble staggered.

The scythe sliced air.

Celebrimble screamed in violated horror.

A heartbeat later the elf struck the ground, the scythe blade rammed through his bowels and into the floor.

51

Uruk heard nothing but his own heaving breath and a man screaming in fear.

Gunsmoke swallowed every other smell, clouding the air and softening the light.

Uruk and the other Tai and Kuru and the false orc alike froze to stare at the most powerful elf in Detroit nailed to the floor like a troublesome boar. Celebrimble clutched the brick with his fingers as if he hoped to dig in the mortar and pull himself away, but the scythe in his gut had to be sunk four inches into the floor and he didn't even twitch his torso. Blood welling from the wound soaked the silk suit.

The war-orc's face flooded with color as Celebrimble's magic faded, but she braced herself on her scythe's bone handle and panted like she had worked three days straight. Her flesh remembered more about war than Uruk had ever known, but was too frail to carry it for long. Her skulls shifted and settled around her waist. Not one, not two, but three failed suitors? She must have been a fierce beauty once, and even fiercer than she was beautiful.

Behind Celebrimble, Earwin stirred and lay still.

Achilles stood with his jaw hanging open like a man, staring at Celebrimble. Blood ran from a dozen cuts all down his shins and calves. Tara must have stabbed him every time he threw one of those crippling kicks.

Tara stepped back, panting. Sweat coursed down his face, but he looked uninjured. Orc blood marked his blade and smug triumph his face.

Kuru fumbled another shell into the sawed-off.

Achilles blinked.

Instinct made Uruk pivot, bringing the Tommy gun to bear on Achilles just as the pistol left the false orc's pocket. "Hold!"

Achilles froze.

"Drop the gun or die," Uruk shouted.

Achilles studied Uruk.

Uruk dared hope he would raise the gun.

Achilles snarled and let the gun fall.

Uruk held. Had they won?

They had.

"Man," Kuru shouted in English, leveling the shotgun. "Stop screaming, or I will shoot your head off just for the quiet."

The man huddled up against the wall wrenched his head up to face Kuru. His face was so pale, he might have had the veins of his legs slashed and been hung up to drain. He drew a shuddering breath and closed his mouth.

"Stay still and silent," Kuru said at the man. "There is blood tonight, but none need be yours."

The man nodded pathetically and tried to shrivel into an even smaller lump.

Uruk nodded at Kuru.

The orcess sucked air, but couldn't seem to get enough into her chest. Had she burst her heart in this fight? Where was her clan? If she fell over dead, Uruk could do no less than let her blood know of this victory. He would bring his whole clan to honor her.

Don't bury her yet. "Kuru," he said in orcish. "Put your gun on the false orc."

"The Tai do not lead." Before Uruk could argue, Kuru swung the sawed-off four-gauge to point at Achilles' heart. "But I *take* this pleasure."

"Remember," Uruk said in orcish. "Last cut loses."

"The Norkosh would prefer that," Kuru said. "Unless this poisoner insists otherwise."

Keeping a close eye on Celebrimble, Uruk stepped up beside the orcess. "War-orc. Alone, we were lost. Together, we won."

The orcess eyed Uruk. "You think war is guns and brass knuckles and tusks. War is in an orc's blood, but you have never learned the most orcish art."

Uruk wanted to bristle, but—she wasn't wrong. He had brawled, he had fought, he had gone on raids to claim his woman and Daka's and Tara's, but this orcess had gone far beyond that. "We honor you."

She dipped her chin, but her eyes never left Celebrimble.

"I would speak to this elf," Uruk said.

Her eyes didn't leave Celebrimble, but her Greater Tusks flashed out. "*My* elf. Mine! He will be *days* dying."

Panting, leaning on the scythe handle for strength, the orcess did not look strong enough to crush a kitten, but Uruk felt certain she could break his throat without taking her eyes from the elf. "Your elf. I would only speak."

"He will not talk to you."

"I do not want him to speak. Only to hear." Uruk bared his Lesser Tusks in a grin. "He *must* listen now. Unless he can will himself into death to keep my words from his ears."

She barked a laugh. "Speak, then. For tripping him, speak."

Uruk nodded and made his way up to kneel by Celebrimble's head.

The elf looked away, as if the sight of Uruk's face would irrevocably soil his eyeballs.

Uruk spoke softly, in English. "It is in the interest of the cor-por-ation that you are dead."

A split second of surprise flashed across Celebrimble's face. Uruk grinned. "This evening, I ordered your child left alive."

Celebrimble said nothing. Uruk had not expected him to speak.

"I would end this marrow feud," Uruk said. "All you must do is leave orcs alone. We stay out of your towers and gardens. We stay in our caverns and docks and slaughterhouses."

Celebrimble kept his gaze away from Uruk, unfocused.

"You do not even need to speak," Uruk said. "You can nod. I know you can nod. I have seen you."

Celebrimble remained still.

"Filth!" Uruk screamed, rage boiling over like a cask of rotten meat exploding. "I give your child life, and you will not even return it?" He shoved his face into Celebrimble's, nose inches from the elf's. "Look at me you arrogant twig! *Look at me!*"

Celebrimble closed his eyes.

"My elf!" the war-orc snarled.

Uruk hissed. "*Your* elf." He spat on Celebrimble's cheek.

The spittle sizzled on the elf's skin. Celebrimble flinched. Was it hurting him? Could you kill an elf by having the whole clan spit at him, for days? What about piss? An orc could piss a hundred times more than they could spit. Would the war-orc let him test that? No, that couldn't work, the stories would have said.

Celebrimble's mouth twisted, like his tongue tasted bad. "Orcs are nothing." His words were just above a whisper. "I do not step on ants, because ants have purpose."

"But you would adopt an orc," Uruk sneered. He pointed blindly towards Achilles. "Would you make us all like that *thing*?"

"Achilles is the greatest of orcs," Celebrimble breathed.

Uruk flung himself back upright to keep himself from ripping the elf's face off with his tusks, wrenching his gaze away to give his blood a chance to cool. You could nail an elf to the floor with a three-foot scythe blade and he still wouldn't admit he was beaten. He caught himself glaring at the false orc instead.

Achilles stared at him and Celebrimble. Uruk had seen the false orc cheerful, and cocky, and even peeved. But his naked rage was as orcish as anything Uruk had seen.

Was the shiny, polished orc truly adopted?

A simple way to find out. Or to learn more.

"Achilles," Uruk sneered. "He calls you the greatest of orcs. What do you say to that?"

52

The rage drained from Achilles' face, leaving him un-orcishly blank.

Uruk's heart still thudded. His blood seethed from Celebrimble refusing to meet his gaze. The only thing that might soothe him would be shooting Celebrimble in the face, Achilles in the gut, or Earwin anywhere. Instead, he kept his gaze on Achilles' eyes.

"What is this?" Kuru said in orcish.

"Keep guard," Uruk said.

"Whatever you have in mind," Kuru said, "he is ours."

"I do not take him." In English, to Achilles, Uruk said, "Well? You claim to be an orc. You claim that this elf *adopted* you. You claim no knowledge of poisoned booze. Yet this arrogant fart says orcs are nothing."

"I will go to him," Achilles said. No orc could have a voice that flat.

"I can kill you any time," Kuru said.

Achilles turned expressionless eyes on him. "You can. I'm still going to his side."

"Hold your fire," Uruk said in orcish. "I would—*we*, let *us* hear what he says."

Kuru bared his Greater Tusks, but held his fire when Achilles took a step. Two more steps, and he knelt at Celebrimble's side opposite Uruk. Up close and unmoving, Achilles looked even more bizarre. His skin was a deeper purple-green than any orc Uruk had ever seen. He might have guessed it was paint, but it showed in the pores of his face and the lines in his hands. His talons, filed not only short and dull but also thin, shone like they had been lacquered. He smelled of orcish sweat, but over that a spicy perfume that reminded Uruk of fresh-cut wood. Could even elvish magic create something so detailed?

Achilles looked at Celebrimble's face.

Celebrimble looked at the ceiling. His face was pale, his lips almost colorless.

"You found me abandoned on the street, too young to walk." Achilles' voice was just above a whisper, but an orc's whisper was still loud enough to carry through the storeroom. "You took me in. Hired men to teach me to read and write and do math. I thank you for those things."

Celebrimble gave a tiny nod.

"And in all those years," Achilles said, "you never once looked at me."

Even with his weakness, Celebrimble still sounded like his words tasted bad. "Orcs and elves were once one. I would bring you back."

Uruk leaned back. *Orcs and elves were once one?* What did that mean? How could an orc and an elf be friends, or even allies? Not even a human claimed such nonsense.

"You brought me as close as you could," Achilles said. "But it was never enough, was it?"

"Maybe your children." Was the elf's voice growing stronger, despite the slash through his gut? "Or your children's children."

"Where were these children to come from?" Achilles said.

"We would find." Celebrimble's voice *was* louder.

"And my home," Achilles said. "You bought me a home. A home built and furnished for orcs."

"So you could be comfortable." Celebrimble's face was quickly gaining color. Uruk glanced up. "War-orc."

The ancient orcess bared her Greater Tusks and twisted the scythe. Celebrimble didn't even flinch.

"And last month, you told me my clan name was Tai," Achilles said.

"You should know that." Celebrimble's face twisted. "My *son*."

Achilles leaned closer, resting a hand on Celebrimble's chest.

Celebrimble flinched at the touch. How could you raise an orc without touching him, without looking at him? Every word Celebrimble had said to Achilles sounded like the elf would rather vomit than speak. Had the elf permanently scrambled Achilles' mind, making him believe these lies?

"I see you," Kuru snarled at Achilles' movement, shifting his grip on the shotgun.

Achilles ignored him. "And the poison?"

"Men break their own laws," Celebrimble said. "Men only learn by pain."

Achilles' lips twisted into a snarl or a smile, flattening again before Uruk could decide. "You call me the greatest of orcs."

The orcess jerked her scythe sideways as if to slice Celebrimble in half through his balls, hard enough that Uruk's guts tightened in unwilling sympathy.

Celebrimble didn't even notice.

Achilles swept his hand towards Celebrimble's neck and yanked.

A small silvery shape swung in Achilles' hand, dangling from a gleaming chain.

"You mean I am the greatest of nothing!" Achilles roared.

Celebrimble's face bled all color.

Uruk lunged.

Achilles already had his other hand at Celebrimble's neck, flexing it far back. A double-edged knife, vicious-looking enough to be a dagger, catapulted out of Achilles' sleeve, punching straight into Celebrimble's throat.

The orcess shrieked. "*My* elf!"

For a split second, disbelief crossed the elf's face. Blood geysered out around the buried blade.

Uruk hit Achilles, knocking him backwards.

"Out of my way!" Kuru bellowed. "He is mine!"

Achilles rolled with Uruk, collapsing onto his back, arms falling to either side.

Uruk snatched Achilles' wrists, pulling his own knees up to either side of the false orc's ribs, crushing the false orc with all his weight.

Achilles lay limp, watching Uruk.

The orcess screamed. "Mine! He was mine!" Her scythe flashed at the edge of Uruk's vision.

Achilles still didn't move.

"I asked what you would say to him!" Uruk snarled.

"What would I say?" Achilles shouted. "I would say that I have blood on my hands. He used me to poison people!"

Kuru thrust the four-gauge up against Achilles' head. "You do not claim innocence? Ignorance?"

"What does that matter?" Achilles' voice went cold. "He tricked me into killing people. I killed him for that. But he admitted it, the whiskey I got through him was poisoned. Any deaths are mine." He met Uruk's eyes. "My fa—" His mouth twisted. "*Celebrimble's* charm. It pins life to flesh. Blocks pain. Take it from my hand before you kill me."

Achilles' words whirled through Uruk's head. He licked his lips, suddenly very tired. "You are an orc."

"Of course I'm an orc!" Achilles said.

Kuru said, "You *are* an orc."

"What else would I be?" Achilles said.

Tara said, "An elvish lie."

"My parents are dead." Achilles scowled. "*He* never would tell me how, or when, or why."

From behind Uruk the orcess said, "He stole a life due me."

"I did," Achilles said. "He raised me to use me, and would never meet my eyes. He did more wrong to me than to anyone else here. And now—" His gaze bounced from Uruk to Kuru, then settled straight in the shotgun barrel. "I pay for it."

"*Your* debt," the orcess said.

Uruk was holding Achilles' wrists so hard that the other orc's hands were growing pale. What would it be like, to be raised by an elf? To have no one to teach you to be an orc? And still, somehow, Achilles understood that ignorance was not innocence.

"Our child is dead!" Kuru shrieked in orcish.

Achilles didn't take his eyes from the shotgun. "Shoot."

In orcish, Uruk said, "He owns his wrong. He fights to own it."

Kuru shrieked wordless rage at the ceiling.

"Do it!" Achilles shouted.

Tara knelt on the other side of Achilles' head. "You have declared that you own your wrong. He cannot kill you."

Achilles' face twisted in anger. "I poisoned people!"

"And you own it," Tara said.

"How many are dead?" Achilles said.

"My brother's daughter," Kuru shouted.

Achilles shut his eyes. "I cannot right that."

"You cannot," the orcess said. "But you can *ktrutcv*." She paused. "Pay what cannot be paid."

Tara said, "There are human words. *Contrition. Redemption.*"

"How!" Achilles' eyes snapped open. "How can you pay for the life of a child?"

"For your whole lifetime," the orcess said.

Achilles glared over Uruk's shoulder, so angry that all his tusks showed. She must be standing right behind Uruk.

Then he sagged. "Death would be easy. Wouldn't it."

Kuru screamed, wrenching the shotgun aside.

"Celebrimble is dead," Uruk said in orcish. "Name your price."

"His life and the life of every elf in Detroit would not be enough," Kuru shrieked.

He whirled to point at Achilles.

"You! Killer of children! Stay there. We have one more elf to kill."

 53

Uruk had forgotten Earwin.

She lay beyond the double doors, in the middle of a human barroom. The walls were rich dark wood, varnished and polished until they screamed of wealth. The bar was gut-high for a man, with low leather-topped stools. Woven rugs in beige and blue marked ovals on the polished hardwood floor. Mirror-backed shelves behind the bar made the space seem twice as large and doubled the number of battered, bruised orcs stuffed into the space. The smell of woodsmoke competed with the gunsmoke, all over the human stinks of cooked vegetables and sauce-tainted meat.

Just as Celebrimble had recovered some strength, so had she.

But Kaba knelt across her, his hand around her neck.

"Well done," Uruk said. His back ached, his eyes ached, even his skull ached. Grandpa claimed that an orc could stay awake for days on end during war, but America had made Uruk soft. Denied sleep, he had let matters escape his attention.

Kaba smiled and said in English, "We are old enemies, this one and I. She knows my law."

Earwin had her eyes closed. Her breath came hard and fast. How long could an elf sustain terror?

"Good," Kuru said. "I claim her life for the Norkosh."

"Wait," Uruk said.

"What?" Kuru said. "You think an elf will own their wrongs?"

"No," Uruk said. "Elves killed another clan of Tai. We avenged them, and killed one of their wizards." The words tasted bitter. "It is as Azok-Snaka said. That night led to this night."

Kuru bared his tusks in a nasty smile. "You brought this on us."

"And!" Uruk said. "The elves would have warred with us anyway. Whatever clan brought draught, the elves would have declared war on. Orcs without draught are not orcs."

Kuru hissed, "When the elves are all dead, we will have all the draught we need."

"Not all the elves are here tonight!" Uruk said. "And why did we win? An ancient war-orc fought for us! How many war-orcs are in your clan?"

Kuru glanced at the orcess, then glared at Uruk. "They declared war on our cavern!"

Uruk switched to English. "The elves have marrow feud with the Tai. An orc who claimed Tai killed Celebrimble. If a Norkosh kills this elf, then the other elves will declare marrow feud with the Norkosh." He tightened his voice. "Would you join the Tai in this war? Or would you demand a blood price?"

Kuru glared at Uruk. "That *suit*. You have spent too much time with that *man*."

Uruk bared his Lesser Tusks. "When this ends, you and I will settle that in the pit. But now, think of your clan."

"She will not pay a blood price," Kuru said.

"Let us see." Uruk tromped over to look down at Earwin's face. "You have a choice, elf. You can—" what was the word? "*Ne-go-ti-ate*. Or you can die."

Earwin squeezed her eyes more tightly and shuddered.

"She will not pay," Kuru sneered. "And we could not trust her if she agrees."

"Orc," Earwin said.

This elf spoke to him? Astonishment froze Uruk's breath.

The stink of a million different flowers flooded his nose.

"My father's power is now mine." Earwin's voice echoed and buzzed. "Release me or die."

 54

Uruk's instincts sent him stumbling back two steps, fear chomping at his bowels. Had they helped kill Detroit's most powerful, arrogant elf only for his wizarding powers to pass to his daughter?

Pinned beneath Kaba, Earwin shuddered. Her fingers shook and pattered on the barroom carpet.

Kuru snarled and thrust the four-gauge shotgun straight at her forehead.

Uruk gagged on the stink of mint.

Kuru pulled the trigger.

The shotgun erupted in a roaring blaze of light, all along its length. Kuru shrieked in pain, staggering back, waving his hands like they were on fire. Earwin let out an agonized shriek. Kaba bellowed.

A dozen white-hot pinpricks spattered across Uruk's face. He swiped at his forehead, his right cheek, finding tiny spots of heat falling free.

Had the shotgun exploded? No, the elf and two orcs wouldn't have faces to scream with.

What was left of the shotgun lay on the floor, smoking. A line had melted along the full length of the barrel and ruptured the bullet. The wreckage had already scorched a ring in the polished wood, and spatters of molten steel lay all around it.

Kaba bellowed again. His hands must have caught part of the metal, but he still had his hands around Earwin's neck and was leaning forward to crush her.

A bizarre smell—something spicy, but—rotting?—erupted.

Kaba toppled sideways, his hands going to his own neck.

Earwin sat up. The top half of her face was burned red and black, with spots of molten steel gleaming among the ruin. Uruk couldn't tell if it had missed her eyes or if the lids had been scorched off. Pain distended her mouth, but she got one hand on the ground to steady herself and raised the other.

Earwin had Celebrimble's power, and the rage of seeing her father's death.

Uruk's revolver would do no better than the shotgun. He rolled his hands into fists, bracing his left around the brass knuckles. They might melt, but they wouldn't explode.

The ancient orcess stomped forward, scythe raised.

Earwin raised a hand at the orcess. "For my father!"

The scythe came down.

Earwin flung herself aside a half-second before the scythe struck, rolling away from Kaba towards Uruk.

No time to bend and punch. Uruk took half a step to drop his knee square on Earwin's face. He was right above her. He couldn't miss.

His falling knee slid sideways in a haze of rose scent, cracking against the floor right above her head. Uruk gasped at the spikes of pain shooting straight up into his gut, but he brought the brass knuckles down to smash square into Earwin's nose.

His hand stopped an inch from her snarling face.

The orcess was swinging the scythe again. This time, the blade slid sideways, veering towards Uruk's sprawled leg.

Uruk threw himself sideways a blink before the scythe bit floor where his foot had been.

The orcess hissed.

Kaba's hands flew away from his throat. He gulped great wheezing breaths of air. She had made him choke himself! Why had she stopped?

The orcess flew backwards like she'd been struck by a car, hitting the double doors to the storeroom to tumble down and through. Why hadn't she done that when the orcess had first struck, though?

The orcess' words. *If a wizard lives through their first five wars, they are dangerous.*

You could have all the world's magic, but not know how to fight.

Or a tiny scrap of power—and not the practice to steadily light a room! The way Uruk had strength, but the war-orc had *skill*.

Uruk bellowed, "She cannot control it yet!" and threw himself at Earwin. His empty hand struck her nose, his brass knuckles her breastbone.

Unfamiliar sweet scents flared, and Uruk was knocked back onto the floor. Scrabble, get up, kick and punch and bite until she died, rip around her neck to find if she had a healing charm like her father and tear it away from her and rip her heart out of her chest and kill her, take the marrow feud to Grosse Pointe and burn down the elven mansions, stack their severed heads in pyres that would light the clouds—

His legs wouldn't move. Or his arms. Even his neck. He could see Earwin from the corner of his eye, close enough to reach out and claw her eyes, and he couldn't move. It wasn't like the thick air Celebrimble had used. His body was ignoring his commands.

The vile stink of cinnamon filled his shallow choking breaths.

The room was still.

Earwin lay facing Uruk, but had her eyes turned deliberately away. She shuddered. "I can. Control. Enough. For *you*."

Uruk couldn't even spit. *Kaba! Tara, in the storeroom! Kuru, orcess, even Achilles! Someone, strike her!*

If he could reach out one hand. Grab her face. In the warehouse, he had broken her concentration and disrupted her magic.

Strain twisted Earwin's face, but the magic held.

Stalemate.

Until Earwin found enough control to stop Uruk's breath the way she did his fists.

"Oh dear," someone said. "This looks bad."

55

Sanford stood just inside the double doors to the storeroom, bundled up in his huge coat and round furry hat. His face looked more pale than usual. Uruk had neither time nor thought to hide Celebrimble's mangled remains.

If Daka or even one of the Norkosh had recovered enough to join the war—but Sanford? The paper man was useless in a fight. He could witness and die, or he could flee.

"Peter Sanford." Earwin's entire body trembled with effort of speaking.

Sanford's eyes went to Uruk. "Are you all right?"

Uruk pushed his lungs, but only a groan came.

"Your pets killed my father," Earwin said.

Pets? Everything in Uruk strained to throw himself at the elf.

"Orcs are people," Sanford said.

Uruk's arm lurched six inches towards Earwin, fingers extended. Triumph flared in his blood, but before he could strike it went limp again.

"Peter." Earwin drew a shuddering breath. "Mister Sanford. I offer partnership."

What had Uruk done—no, it had been Sanford's ridiculous statement that orcs were people. It had distracted Earwin. Would the paper man even realize that? Trapping the orcs had exhausted her, or maybe the magic didn't work on humans, or perhaps she couldn't change the magic to add another person, but Sanford was free. If he broke Earwin's concentration, Uruk could strike.

"Partnership?" Sanford said. "Indeed. Tell me more."

Sanford will betray you. Kuru's words.

Uruk wanted to howl.

Despite all Sanford's words, he had always known that a man would never truly partner with an orc.

"What do you..." Earwin gulped air. "Desire? Aid me. Name your reward."

"And what aid is it that you want?"

Uruk had saved Sanford's woman, and he talked with this elf? Rage at the man's betrayal made him want to scream.

"My father's ring," Earwin said. "Take it from his finger. Put it on my hand."

Whatever that ring was, it would doom the Tai.

Uruk had failed everyone.

"Your father? I take it that's the deceased elf in the next room?"

Earwin nodded. The burns on her face were fading from red towards pink. She must own a healing charm like Celebrimble's.

"You want me to rob the dead?"

"Inheritance," Earwin wheezed.

The paper man hated violence. Even glimpsing the blood trail left by the dead had unsettled him. He would not have the marrow to take a ring from a dead elf.

"Just a moment," Sanford said.

To Uruk's astonishment, the man strode through the double doors.

Could that smooth soft elven voice make Sanford betray not just Uruk, but his own nature? He strained harder, trying to roll towards Earwin.

Not one muscle twitched, but Earwin gasped. The awful cinnamon smell grew fiercer, violating his every breath.

Sanford returned. Whatever he held was just out of Uruk's vision. "This?"

Uruk's body obeyed him for another split second, letting him roll from his back to his side, arms outstretched. He heard Kuru snarl at the exact same time, and caught a glimpse of Kaba raising an arm.

Earwin's back arched, and Uruk went limp mere inches from her. His head was turned towards her, though. He had a better view of Sanford's betrayal. The man didn't even have the courage to look at Uruk, instead holding a tiny circle of glittering diamond aloft between his thumb and forefinger.

"Yes," Earwin said. "Give it—to me."

Sanford scanned the room. "Just a moment."

Betrayal. Uruk ached to shriek, to rend Earwin and Sanford alike, but his muscles sagged.

Sanford shrugged out of his coat, laying it on the bar. "Excuse me." He put a foot between Uruk's sprawled arms, and Uruk couldn't even claw his ankles! Watching his footing, he picked a path through to stand by Earwin's head.

Earwin shivered. Greed?

"I am curious, madam elf." Sanford's voice got softer. "Who cursed my wife?"

Doubt shivered through Uruk's rage. Sanford *knew* that.

Earwin's lips tightened. "Explain after." She shuddered. "Ring now."

"Uruk said you are a wizard," Sanford said. "How many elven wizards remain in Detroit? Rumor says only two, now." He glanced at the double doors. "One, that is."

Earwin's fingers clawed the floor. "The ring!"

"I can't see the chief elf of Detroit cursing my wife." How could the man speak so lightly of an attack that had nearly killed his woman? "I think he sent you."

Understanding flared through Uruk.

Sanford drew a foot back and kicked Earwin in the head.

Uruk's body woke.

He threw himself onto the elf, even as from her other side Kaba's big feet kicked her ribs and Kuru rolled in.

Kaba's hands around her throat had not been enough to stop her, especially with that healing charm.

Uruk used his tusks instead.

Elf blood was the richest flavor Uruk had ever tasted.

 **56**

Despite Uruk's best bite, Earwin lived.

Achilles hadn't called it a healing charm. He had had said it *pins life to flesh*.

Uruk could take the charm and rip her throat out again.

Or he could let her keep the charm. Watch the flesh reform, then rip her throat out again. Let Kaba and Tara have a try. No, the Norkosh were allies. Kuru should go next. Each clan could take turns in a magnificent Greatest Dark feast that no orc had ever enjoyed.

Instead, Uruk had taken the charm from around her neck. Kuru stood at her back with a long knife stolen from the bar against her carotid.

"If you smell anything," Uruk said, "cut."

The barroom now stank of burned wood and scorched varnish and gunpowder and ripped bowels. Elf blood drenched the front of Uruk's fancy suit.

Tara and Achilles trailed the orcess into the room. She leaned heavily on her scythe's bone handle, and somehow limped on both legs, but her gaze burned and a tight smile showed a broken-off tusk.

Excitement had burned away Uruk's exhaustion. They had fought, and won.

Behind the bar, Sanford retched into a bucket. How much vomit could come out of one man?

The doors swung open. Daka and the two Norkosh charged in, stumbling to a stop at seeing Kuru with a blade at Earwin's throat.

Daka frowned. "Did we miss the war?"

"The good part," Uruk said.

"Shurka!" Kuru said, looking at the shorter Norkosh. "Gushbaz! The enemy has fallen."

"And we missed it!" Daka snarled.

"Is it time to piss on the corpse?" Shurka-Norkosh said.

"I like pissing on the corpse," Gushbaz-Norkosh said.

Earwin shuddered.

"And now," Uruk said, "we end this war."

In orcish, Kuru said, "Last cut loses."

"Hold," Uruk said.

"Why?" Kuru said.

"We kill her and the other elves come for us," Uruk said.

"Let them," Kuru snarled.

"They will bring men," Uruk said. "Police. We cannot win."

"We are orcs!" Kuru said. "We do not surrender!"

"We do not," Uruk said. "But we can change this war."

"Un-orcish," Kuru sneered.

"An orc endures!" Uruk said. "I will endure a different war, if it means my boys and my woman and the Tai survive. I will endure this. This is not our cavern, our basement. America will not let orcs be orcs—so let us *take* what America has. Let us take chairs that fit us! Rooms where we can stand straight! My brother, a builder of cars! Your brother *takes* electricity! Let us take more, fight for more, make it mine and yours!"

Kuru stared at Uruk.

Uruk stared back. More words would not help.

Kuru inhaled through his nose and said in English, "I can always cut her throat later."

Uruk tightened his gut against the bruises. A new kind of war. He could do this. "I offered to *ne-go-ti-ate* with you once. I offer again. You leave us alone. We leave you alone."

Behind the bar, Sanford groaned. "Let me do the talking."

"You have been useful, man," Kuru said to Sanford. "But this is orcish. Do not meddle."

Sanford poured himself a glass of water.

Uruk said to Earwin, "Would you rather we kill you?"

"An elf does not negotiate with orcs," Earwin muttered.

Sanford spat vomit-stained water into his bucket. "But elves negotiate with men all the time."

Kuru said, "She is ours!"

Sanford swallowed another drink of water. "You need a middleman." His face was a bizarre combination of white and green. Thick sick-sweat dripped down his forehead. The man was no stronger than the day Uruk had met him.

Yet he'd kicked an elf in the head.

And he still clutched Celebrimble's ring.

Uruk said in orcish, "He chose us over an elven reward. Let him try."

Kuru glared. In English: "Fine. Attempt a blood price, man. You will fail."

Sanford straightened his suit jacket and staggered around the bar. "You see, madam elf? I am your best hope for life." He limped. A paper man didn't know how to kick without hurting himself, but Uruk liked him better for trying. He sank onto one of the bar stools and let out a tiny groan.

How could Earwin glare so fiercely with a blade at her throat? "Give me my father's ring."

"What will you give me for it?" Sanford said.

Kuru growled.

Uruk said in orcish, "He has shown his loyalty."

"We will not surrender our prizes," Kuru said.

"We do not understand word wars," Uruk said. "Let him work." In English: "If we do not agree, cut her throat."

Sanford's gaze flickered between Uruk and Kuru as they spoke. When they fell silent, he said, "I may proceed?"

Uruk grunted. "We must all agree."

"I expect nothing else. Now, ma'am." Sanford took a drink of water and rubbed his stomach, wincing. "You cursed my wife to keep me from defending Mister Dodge's company. Why was he so important?"

Earwin said nothing.

"It is said that elves never lie," Sanford said. "Orcs, on the other hand, always tell the truth. Uruka, what will you do if these talks fail?"

Not even close. "Uruk-Tai," Uruk said. "Cut her throat out."

The orcess said, "Eat her."

"I dislike negotiating under duress," Sanford said to Earwin. "But here we are. My friends are most intent on ending this feud. One way or another."

Friends?

Yes. Sanford had fought by Uruk's side. Friend. *My* friend.

Would Grandpa have ever dreamed of this day?

Earwin drew a deep breath and fixed her eyes on Sanford's face. "Dodge is too successful. He gains too much power."

"Someone will be successful," Sanford said. "Why not Dodge?"

"He owns his company." Earwin's face tightened.

"So do many men."

"Without stockholders."

Stock holders? What were they, people who managed cattle? The way Sanford drew his chin up told Uruk that the paper man knew a different meaning. "So you elves have no say."

Earwin held Sanford's gaze. "Left on their own, orcs would murder the world. Men would devour it. Only elves live long enough to guide a country. We must be free to make the right decisions, for the good of all."

"Decisions like tearing down tenements where orcs live?" Sanford said.

"Those buildings are unsafe and unclean. Nothing should live like that."

"Our home is clean," Uruk growled. "My woman battles roaches every day."

Sanford did not look from his word-battle. "So you're having the city build fine new homes for orcs?"

Earwin fell silent.

Sanford shook his head. "It's like this. Humans and orcs and elves and dwarves, we live together here. We have our own ways of life, but we build the world ourselves. We rule ourselves. You either sign a binding agreement right now surrendering the tenement to these orcs, stopping all interference with my family and all orcs, or I will cut your throat myself."

Uruk blinked. Kuru had tried to insult Uruk by declaring that he had learned too much from the paper man, but Sanford had learned as well.

Kuru tightened his grip. "Her throat is mine."

Earwin said, "Peter Sanford. If they kill me, you and your wife will die along with every orc in Detroit."

"For that, we're adding Mister Dodge into the covenant," Sanford said. "You leave him alone, and if he ever goes public, you don't buy any of his stock."

Earwin did not answer.

Sanford studied her face.

Why didn't he speak? He was the word warrior. Was he out of words?

Uruk opened his mouth to demand Sanford strike.

"It's like this," Sanford said quietly. "I am a peaceful man. You cursed my wife. Your existence is an unacceptable threat. Without an agreement—it's you or my family."

"No." How could anyone, even an elf, sound so definite with a blade at her throat? "You will not dare."

Sanford winced as he stood. "Urka-Tai!"

The man should stop *trying*. "Uruk-Tai."

"When we first met," Sanford said. "You told me how to roast a man. How do you roast an elf?"

Uruk had never heard that tale. He glanced at Kuru, who shrugged.

The orcess declared, "Elf is too weak to roast. It must be stewed. It needs much spice to cover up the sweetness and to give flavor."

That made Earwin flinch.

Sanford didn't notice, though, instead looking to the orcess. "Thank you."

The orcess hefted her scythe. "Brains are delicious fried with garlic. They should be fed to the young, to give them a taste for elf."

"My wife is still recovering from the curse they laid," Sanford said. "What would give her strength?"

The orcess peered at Earwin. "Spleen, fresh-stewed, with onions and the hottest peppers."

Surely Sanford should look at the elf, to drive home the threat? He ignored her, instead turning to Uruk. "I have done my best to negotiate. She refuses. You say that we must agree on what is done to her?"

"Yes," Kuru spat.

"As Urka says, I have cause for marrow feud."

Earwin said, "You will not."

"I will settle any claim I have on her for her spleen," Sanford said. "Fresh."

Kuru said, "Why should we share? His blood price failed!"

Uruk held his groan. "He allied with us. A spleen is small."

"You *do* side with him!" Kuru said.

"The only man to choose an orc over an elf?" Uruk said. "I will give him a dozen elf spleens."

"You will talk to me, man," Earwin said.

Sanford ignored her. "What about the other elf? Does he still have a spleen?"

"You bluff!" Earwin said.

"I ripped his liver," the orcess said. "The spleen is whole."

Uruk said, "Daka. Do you know how to cut out a spleen?"

Daka said, "I have seen it done."

"If you butcher like you fight, you will ruin it," the orcess snarled.

Gushbaz-Norkosh said, "The Norkosh work in slaughterhouses. *I* will fetch his spleen."

The orcess sniffed.

"Two elf spleens, then," Sanford said.

"Why would you choose an orc?" Earwin snarled.

Sanford sighed. "Do you know what *partner* means, madam elf?"

She stared at his face.

"It means that the Tai and I are stronger together than we are apart. I stand with him, as they stand with me." Sanford shook his head. "Either you settle with me, with the Tai, with these other orcs—excuse me, mister orc?"

Mister again? Sanford might have earned Uruk's trust, but Uruk did not have enough patience for this.

Kuru furrowed his eyebrows at Sanford.

"You said blood price," Sanford said. "How much is that, in dollars?"

"There are no dollars for this!" Kuru snarled.

"For a child?" Uruk said slowly. "A shaman would say one hundred dollars."

Kuru bared his Greater Tusks and hissed, but did not argue.

Earwin dared to smirk.

Sanford nodded. "That's a lot of money for an orc to raise." He looked back at Earwin. "So, the tenement, and shall we say... ten thousand dollars?"

Earwin's eyes went wide.

"A hundred dollars would hurt an orc," Sanford said. "Losing the building, losing the money, and losing a battle with orcs? *That* will hurt an elf."

Earwin shook her chin as far as she could. "I will not agree."

"And water," Kuru said. "Power. Celebrimble had it turned off."

"Oh, that's low," Sanford said. He shrugged at Uruk. "I apologize. The rest of the night is orcish business." He glanced at the blood on Uruk's jacket and turned even paler. "Do you mind if I take my first spleen and go? You can bring the other spleen when you're done."

Still stunned, Uruk said, "Go. Nobody wins against an elf." An end to the marrow feud would have been good, but a man who would stand by agreements with an orc was a clan's treasure.

Kuru grinned. "We do. Tonight, we do."

Uruk looked to Kuru. "Last cut loses?"

"I grant you first cut," Kuru said. "Show me your subtlety."

"Wait!" Earwin said.

"Can't wait," Sanford said, scooping up his coat. "I have to stew that spleen while it's still fresh. I hope we have peppers."

"I agree!" Earwin shouted. "I agree!"

Sanford paused. Without turning around or setting his coat down he cleared his throat and took a deep breath. "Uruk-Tai." A burst of coughing made him double over.

Uruk stared. The pronunciation hadn't been perfect—but it had been enough.

"Do you and yours agree?" Sanford wheezed.

Uruk looked to Kuru.

"Ten thousand dollars and the tenement," Kuru said. "Power and water."

"Leaving us alone," Uruk said.

"Wait," Achilles said.

"You own debt!" Uruk snarled.

"I do," Achilles said. "Yet Celebrimble claimed me as his son. One of four children. I demand my fourth of his estate."

Kuru burst out in bitter laughter.

"You betray us and demand this?" Earwin said.

"You used me," Achilles said. "You used me to kill innocents."

"Lawbreakers are not innocent!" Earwin said.

Achilles said, "You used me to *kill*. If you would have me forget that, you will treat me as your father claimed. One fourth."

"I am your family," Earwin said.

"How many times did you say you didn't need me?" Achilles said. "Did not want me around? That I smelled bad, that I was stupid?" His voice grew tight. "And how many times did you show up at my warehouse, using your wizardry to taint unopened bottles?"

"All that you have, my father gave you," Earwin said.

"He showed me that all I have is what I take," Achilles snarled.

Uruk glanced at Kuru.

Kuru grimaced. "He is an orc."

"Elven treasures are not for you!" Earwin said. "No property. Only cash."

"My home," Achilles said. "And one quarter of all cash, stocks, bonds, and financial assets."

Sanford coughed. "It seems highly fair. He didn't even request a fiscal evaluation of your famous sacred grove."

Earwin flinched.

"Why should he get anything?" Kuru said. "I grant him courage, but he fought for them!"

"It's not about him getting," Sanford said. "It's about elves losing."

Sorrow flitted across Achilles' face. "Celebrimble made me—not orc. Not elf. Not man. I belong nowhere. But I have a debt to pay. I demand my inheritance. For that."

Kuru grunted.

"Easy enough to add," Sanford said. "Or I'll take my spleen and leave."

"The ring," Earwin said. "I must have the ring."

Sanford paused. "I don't think so."

"It is *ours*."

"Madam orc," Sanford said. "My wife does not like her food very spicy. Can we add sour cream, to make the peppers less hot in that spleen?"

Earwin screeched, "You will not eat my father's body!"

The orcess frowned. "Only if you are weak."

Sanford nodded. "I fear she is." His voice turned hard as he faced Earwin. "Decide. Now."

"The dead elf is *mine*," the old orcess said.

Sanford nodded at her. "True. You have not stated your price."

She pursed her lips in thought. "The elves lose much tonight. He is yours." A smile broke her face. "I already pissed on him."

A bizarre war, Uruk mused.

But no orc had ever witnessed an elf wizard break down sobbing.

57

Sanford sat at the bar, writing on loose sheets of paper fetched by the barkeep. The barkeep himself cowered behind the bar, twitching any time an orc farted.

Uruk weaved around Kaba and made his way to the ancient orcess. "War-orc."

She nodded. "Uruk-Tai. Foolish child."

Even she had understood Sanford well enough. "You turned the war."

She snorted. "You boast."

If Uruk denied her claim, he would have to fight her. She looked fragile enough to crush with a sneeze, especially with the bruises forming on every scrap of exposed skin, but his marrow said he would lose. "It is the Greatest Dark, and we have won war with the elves. It is a night for boasting. For sagas. For celebration."

She gave him a cool stare.

"I would know your name," Uruk said. "I would honor you for your battle."
She raised her chin. "I am Mha n'Tass."

Uruk stopped. Fifteen-year-old memories of claiming Vara flashed through his mind. Could this orcess have sent him tumbling down tenement stairs five times, one after another? She looked nothing like his dim memories of Vara's mother.

Except her rheumy eyes. An orc did not acknowledge defeat, but her gaze said everything.

Uruk would not shame her by speaking of defeating her. "I would tell your clan of your prowess."

"I am alone."

Uruk drew a deep breath. "Then I would offer you the shelter of the Tai." This much he could do. "My two fine boys and my woman Vara would welcome you."

A tiny tension left Mha's face. "I have labor I cannot abandon."

"Then tell me where you live," Uruk said. "The Tai will come to you. You have earned what we can give."

"And the Norkosh!" Kuru said, coming up. "We honor you as well."

Mha looked from one to the other. Was that hunger in her eyes? "Half a mile east. The Harrison farmstead."

"We will be there," Uruk said. "Me, and all of mine."

"Do." Mha's stare seemed to punch through his skull. "Do not speak. Do."

Mha was harder than Grandpa. Uruk nodded and turned away.

Kuru said, "We will need transportation. Tara-Tai. The Orcsmobile. When you finish it, will you sell it?"

Tara straightened from his rummaging, setting two bottles of Canadian Club on the bar. "This car? No."

Kuru grimaced.

"I build two," Tara said. "Selling the second will give me the money to build two more."

Kuru let a smile creep across his face. "I will find the money."

"You become a landlord tonight," Sanford called without looking up from his scribblings. "You will collect rents from the other orcs in the tenement, and use part of that money to pay the heat and lights and water. The rest is yours."

Kuru cocked his head. "I get money for no labor?"

"It's called *capitalism*," Achilles said. "I'll try to explain it later."

"You take the responsibility for the tenement," Sanford said. "In exchange, you get money."

Kuru shook his head. "But no labor? How can that work?"

Uruk laughed. "At least bootlegging is labor."

"Done." Sanford dropped his pen. "All cash payments are due tomorrow." He yawned. "Today, really. Ur—" he coughed.

"Save your strength for when you most need it," Uruk said. "Call me... partner."

Uruk had seen Sanford smile more broadly, but only when his woman was involved. "Partner. Before signing this, you should read—" He stopped. "Er... I guess you have to trust me?"

"Give it to me," Achilles said. "I will read it aloud, for all to hear."

Uruk listened in astonishment. An orc *could* read.

One day, his boys would do the same.

Achilles spoke in a monotone, fumbling the longer words, but Sanford kept nodding so he must have done it right. When Achilles finished, Sanford took the papers back. "Madam elf. You sign first."

"I cannot with a knife at my neck," Earwin snarled.

"Reasonable," Sanford said. "Mister orc, would you bring her over here?"

Kuru inched Earwin forward. Seconds later, her belly was pressed against the bar.

Earwin studied the page.

Sanford handed her a pen.

"No!" Kuru snapped.

"They win—and dare refuse?" Earwin said.

Uruk should have expected this. "Agreements with orcs are in blood."

Sanford blinked. "I should have expected that."

"An elf does not sign in blood," Earwin said.

"You sign in blood," Kuru said. "Or I drown this paper in your blood and we ask again."

She tightened her jaw. "Fine!" She rolled the tip of the pen in the blood soaking her shirt, to scrawl a few letters at the bottom of the page. "If you break this, we will destroy every orc in Detroit!"

"We are too busy living to bother with you," Uruk said.

"You may go," Sanford said. "I will deliver countersigned copies tomorrow, if that suits you."

Earwin said, "Release me."

Kuru looked to Uruk.

Uruk nodded.

Stepping free, Earwin glanced at Uruk. Violet eyes met his for a fraction of a heartbeat. Uruk had never seen such pure loathing before.

Then the elf whirled towards the door and took a step.

Mha n'Tass happened to be blocking her path.

Earwin waited.

Mha stood still.

Earwin gave a nearly orcish spit and swerved around Mha, disappearing out the doors.

Uruk grinned.

Sanford said, "Partner. Make your mark, here. You—" He pointed at Kuru. "You next. Right here, that's it. Mister Achilles, now you, yes, there. A signature, good. And my witness mark." He scribbled.

"And done," Sanford said.

"Tara!" Uruk said. "If there is no draught, the whiskey must do. We must drink to shaman Azok-Snaka! To his power, to his life, to his death!"

"You must eat him," Mha said. "It is the only way to show respect."

Uruk tried not to flinch. Orcs had not eaten their dead in generations—and besides, Azok-Snaka had been all gristle.

"Use his hide to clothe your young," Mha said. "His bones as tools. You endure something new, Tai, but this is the way of the proper orc."

Tara bellowed a laugh. "All know that Uruk is a proper orc. He deserves first bite."

Kuru chortled.

Uruk snarled, "A toast!"

"You would do me honor?" Mha said. "I will teach you how."

Tara handed out bottles. "To Azok-Snaka!"

Uruk raised his bottle and swigged.

Kuru followed. "Tai!" Uruk had to return the toast, of course. Whiskey wasn't draught, but it was warming.

Sanford contented himself with ridiculously small shots, but drank along. Uruk went to slap his back, but caught himself and hit the bar instead. "Partner."

Sanford raised his glass. "Partner!"

"This cor-por-ation."

Sanford nodded.

"Make the papers."

Sanford raised his glass. His hand shook—was he drunk already? "It is in the interest of the corporashunnn..." Yes, those few shots had finished him. "That we toast that!"

Uruk laughed and raised his bottle.

"Uruk-Tai!" Achilles said. "I must ask a question."

Uruk eyed the un-orcish orc. "What?"

Achilles plucked his lapels. "This suit is awful. Who's your tailor?"

ABOUT THE AUTHOR

https://mwl.io

Never miss another new release!
Sign up for MWL's mailing list at
https://mwl.io.

NOVELS AND COLLECTIONS (AS MICHAEL WARREN LUCAS):

Immortal Clay
Kipuka Blues
Butterfly Stomp Waltz
Terrapin Sky Tango
Forever Falls
Hydrogen Sleets
Drinking Heavy Water
$ git commit murder
$ git sync murder
Prohibition Orcs
Frozen Talons
Vicious Redemption
Devotion and Corrosion (coming 2023)

NONFICTION (AS MICHAEL W LUCAS):

Cash Flow for Creators – Relayd and Httpd Mastery – PAM Mastery
FreeBSD Mastery: Advanced ZFS – FreeBSD Mastery: Specialty Filesystems
FreeBSD Mastery: ZFS – Tarsnap Mastery – Sudo Mastery – PGP & GPG
Networking for Systems Administrators – DNSSEC Mastery
FreeBSD Mastery: Storage Essentials – Absolute OpenBSD – Ed Mastery
SSH Mastery – Network Flow Analysis – Absolute FreeBSD
Cisco Routers for the Desperate –FreeBSD Mastery: Jails
SNMP Mastery – Letters to ed(1) – Domesticate Your Badgers

The Networknomicon
Only Footnotes

See your favorite bookstore for more!

MY FANTASTIC KICKSTARTER BACKERS

Ada Kerman
Adam Thompson
AFresh1
Alexander Shendi
Alexandra Brandt
Alexandra Fluskey
Algot Runeman
Alyssa Rose Farver
Ami Parikh
Amy Claflin
Andrew Wainwright
Ann R. Kist
Annie Reed
Anthea Sharp
Appalachian Orcish Outpost
Author Amy Campbell
Ben Korvemaker
Berat 'The Tornado' Arik
Bill Albertson
Bill Kohn
Bonnie Elizabeth
Brad Ackerman
Brigid Collins
Brooks Davis
Caleb
Carolyn Rowland
Ceredwin
Charles B
Charles Childers
Chris Pullen and Mia Tokatlian
CJ Jones
Claas P.
Craig Maloney
Craig Small
CrispyMayhem
Cyberfossil
D. Moonfire
Dan S.
Dave Cottlehuber
David "Handsome Dave" Bishop

David Bowden
David H Hendrickson
DeAnna Knippling
Dustin Laughlin
earless wondercat
Eric Barry
Ericka Kahler
Erik DeBill
Erin
Eva Holmquist
Fatima Fayez
Felicia Fredlund
First Wildebeest
Florian Obser
Fshhhbone Spineshiver
g
Gaël Vander Schelden
Gaston Phillips
Gergely "algernon" Nagy
ghostDancer
Gil André
Gordon Carrie
Grawg Skullaxe
Jay Hannah
Jeanette Brewer-Loebig
Jeff Marraccini
Jessica Marquardt
Jim Cheetham
Jim Kosmicki
Johanna Rothman
John Gilligan
Jonathan Mendonca
Josh Grosse
Josh Washburne
Karen Fonville
Kate MacLeod
Kate Sheeran Swed
Kelly Hays
Kelly Smith
Ken Strong

krinsky
Kristine Kathryn Rusch
Laura Bickle
Laura Ware
Leigh Saunders
Linda Jordan
Lisa Owen
Lisa Silverthorne
Loren L Coleman
Louisa Swann
Lukasz Bromirski
Luke Kolata
Mark Damon Hughes
Mark Moellering
Mary Jo Rabe
Mary Sue
Mason Egger
Matthias Schmidt
Merrie Destefano
Meyari McFarland
Michael "You *Wish* You Were Half-
    Orc" McComas
Michael A. Stackpole
Michael Cieslak
Michael Hannemann
Michael Mock
Michelle A Freeman
MJ Silversmith
Ms. Anonymous
Murray Bollinger
Natasha Swift
Niall Navin
Nic Neidenbach
Niels Kobschätzki
Olivette Devaux
Pam A. Herbster
Patrick Muldoon
Phillip Vuchetich
Prince Eric Vickers
R.S. Kellogg
Ranthoron
Ray Percival
Rebecca M. Senese

Rhel ná DecVandé
Rhonda Lane
Ricardo M.P. Martins
Richard "President of the MWL
    Depreciation Society" Jones
Rob Szarka
Rob Vagle
Ron Collins
Ruthenia
Ryan M. Williams
S. J. Schuchart Jr.
Sarah Clark
Scott Murphy
Scott Peters
Sean Watson
Seth Hanford
Shaun Davidson
Shawn K. O'Shea
Shayne Power
Sherry D. Ramsey
Stefon Mears
Stephannie Tallent
Steven Martindale
Steven Saus
Stinkthorpe Bogwoncher
Stuart Griffiths
sungo
Tao Wong
Tifaine Highly
Tobias "rixx" Kunze
Tom Rini
TommiP
Trip Space-Parasite
Veo Corva
Walter Parker
Wes Frazier
Willard Goosey
Wolf Duttlinger
yam655.com

and the Anonymous Thirty-Seven